A Fling with a
Demon Lover

Also by Kelvin Christopher James

Jumping Ship and Other Stories

Secrets

A Fling with a Demon Lover

KELVIN CHRISTOPHER JAMES

HarperCollins*Publishers*

A FLING WITH A DEMON LOVER. Copyright © 1996 by Kelvin Christopher James. All rights reserved. Printed in the United States of America. No part of this book may be used or reproduced in any manner whatsoever without written permission except in the case of brief quotations embodied in critical articles and reviews. For information address HarperCollins Publishers, Inc., 10 East 53rd Street, New York, NY 10022.

HarperCollins books may be purchased for educational, business, or sales promotional use. For information please write: Special Markets Department, HarperCollins Publishers, Inc., 10 East 53rd Street, New York, NY 10022.

FIRST EDITION

Designed by Nancy Singer

Library of Congress Cataloging-in-Publication Data

James, Kelvin Christopher.
    A fling with a demon lover / by Kelvin Christopher James. — 1st ed.
      p.   cm.
    ISBN 0-06-017350-5
    1. Man–woman relationships—Greece—Fiction. 2. Americans—Travel—Greece—Fiction. 3. Young women—Greece—Fiction. I. Title.
    PS3560.A386F58   1996
    813'.54—dc20   96-1300

96 97 98 99 00 HC/❖ 10 9 8 7 6 5 4 3 2 1

Acknowledgments

Sincere acknowledgments to my most gracious and lovely posse who helped in making this book happen, and who—bless their beautiful souls—may ride under these (or other) noms de guerre:

Dame Joy-O-Joy and La DianRe and Jqui-D and Jeenie-K and Jo-deH and JenLa and Jay'nB and Nellie-V and Kris-10 and Des-Po and Blushé and DiM6 and a very loud extra-special shout-out for Gitte-B.

Love y'all,

so many thanks

. . . to our daemons, laughing in their sleep . . .

1

Out of the corner of her eye, Sassela caught the instant. As if he were a veteran tobacco-chewer, Tiago Marin's gob hit Zwezi Johnson *splat!* on the back of his neck. And reflexively, Zwezi's hand slapped at the spot, squishing the spit through his fingers. Then realizing he was the victim of a wickedness, in a disgusted voice, he snapped to his feet screaming: *"Miss Jack! He just spit on me!"* And those close enough to witness the offense in concert went: *"Ugghh!"* while the rest of the class turned their ready, rabid focus to the fracas.

Sassela saw it all. Too fast to make a difference, she saw the last straw fall, felt her final nerve unravel. *"Tiago Marin!"* she yelled, then catching control, shifted to a seething hiss: "Right now! You are out of this class. Go stand in the hall. And don't you return without your mother!"

That mother would be Mrs. Marin: a squat, brown-skinned Latina. Early thirties, yet fast becoming a bulgy sack on stumpy legs. A determined, always-busy, bunch-browed woman who glared with fierce black eyes each time Sassela called her in. Sassela was well aware of the logic of Mrs. Marin's anger. Understood it meant time off from sweatshop work; meant loss of already low income; meant less for Tiago's two younger siblings she was raising alone.

On the other hand, Sassela knew that just such a severe bother would frustrate and fire up Mrs. Marin to the point of administering upon Tiago the proper whipping he deserved. Since becoming a public school teacher, Sassela had concluded that a few justified lickings never hurt the soul.

Thoughts aside, she grabbed Kimwipes from her desk and was quick to clean up Zwezi's neck and dignity. Satisfaction flooded warmly as she noticed the sudden wetness in Tiago's eyes as he sullenly shoved books into his bookbag and slouched out of the classroom. The nasty little bully. Out of spite she hoped that Dr. Gruder, or one of his policing assistants, would happen by and question him standing in the hallway. Since students saw it as the ultimate diss, the principal's expulsion policy could be a potent threat.

A tentative titter tested the wobbly stillness Tiago had left. Sassela whipped a searching glance around, and the would-be toppler kept cover. Wary quiet crept back to ascendance.

Sassela glanced at her watch: but ten more minutes left until the end of today's attempt at culture-shaping.

Home at last from evening classes, she unlocked her apartment's door, pushed it open. Her mood worsened as empty quiet and the flat scent of plug-in lemon air-freshener met her. Harry had not cooked, was not even there. She kicked off her shoes, dumped her pocketbook on the table, went into the kitchen. Opened the fridge to find leftover pasta, half an apple pie, cold disappointment. She microwaved a cup of milk, added a few drops of vanilla, drank the brew down in a draught. Then she lay her melancholy self down on the couch.

They used to be like Jack Sprat and his wife: he loving to cook, with a special touch in pot with spoon and spice; she unable to suppress drooling for his delectable creations.

Now he had stopped, and instead stooped to deliveries from whichever menu was stuck under the apartment door. To Sassela, it was a rank betrayal of their unspoken bargain. When challenged, his defense was that cooking made him fat, and that made him lazy, and so he had to stop. Didn't stop his belly from barreling, though. All it ended was her knowing the pleasure of his kitchen: his breakfasts, sometimes just being awoken by finished aromas—of chocolate with milk and cinnamon, of buttery fresh-made rolls, hot right from the oven. Each mouthwatering breakfast a promise delivered, a tease unstripped.

As good, but different, were those times she watched him cook: making bread, the rhythmic play of hips and shoulders as he leaned into the kneading. His hands certain, deftly catching and turning and molding the firm shiny dough. A peacefulness to it. A strength, too. A suggestion of competence beyond skill, that he could so transmute basic foodstuff. The idea beguiled, meandered her mind to other masculine mysteries. She never let him know it, but her eyes on him cooking was always his best seduction tactic. Sighing at the memory, Sassela got up and headed for the bathroom.

Her tension sprayed away under the rushing flow of hot water, Sassela stepped out of the shower, stretched her neck backward hard until the feel was good, then shook her head side to side, making the thick, wet, sultry hair tickle her shoulders. And that was good, too. Good hair, loose curly to almost straight—depending on Harlem's humidity. She used to perm it crimpy during her teenage politically aware days.

Right now, though, it was merely dripping a puddle on the bathroom mat. So she pulled down a towel, dammed away the stream into a blue turban. With a washcloth she demisted the mirror, then dabbed at her face with a gentle, careful sponge, scrutinizing critically, squarely facing the evidence.

Didn't look bad. No! Definitely didn't look—as her psyche suffered a familiar wince—didn't look her thirty-eight years.

Her skin, water-beaded, still soaked, was a smooth rich chocolate brown—about one-third cream. At any age, all-purpose, prime, American skin.

Reminded, she applied a light moisturizer. Older skin is fragile, especially around the eyes. Although not a bother for Sassela. She had her mother's Asian eyes. The Apache in her, Mams always said. Whether in truth, Sassela didn't really know. Whatever. Sassela Jack's upslant eyes—deep and black, incongruous above her narrow nose with its saucy African flare—proved magnetic. Attention she had learned to handle, to keep unsticky, sometimes with a harpy's tongue. She had survived being a scrawny only child among dozens of cousins in her parents' hyperactive household. People who knew her then also knew that her nickname, Sassy, was ruggedly home-proven.

Until a few years ago, she'd considered her mouth too wide and her lips too . . . well, prominent. But she always could produce a broad, genuine smile filled with strong, even teeth, and glitter.

Yes. Hers was a good-looking face. An honest place where beauty had visited. Camped out, even.

A turn of her head, a glint in the mirror, and she looked harder and saw the streak. Fine, silvery, right behind her ear. Automatically, she reached for the tweezers, caught the bad news by its root, firmly pulled it out.

A careful search found no other traitors. Her mane was again black as a midnight river. Black as it was at sixteen. Sassela snorted with immodest recall of the time she won the national high school debate. The competition, prize, speech, the handshakes—it was all radiant, and glorious. The keen thrill at the envy in her rivals' stony eyes. And then, during the party and the whole of the afterward, she had become consciously beautiful. Not at all shy about it. In the mix of pleasurable sensations, awareness grew upon her, and she had known certainly. Everyone showed, proved how beautiful she was. Her boyfriend Afemi did in whispers—she loved his name, Afemi Evenin Nelson—minty breath, shining eyes, kissing her beauty into her ear, his damp warm hand squeezing.

Her Mams did, too. Above the jamming music, bragging to everybody in the jostle, "Ain't my girl a wonder!" And they—family or not—all replying like chorus, "True beauty, Missis Jack! Real beautiful!"

Not to mention Shaquina BeaAnn Johnson, team captain, hugging and crying and stomping hysterics all through the craziness, testifying: "Oh yeah! Sassy! That was beautiful." Even years later, in a high school reunion, when she added how that celebration excitement had made her wet her pants—which story renamed the prize the Spritzer Trophy—even then, Shaquina still spoke about how beautiful Sassela had been.

Sassela sighed nostalgic. Yep! Hers was a face that had *celebrated* beauty. She set to drying herself, turning her back to the mirror, scrubbing briskly across her shoulders with the big towel. Good for firming the bustline. Though she couldn't but notice her buttocks jiggling loosely, the puffy extra there, like sponge, or jelly—

A hard knocking on the door interrupted. "Gotta piss, Sassela!" Harry called, exasperated.

A thought zapped that some time ago she'd heard the muffled slam of his return; while, starting guiltily, Sassela answered, "In a minute—" aware she had got to daydreaming again.

"Goddamn it! Yu'know how long you been in there?"

Reflexively Sassela bristled at his swearing. "I *said* I was coming out!" she called back, sharp on the "said." And, draping the towel around her, holding it securely, she opened the door.

Was barely out as he brushed roughly past, grumbling about the "goddamned" steam.

Later, in her favorite cuddly-soft dressing gown, ready for bed, she went into the study, took her diary out of the Hammacher Schlemmer house-safe set beside her desk. She glanced at her table clock. Nine thirty-five, a mere twenty minutes to do her daily entry before strict beauty rest.

Today had been an especially exhausting one, tension clammy like humidity, and every living body—pupils, staff, even the bus driver—affected. Sassela began putting down a few details:

Dear Di,

*Today Neal Dadson and Drew Larosa got in a
dissing contest. Drew said that Neal was so
"stoopid" he thought collard greens was a
football player. Then Neal said—*

She reached down into her pocketbook on the floor, retrieved a slip of paper, scanned it before proceeding.

*—that Drew's mouth had "lips like a whale's
asshole, and those lips were restraining some
seriously spronged and spraggled buckteeth*

hopelessly trying to escape from his poisonous breath." Don't know how he came up with it, but swear this's a direct honest quote. And check imagination. Check use of language. This from a kid failing to read 4th grade. Laughed 'til I cried. As they'd say, "Word!"

Sassela grinned and sniggered as she wrote, the pleasant expression remaining fixed as she turned the page, scribbling on:

That's the extent of my rollicking, though. Matters went downhill from there. Not to mention Tiago Marin, the girls' lunchroom cuss-out, etc., and as usual. Rest is the same old same old, came home today to my so-called helpmeet who's been reading more and more on Middle Eastern doctrines. Don't know if it had to do with it, but yes'day he's so pissed I came home late, 9:15, he ordered Chinese, ate his fill and dumped the leftovers. When I saw it in the garbage and asked, he said he thought I'd have "filled up" wherever I was. So heavy on the "filled up," you didn't even have to imagine the innuendo. Made me feel like murder, so I walked. But one day, who knows? Of course today, again no meal. All I have to say is, Mammy well did warn me. "How long is too long!" she used to say. So guess I'm a coward playing martyr, and I'm all right only if my screaming is quiet, undisturbing. But I gotta do something, right? Right. Though, right now, I'm only choking back yawns.

Bfn. Another school day. Sss.

Done with it, she returned the diary, shut the safe, and spun the combination lock. Then, stretching close to painful, yawning like a lion, she went into the bedroom.

Harry lay on his side watching a talk show. He had the earphones on, had rolled the TV halfway up the bed. He didn't see her come in, although felt as she got into bed, and turned her way. Compensating for the volume in his headset, he yelled "Hi!" Too loud, but toned pleasant enough.

"Hi and goodnight," Sassela answered. Neutrally, shutting her eyes and curling up under the covers in one continuous motion, her back to him. Soon plain tiredness dropped her off into her usual sound and dreamless.

2

Morning come, well awake, Sassela jabbed the snooze button before the clock went off. Her need was some extra quiet for thinking through her day's outfit. She had started the week gallerying blues: total mauve on Monday. Tuesday was nautical, with sea-blue silk bodice under a sharp navy jacket, a full skirt. Then the children had been good, and two days straight, it was bright as spring, so she'd accepted that her blues depression had been due to PMS—her friend being due. So Wednesday morning she'd stepped out rosy. Flagrant throughout, from full-sized cotton panties to galea head-wrap, she sported shades of rebellious red. Cool A-line dress, floral—carnations—chiffon scarf. Blood was a happy color. Red was beautiful. Rounded off with silver hoop earrings with pearl drops. Everything framed by her milk-chocolate tint. She was looking the renegade beauty.

Today, Thursday, should be drama all the way— either out-and-out black, or the beige poet's blouse and coffee-brown flare skirt—

Harry rolled over, yawned mightily, stretched—his flying right fist missing her jaw by a breeze. The radio popped back on into the seven o'clock news. In one swift, smooth movement, Sassela rolled off the bed onto her feet. Automatically, she picked up her watch from the dresser, strapped it on. Thursday had begun.

Without knocking, Harry entered the bathroom bearing that sour aroma of microwaved instant, and brimming over with free advice. "Sass, morning sweetheart. Got this hot byte for you."

Hearing "bite," Sassela glanced in surprise to his empty hands, face.

He shook his head, dense morning beard framing a tentative smile. Answering her eyes, he went on, "It's this pattern of daily hairdressing you could adopt and get over, yu'know, psychological advantage, yu'know, power and so on—"

His nodding head faltered as Sassela screwed her lips wry, gave him a pull-my-other-leg look.

Harry gazed puppy eyes at her. "Anyhow," he said, "it sounded good on TV. But, but hear this one—" And he was off.

Mute under the unregarded flow of words, she eyed him askance in the mirror, earnest, gesticulating, glib. In her three years with him, she mused ironically, she had learned a lot about herself. Her tolerance, for one major thing. Yup! Did she ever discover how much she'd tolerate for companionship! She who bragged how she preferred good books to good-looking boors. Same she who was never fooled about Harry, five years her junior and already overweight. His cooking aside, he was lazy, selfish, greedy, and would readily barter self-respect. Sure, his packaging was an effective lost-puppy manner, plus steady sitcom company, and a job teaching philosophy at the City University.

Partly catering to that prestige package, she had

tried to match his light wit, his prosaic banter, although knowing for certain that dull humor was never her forte. And from their outset, she saw his laughter come too quick, spread wide but thin. A jackass's ready laugh at anything she threw out; although, since jackasses have the integrity of a stubborn spine, his was nearer the dutiful yap-yap of a lap dog.

Though he never lacked for others, this essential fault she always most despised. Yet still she put it aside, let him move in. Because she so craved companionship, was why. Perhaps what she suffered now was the gods saying, "Okay, wish granted!" then laughing themselves silly.

For it was she who'd instigated them toward being a unit. Shifted them from a once-a-week sleep-over date to this live-in arrangement. It was she who had broached the pregnant moment—that sleep-in Sunday, Esther and Dinah grating out edgy blues and raspy soul on FM public radio. He had made breakfast, delicious, the usual perfection. Then they lolled around naked under identical terry-cloth robes, Sassela on the couch, Harry on the carpet, close to his instant, newspapers in discard about them. A rustle as Harry scanned newsprint, then grunted, "Yeah, right! As if God created Africa, too—"

"Huh? What?"

"Another war in Ye Olde Country," he muttered, "and whether we should intervene. What's the difference, huh?"

Without comment, Sassela had watched him, smiling fondly. From banal to brilliant, never knew what'd come out of his mouth. And what with the bright spring sun and soothing sounds and all, a gentle warmth charged her as she became privy to a perfect moment—a glistening bubble wavering rare and raw, sparkly and precious above plain, flat time. She sighed, took deep breath of the moment, holding on to it, as she fancied what home might be, and that Harry being there made it so.

Just then, ballad ended, the deejay mellow-voiced: "At the tone, we have exactly twelve o'clock. Midday for you sports fans. One bare hour before the ball game." A musical laugh, full of mischief and macho conspiracy. Then he began the latest news reports.

But right away Harry's eyebrows had raised alarm. Round browns bulging somewhat, he exclaimed, "Damn! Time went past fast. Slipped on through to whenever, didn't it? Still, the man in the box is right. I just gotta git, girl."

No thought but a heart-leap, Sassela reached her foot out, halted his straightened, intent shoulder. "You know, Harry," she began softly—as he caught her foot, turned his head away and began stroking her instep absently, paused, giving her attention but not his eyes— "you don't have to be, I mean, you don't have to go, you know, like—" She hesitated, waiting for his eyes, for help.

But he said nothing, just kept stroking her instep more and more slowly. With each stroke his fingers ever gentler, going from caress to tickle and drawing nearer irritation.

She pulled her foot away, sat up, said it straight out. "You can stay if you want to, you know. I mean, move in."

Harry looked at her then, eyes diffident, not fixing with hers, said, "Sure, if you like. It could be great. And cheaper, too."

She knew the last to be his toss at banter, a chance at cool comedy easing the strained moment. Instead, his shifty eyes chilled her heart. For his response had no real fervor. And how he had turned her gesture around: accepting, rather than expressing, gratitude. Or even sharing, for it wasn't thanks she wanted. What quaked her so was just that already, that so immediately, she felt used. And a certain coolness within was admitting ruefully that she had saddled herself with a burden.

Though what she actually did was reach down, hug him, say, "Well, let's give it a try and see."

Although as they hugged close to seal the pact, the stiffness to his embrace had never relaxed—

"Hey, now," Harry's voice recalled her, "stay with me on this. It might work. Really—"

And like a salesman, he went on detailing how best to tend her thick hair: how to brush it, and with which brushes; how to hold her special wide-toothed comb to address a single line of morning-hair snarls; how to irritate the scalp for improved blood circulation. Half and half, she picked up that his data came from a public access TV show he'd viewed before the basketball game. The time, as she recalled, he had excused himself as being too busy to cook. But Sassela kept her breathing steady, her demeanor bland. Just slowly looked at him caught up in his spiel: gesturing and smiling conviction at how simple and effective the techniques were. "Excellent. Elegant. Not elaborate at all." Like gospel, he sang their praises.

She closed her eyes and mind, shook her head. Then, putting her lipstick down, she bustled him out like an out-of-place Boy Scout, shut the bathroom off from his irritation. Wouldn't let his foolery spoil her mood.

Into the mirror, she coughed up a wry chuckle. Mused: This was all her own choice. He was a pet, a child, this man. If nothing else, this definition of him provided rare irony. For certainly no pet or child'd be here expounding the ways of hair; at least, not to one who'd sported a mane all her life. It was funny, Harry in the role of hair-management database; him, cropping his own scalp-short to mask a fear of baldness.

She caught herself, studied her watch blankly and did the arithmetic. With all his bothering, she was close to late for morning assembly.

3

Her class dismissed promptly at 3 P.M., Sassela went through the school's back door to a near and tiny corner of the parking lot where she had put her Bug. Outside, the world was gray, air foggy and close, the clouds like heavy smoke, threatening. From somewhere inside the floating, urgent mass, thunder like labor contractions rumbled constantly. A car squished by, headlights glaring, horn beeping byes.

Sassela waved routinely. Core twisting to a vague tension, she got into the ancient Volks, started its huffy, can-do putt-putt, and drove off as if toward crisis. Namely, the last six credits toward her doctorate in education. After which, there'd only be the task of a written original thesis.

Waiting for her next to the bus stop, she found a legal parking spot exactly her car's size. Praise be! a reverent she offered, then locked up and rushed through the college's door, relieved she'd made it before the city's fourteenth snowstorm—a twenty-year record—burst.

An hour later, around four, it did. At six, changing

rooms for her second class, she heard someone's radio reporting six inches and steadily piling up. Ten inches were expected in the city, twice that in suburbia. Sassela grimaced distaste, tried recalling the last time she'd serviced the Bug, hoped it wouldn't act up.

The second class, Innovation in Teaching Science, was canceled, the professor having to rescue her children from a nursery aftercare crisis. Of course, outside was still coming down like wool. Two, three souls—maybe of Inuit heritage—braved it from the college's door, and promptly disappeared, absorbed into the whiteness. Everyone else remained stranded, the class breaking into groups to wait it out with small talk.

A dark-skinned West Indian, Nollis Pabois, was holding forth entertaining the largest group. Curious, she drifted closer, heard his singsong island accent:

". . . La Diablese beautiful as wishing well, thrill you more than danger, some say she hair like the ride the moon take in the blackest sky, she so pretty and sweet in she eyes, but she feet, they put on backward, and she teeth, they arrow-file, and she fingernails like spikes could slice your manhood gone like lightning flash . . ."

Suspicions confirmed, Sassela walked away. She didn't like this Pabois fellow, found him annoying, with a slyly amused, superior manner. Saw him as typical of those black folk who, driven to pander to white people's needs for nativeness, become singer, dancer, or, like Pabois here, black magic storyteller extraordinaire with antic eye and face mobile from grin to growl. Their purpose always to wowing the white folks, pushing the darkest connotations of blackness, and making her heritage hard to wear. She scanned his group impatiently. It piqued something in her that he should so enchant his audiences. Her white classmates were always wonder-rapt attending to his outlandish stories of superstitions. Sighing sarcastically, Sassela dawdled to the over-size window, propped a hip on its sill, stared out.

Pure awesome white was everything out there. Solid wind blowing white. Street matte white, lined both sides with white humps and hillocks. Hulking white mountains of buildings. Her irritation diffused before the completeness of the billion-flaked constant outside, Sassela got to daydreaming. Her mind sought sand, and sun, and sparkling fun. She thought afford-able, like maybe Mexico. Margaritas and mariachi music. Miles and miles of brilliant beach. Blue-green waters but a footstep's reach away, wavelets, puny but aggressive, rushing the beach, playfully nipping her bare toes. She'd hold off on going in. Though when she did, the water would be just right, beading on her oiled, tanned skin, sparkling like gems. Like liquid pearls or diamonds trapped in temporary nets of sun-light—

A touch on her shoulder. "Hi, Sassela, isn't it terri-ble?"

It was Cathy Pianin—Cat—her best buddy in the class. Destiny, it seemed, as they both had happened into these two evening classes, and years ago as begin-ner teachers, had subbed together in several schools.

"Yeah, but sort of pretty, too. Don't you think?"

"Not to me, it isn't," Cat said firmly, shaking her head. "Cold and wet and inconvenient—that's snow to me."

Sassela chuckled at her vehemence, which tugged a memory. "Remember that day Gruder ordered you to take your class to the playground for exercise?" she asked.

"Right! And in the middle of a bleeping snowstorm," said Cat with high-pitched indignation. "Remember? How can I forget! Though it only got me written up by the good doctor of discipline, and got me out of kindergart—"

"Doctor Fart!" Sassela interrupted, chortling. "You called him 'Doctor Fart' right there in front of the whole assembly. I can tell you, it was the high point of your popularity in school. Definitely with the students."

"I was just young and brave then. But it was funny, wasn't it?"

They watched the snow.

From the start, they had got along, and had been friends ever since. Mother light-skinned Jamaican, father Irish, Cat was very fair, could pass for white, but for her crimpy hair—she called it "curly." She kept her maiden name when she married a Jewish guy, a doctor. Sassela, introduced at a school function, remembered him as deep-voiced, of medium height and slim build, with a tight, aloof smile and a manner of speaking in ponderous sentences. Seemed he said "laymen" a lot.

"The radio says at least another hour," said Sassela.

"Then double that right off. You know they never know. They just play us for the excitement."

"Yeah! Ain't technology wonderful."

"Right! Wonder-full of shit," replied Cat, with unexpected fierceness.

Sassela measured her, said calmly, "Can't fight Nature, girlfriend. Anyhow, it's Thursday, nowhere to go but home to huzz."

The loaded look Cathy cast made Sassela quickly recall how she'd confided romantic interest from classmate Nollis Pabois: the man with opinions on everything under the sun, whom Sassela disliked, and pointedly avoided.

Cathy grasped her hand, stared earnestly. "Look Sassela," she said. "Something important I want to ask. That's if you want to do your girlfriend a favor. A personal secret favor."

Sassela's heart throbbed, intuitively guessing the

nature of Cathy's request. "Something to do with Mr. Caribbean?" she challenged.

Cathy nodded, her neck, ears flushed even in the dim light near the window, eyes shining promise like gold-flecked crystal balls.

"How can I serve the cause of stricken love?" Sassela said.

"Oh! would you, Sassela? That'd be great. And there's a free trip in it for you, too. To Greece."

"Say what?"

"I've told Paul that I'm signed up for the three-week ecology trip to Greece. It's the university's yearly ecology trip to Greece, Mineros. A fat ticket. Twenty days for about two hundred dollars and college ID. Well, I've got both. Don't I? Except"— her voice dropped conspiratorially —"except that Nollis has tickets for a trip to Tobago. For two. The two of us. Same time as the school's trip. Get it?"

"Lemme guess. You want me to cover for you in Greece while you go play nooky hooky in Tobago with your West Indian sweetman, huh?"

"Say 'Caribbean.' But exactly," said Cathy, triumphant, with a compressed there-you-have-it smile.

Despite her automatic nag of moral objection, Sassela smiled. Cathy Pianin might be selfish, but she was straightforward about it, and spunky, too. "When is this big fling?" she asked.

"Third Monday in January, about a month away and counting, if you say yes to the trip. It's all paid up, and everything. So please say yes."

The firmness of her expectation startled Sassela to protest, "But I can't say, girl. I don't know what'll be going on. Haven't looked at lesson plans that far ahead. Then there's notice. I'd have to get leave. We teach public school, Cat, remember?"

"No, no, no," said Cathy, "don't try that. You have

the leave, of course. Sick days, and since this is work-related, you could get special sanction even if you didn't have leave. I checked it all out with Board of Ed. It's no problem for them. For bettering our teaching skills and potential, we can go anyplace anytime. You just gotta show them it's a legitimate trip. And it is. It's the truth, you really can go. Union contract permits it. You'll get the time. You just gotta want to, and decide."

"Did you check, really? And it was okay, clear?"

"As water. Swear!" Cathy said fervently.

Still doubtful, Sassela looked at her.

Cathy pressed full-court: "Look, Sassela, I'm going to go with Nollis to Tobago anyhow. So if you go to Greece for me, you'd be mostly saving me from wasting money. And that way I'll have some notion of the place to bamboozle Paul with. And anyways, what do you have against a found vacation? Huh? Thought you were my friend," she ended petulantly.

For a long moment Sassela considered the snow steadily falling outside. She turned to Cathy, said, "I'll check my end, and if it's any way possible, you got a deal." She thrust out her hand.

"Atta girl!" cried Cathy. They clasped hands and hugged.

Nollis had been watching, and came over to Cathy, close. Expectantly, bright-eyed, black coffee searched vanilla wearing a coquette's grin. Something potent charged between them. Then Cathy nodded, smiled like a strum to the tension. Clear was their blissful lust, or love, or whatever stronger drive.

Self-consciously, Sassela started away from their passionate aura. Cathy called after her, "I'll bring the details Tuesday. Okay?"

Sassela looked back. "Sure," she said softly, mentally wishing them magic.

Away from them, Sassela's mind roiled with mixed

feelings: encouragement spiced with envy. Although quite heavy on the envy when she compared her own live-in love affair. More recently, hers was better a record of reconciliations from mess-ups, mutual mis-reads, and misdirections. In hers and Harry's fireside romance, every ember of affection seemed being smothered. Hot as their first fires had been, passion seemed now reduced to ash, white as the steady snow outside, passive and stifling.

Fairer promises notwithstanding, for another half hour or so, with mocking gentleness, the storm spread its chill confetti, firmly muffling fun, playing cold quicksand to any light-stepping intent. Musing at her window, passively waiting, wondering if the Bug would start, Sassela suffered the city's latest record snowfall. Then around seven-thirty, the weather cleared, and flocks of penned students poured from the college doors as if escaping.

Sassela made tracks to where she had parked the Bug, and found it forlornly half-buried under dirty slush: the culprit, the snowplow clearing the streets. In swift rage she kicked at the freshly piled snowbank, lost balance and barely recovered by snatching at the Bug's frail radio antenna. Breathless with her futile effort, she was forced to lean on the car and deeply inhale her own stale-sweat smell. "Control, control," she murmured. Although what she really wished was that she was at home, warm in bed, and merely dreaming this nightmare.

With thoughts of suing the city for aggravation, she decided to abandon the blasted car right there and stomped under the bare, well-lit bus shelter. If need be, to express her frustration, she would stand there forever, adamant and frozen. She'd await the damned bus, show her mettle. But after a little, a chill shivered through her bones, and a leak of tears confessed her heartfelt frustration.

Eventually she made out a phone booth up the street a bit and, chagrined that it'd taken so long to marshall composure, set off toward it along the snow-plow's tracks. It was hateful bringing Harry out to this freezing morass—him being such a baby about cold, too—but tonight was extreme, and desperation was her warrant. This was real distress, he had to be her may-day man. Especially him, equipped with his six-cylin-der, four-wheel-drive Range Rover. Regrettable, but she had to bust him out. Who else?

She got to the phone booth, found it also marooned by the snowplow's cast-aside slush, the door banked in halfway up its length. No way could she get in. Too beaten even to try, she just pulled up her coat collar against the chill wind, glumly headed back to the bus shelter.

Standing there, giving the car evil looks, it occurred to her that she might get the passenger-side door open, and get out of the growing wind. Nothing else to do. Plus the activity would be warming. Looking about the barrenness, up and down, the snowbound avenue seemed abandoned, putting paid to her self-conscious-ness. So, pocketbook as shovel, she began making clear-ance.

After a few minutes, she straightened up to catch a breath, survey her progress. All at once, she sensed eyes on her.

Startled, she turned around, and there was her watcher. Under the bus shelter, dark jeans, hands stuffed into a warm-looking oversize jacket, he was steadily regarding her.

Swiftly her New York eyes judged, intuitively deem-ing him okay: especially since, accommodatingly, he looked away, conceding to her scrutiny, then squarely remet her eyes. Sassela figured him a college student on a late run, and returned to her labors. Only now, aware of his silent masculine supervision, her effort was more elaborately awkward, her distress more finely accented.

Wasn't long before, hands deeply pocketed, he sauntered nearer, observed, "Got you a car somewhere under that pile, ma'am? Or is it treasure?" A definite West Indian accent, tones genial, bantering.

Neutrally, Sassela looked up to a broad grin, nice teeth. She said, "You might very well stand and guess like the paying audience, or you might help find out. Huh?"

Under impertinently arched brows, he eyed her battered pocketbook and, still grinning, said, "Equipment looks expensive, but is it efficient?" His hands remained snugly in his pockets.

Firmly holding her soggy pocketbook, Sassela straightened fully, looked him over. Brown-skinned, medium build, not much taller than she. Sporting that fresh smile. His light-brown eyes teasing, playful. Still no unpleasant undercurrents at all. She emptied tension from her lungs, stretched her unpracticed shoulder muscles, said boldly, "In this game, Sonny, you gotta play to learn."

The guy laughed outright, "Heh heh heh!" A gaudy old-timer's laugh, suggestive of a good-times paunch. His teeth were beautiful. He said, "Not to worry, mi'lady. Yuh savior's here." He raised a foot, shook it. "These heavy-duty clodhoppers here are really bulldozers incognito. Make room and watch them work your miracles."

They were those thick-leathered, hightop boots with treaded soles that seemed designed for extravagantly rough terrain or combat duty. Might've come with solid fuel boosters, they certainly did a job on that snowbank. A few kicks and tramples and the snow pile was gone from the door. Then her key, borrowed, was turned. Then a vigorous tug, and she could enter the

Bug. A scramble over to the driver's seat. Then, after a reluctant turn or two, the engine fired, raced, and settled to a steady heat-generating chug-a-chug. Out of plain old-fashioned courtesy, Sassela couldn't but ask her hero out of the cold. "Want to get in?" she invited.

His rescuing had roused a sweat, and in the closeness of the car, his strong funk was inescapable. Primal, coarse, intimately of unwashed male. Nothing artificial, a fine notch beneath offensiveness, it caught sharply in the back of her nose. Suddenly, guiltily, Sassela was overwhelmed with a sense of debt to this smiling young man. With an effort to breathe through her mouth, she said, "I'm Sassela, and I'm very grateful, yu'know, for all you did."

"My pleasure, ma'am. No problem at all. I'm Ciam Turrin. And I know your name. I work in the library evenings. Returns and stuff. I've seen you around."

"Oh," said Sassela, taken aback at the one-way acquaintance.

"Is okay. I took my time to look. And you as Beauty don't have to witness every admirer."

Very much the gallant, thought Sassela, and flushed warmly in the darkened car as a memory of Cathy and Nollis and their romance slipped forefront.

Right then, streetside, a car's horn blasted, startling away the awkward mood. Deafened heart a-thumping, Sassela lowered her fogged-up window. And yes, Praise be! it was Harry's Range Rover alongside. Through his barely lowered window, angry, accusing eyes glared at her, and past. Just as immediately, her surge of relief at his arrival shriveled.

Coolly, even-voiced, she greeted, "Well, hi, Harry. I'm so glad you're here."

Harry glowered silently.

Sassela rolled up her window some, glanced defensively at Ciam, fiddled with the steering wheel, raced the engine. Well reading the insinuation stabbed at her companion by Harry's sharp, red eyes, she was pissed. Very and uncontritely. Where did he come off with these possessive, strident looks? On what basis? No matter that he had volunteered as savior, this kid here had already attended to her distress, and without benefit of four-wheel drive—

Harry blasted the horn again. Sassela lowered her window, rolled baleful eyes his way.

He lowered his window some more, said coldly, "Well? You want a ride, or what."

"What do you think?" Sassela shot back, rolled her window up sealed tight.

Ciam was looking between his knees, shaking his head. He glanced up, caught the end of her look. "Look, er, ma'am, I'm sorry—"

Flustered, unexpectedly chagrined at the impressions she knew he was forming, Sassela reached out— was it the gloom that made her touch his face? "No, no. This has nothing to do with you. Please. Let me say thank you for helping out." She heard herself sounding courteous, rushing. Mouthed a defensive smile, knowing it had formed awry.

He looked at her with clouded eyes, cocked his head mocking, impudent. "Sure, anytime. So look, I'm outta here." He pushed the door open, started out.

All at once, fearing he had listened to the rush in her voice and misinterpreted, Sassela couldn't let him leave. She grabbed his coat sleeve, tugged. His eyes so cool on her, it put her off. "Look—" She shut her eyes to help recall, and couldn't. "What is your name, again?"

"Ciam," he said flatly.

"Sorry, thanks. I mean, yu'know. Listen, Ciam, can we meet? Dinner? Coffee? In the coffee shop? So I can thank you better, and talk."

She couldn't account for her huge relief as his eyes

softened, his smile flashed. "Sure, I'd like that," he said. Then climbed out of the car into a blast of wind that tugged open his fat, fat coat and bared only a thin T-shirt underneath.

Sassela clambered over the gearshift to the still-warm passenger seat, and out into the gusting cold. Instantly chilled, she hugged her warm coat close, thought of his thin T-shirt, the warmth left inside the Bug. "Ciam," she said, "if you'd like, you can stay in the car until your bus comes." She proffered the keys.

Well swaddled in his coat again, he shook his head. "Nah, I'll hit the subway before too long, anyhow. Thanks all the same."

But in his eyes, a lance of grateful surprise had flicked toward the offered Bug. And at the same time, his strong smell, and the conditions outside, and the location, and other intangibles all tied together into sense. Sassela somehow knew that here was a proud young man at grievous ends, and needy of shelter. She said, "Listen, you say you work in the library?"

"Sure. Tuesday to Friday, evenings."

"Well, you can give me the keys on Tuesday. 'Cause certainly this," she nodded toward the car, "won't be thawed out before then."

His eyes, intent on her face, flickered at the keys in her hand and back to hold her eyes. "You mean it?" he asked, hand tentatively edging from the deep pocket.

"Sure," she said, as lightly as she could make it.

Very gently, he took the keys, murmured, "Thanks," and quickly looked away into the cold, crying wind.

Harry's impatient horn blasted again. Sassela said, "Take care," climbed the dirty snowbank to the Range Rover.

Except for a NutraSweet "Thank you" when she got in, silence was her strategy on the way home. When he started with, "So! Don't you think you should say something?" she only looked the slap to his face. When he began a soliloquy about his wounded manhood, she snorted derisively, once, and he shut up. The heater hummed quietly, filled the air with soothing warmth. Her mind turned to Ciam in the close Bug. She hoped he was warm.

Fed, showered, diary done, ready for bed, Sassela went to the bathroom for her last glass of water. Gazing blankly in the mirror, she got to comparing Ciam's rude man's scent with Harry's. Realized she didn't know Harry's real, actual smell; he normally smelled of whichever popular man's perfume she got him. She wondered if the harshness of Ciam's odors would remain in the Bug. And resisting a whisper that she was dwelling too much on it, admitted a tiny, kinky surge that she was eager to find out.

She got into bed without saying goodnight, curled up in a second comforter with her back to a cocooned Harry, and was soon fast asleep, without even remembering Greece.

Somewhat before seven the next morning, Harry rolled her way penitent, wanting to make up. He hugged close, and through the thick comforter she could feel his bobbing hard-on. Unexpectedly needful of solace, she whispered, "Hold everything"—their code words—slipped out of bed, went into the bathroom, reached into the medicine cabinet. Quickly returned and ready, she burrowed under the covers as welcoming of the wake-up call as he was eager.

On time, pepped and jaunty, she wore to work a fashion statement: rough dark-green woolen slacks, one of Harry's white dress shirts under a thick made-in-Ecuador patterned sweater, and laced-up pro-hikers. She was just into the school's door, stamping off snow from her boots, when it came to her that she would do the Greece trip after all, that she would not mention details to Harry. No reason, she just wouldn't.

The weekend turned milder, and so did Harry, seeming to make up for his cyclone of jealousy. Just his effort to address her pique compensated somewhat, made her soft to him, and she was graceful accepting. So Saturday evening, despite basketball on cable, he took her out to dinner, presented a gold bracelet, and, charming as contrite love, said he was sorrier than the fly that challenged stick-um. Afterward, they walked the Apple some. He bought her roasted chestnuts, then a red rose from a hooded street hustler. Chatted a deal from the guy, then gave him a dollar tip anyhow. The guy said, "Way to go, Blood," and clenched a fist high. Eyes agleam, Harry smiled at her proudly. Then they snuggled close in the taxi home, and later on was nice— playful to a buildup, then a quick, sweet crash.

Sunday was different, but as pleasant. In her weekend's final entry, she told her diary,

Seems another of our storms has blown over. Until next time.

4

Her first class broke late, so it was near six-thirty when Sassela got to the Returns desk. And her heart sank. Pencil like a bit across his mouth, both-hands busy, another young man sat there whipping his concentration with pen, protractor, and ruler. Sassela cleared her throat. The desk-jockey jerked his head up, queried with hoisted brow.

"I'm looking for Ciam Turrin," she explained.

Thoughtful to that, but unconvinced, he pointed the pen at her, growled, "Whooorryuu?"

She figured, said, "Sassela Jack."

Rightly answered, the desk-jockey nodded vigorous approval, turned his pen to probe the pigeonholes before him. He pinched out an envelope with pen and thumb, examined it, eyed her once more. "Gorraidee?" he challenged, passing fingers over his heart, where a large button reminded: LAZARUS DIED AGAIN!

Sassela searched her pocketbook, took out her college ID, spread it for him.

He glanced at it with knotted brow, passed over the

wrinkled envelope, and was back to his homework, curtly acknowledging her "Thank you" with a nod.

Sympathetic, but amused by his effort, Sassela said, "Hope you corral that A," two-noting the "A" sweetly.

Suddenly dynamic, the kid dropped the pen as he grabbed the pencil from his mouth, stared as if she'd just now magically appeared, and blurted dramatically, "It's do or die, Sister. I gotta do or die. But thanks anyway, and take it easy, okay?"

Wasn't what she expected, but accommodating the eyes she knew she'd caught, Sassela strolled off, adding extra hop to the natural roll of her hips.

She shook the envelope, felt the bulge, got the sound of keys. Stuck it in her pocketbook and, with a glance at her watch, headed for the coffee shop. She turned into its hallway, and who should be cockily strolling toward her but Ciam himself. A fleet quaking within caused her to misstep. Compensating, she stopped altogether, greeted, "Well, hello there! I, I just, er, picked up the keys," flushing self-consciously, tones falling lame.

He stopped, eyes bright, beautiful teeth glinting. She felt her hand grasped in damp warmth, not realizing she'd offered it.

He said, "Yeah, my shift was done. Thought you had forgotten, or—"

"No," she squeezed his hand, "I wouldn't have forgotten. I didn't. My class broke late, that's all." She realized she was holding his hand in the hallway, let go guiltily. "I was heading to the coffee shop. Want a java?"

Too close, he stood regarding her cheekily, said, "You mean a mocha java, or maybe a Jamaican Blue Mountain cappuccino, or even a Hawaiian Blend one-hit latte? You know plain java ain't that exotic a caffeine no more. You following?" He hooked his arm in hers, marched her down the hallway.

"So you're a coffee expert, too." She laughed delightedly, rousing her spirits to the bounce of his extravagant strides. Like Cinderella on the Prince's arm, she walked into the coffee shop feeling every eye on her. Felt proud to be in their envy. He led them to a table, and instantly a waitress was there.

Ciam accepted the prompt attention as if accustomed. "For the lady," he said grandly, "I have recommended the special roast latte." He looked a question at her. Sassela nodded acceptance. "And for the gentleman, we shall have a steamed milk, with a scrape of fresh-grated nutmeg."

The waitress, smiling familiarly, chorused this specialty along with him. Their friendliness prompting vague challenge, Sassela reached for her pocketbook. "I'll get it," she said to Ciam, and anyone else interested.

"Of course, your graciousness," said Ciam, grinning broadly.

They chatted while their orders quickly came. Then they sipped and chatted more. What of, Sassela was uncertain, as all passed in a wrinkle of smiling time: she flirtatious for being admired by such a fine young guy.

Too soon, he was the one reminding her of her second class. Then, as she scrambled up, grabbing her books and handbag, he casually offered, "If you need a hero to rescue your trusty Bug later on, I could be the fella."

Surprised but gratified, Sassela said, "Sure, and thanks."

"So I'll meet you in Main Hall after class, front door," he suggested.

"See you then," said Sassela and rushed from the coffee shop.

The class went by in a fugue. As soon as it ended, self-conscious about her hurry, Sassela started for the main exit.

"Sassela!"

She turned around to Cat's call, stopped.

"What's up, girlfriend? Didn't you say you'd wait here for me after class?"

Oops! went Sassela's memory; she'd clean forgotten. "No," she lied smoothly. "Thought we agreed on the front door. My mistake."

Cat looked at her skeptically. "Hmphh," she grunted, took an envelope from her briefcase, handed it over.

Barely glancing at it, Sassela put the fat envelope in her pocketbook. "Cut the dirty mind, Cat," she said. "I'm taking the tickets, not so? Thought we'd said here, that's all."

"Well—" said Cathy grudgingly, as they walked down the hallway to the main exit.

And there, lounging hunky against the doorpost, was Ciam. "Hi, folks," he greeted.

Cheeks burning, Sassela said, "Hi," and stopped beside him, ignoring the arch look, the one raised eyebrow Cathy cast her.

"Cathy, Ciam. Ciam, Cathy," Sassela said, crow mixed with crawl in her tone.

Ciam said, "Hi to you, too, Cathy," shedding on her a brilliant smile as he reached for Sassela's arm to lead them away. And, grasping him in sufficiently possessive manner, Sassela smirked at her girlfriend's gossip-greedy eyes, gave a careless wave as they strolled away.

The car was fine. The engine revved steadily after a lazy turn or two, and Sassela was ready to roll. Except for irresolution about Ciam: he was fun, but seriously. . . . She was just about deciding absolute negatives, when he said, "Well, so long, Cinnamon. I eat in the coffee shop as much as I can. Maybe we'll connect on a dinner, eh?"

To her surprise she answered, "Sure, the coffee shop. I owe you one. See you, Mr. Cinnamon yourself." She drove off smartly to hide her sophomoric fluster.

*   *   *

She made one stop at the greengrocer, then got home to Harry sitting at the blank table in the living room. She said, "Hi, hon," dropped her keys on the counter, stepped out of her shoes, then went over to buss his cheek as usual. As she leaned down, though, he pulled his face away, said haughtily, "No thanks, baby. Better keep 'em fresh for your mechanic." Then he picked up his keys and was out of the apartment with the door's slam.

Stock-still she stood. Shocked. Lips feeling empty where the kiss should've been, electric with missing. The process of his meaning soaking into her. The how it came about: him playing spy, surveilling her. Probably saw Ciam walk her to the car, arm-in-arm familiar, happily at banter. And, as if it were ever close to that, Harry had tied all together to create an infidelity. Like stone shattering, some core in her middle recognized his recent niceness as a ploy. All playacting, put on to confirm his scientific suspicions. And that she had been so disarmed now made her sick. Self-pity maybe, her wounded heart recoiled against the unfair strike. Tears welled silently, choking, bleeding away a precious, fragile balance between them.

Absently, aimlessly, she wandered to the bedroom, the bathroom, the kitchen. She stared about, seeing memories sunder, touching things as if finally. As if in grief for never again.

Later on, she wrote in her diary:

Dear Pal,

As the song says, Sing us a sad song of parting, one of broken ends. That's how it goes around here. Tonite a spider's web was stretched too far. Hindsight makes all flaws obvious right now. No

blame to cast tho. But no pretending, things were
on the downslide. So this, in truth, might be a
better way.

Bfn. Sss.

She slept through his coming in.

5

Still in his huff, next morning Harry rose early and was gone by seven, allowing Sassela to relax her pose of granite, oblivious to whatever he might do. With the space free of him, she dressed her usual smartly, and left for work, her mind absorbed with techniques to teach kids standard English.

After a fruitful day she went home tired, ordered pizza, watched a sitcom as she ate. Then she did her diary, not much to say, and by nine o'clock was settled into bed. Soon asleep, once more she knew not when Harry came in.

Again next morning, without a word, Harry was out of there early. Head under the covers, she pretended sleep while he dressed and left. She halfway welcomed his snotty attitude; she felt as aloof and adamant. Decision close-lurking in her mind, already Sassela was near indifferent to his antics. When he was gone, she did as usual, left the house in sober spirits. Indeed, a small anticipation tickled: at the college this evening, during class break, she intended to visit the coffee shop.

As she knew he'd be, Ciam was there. She offered to spring for dinner.

He said, "Sure," and they ate, although she hardly noticed the fare, her bracing diet more of swallowing his flattery, absorbing his glow, feeling the focus of attention, and triumphant, and beautiful as she couldn't remember when. She passed on her second class, and they chatted away into evening—he doing most of the talking.

". . . ten points a term, budget depending. Majoring in chem and bio. From the Western Scientific Method point of view, that is. Not, for example, the native bushman in the heart of the Amazon perspective, if yu'know what I mean."

Sidestepping that tangled trail, she asked, "Intending medicine?" While her other, more serious self was wondering where he lived, if he worked somewhere else, who he was seeing.

". . . Me. I just couldn't stand it. I'll get sick of sick people. Nah. I just studying to know more, and too, because it easier than hard work—"

"Is that a West Indian philosophy?"

"Nah, it's personal, mine. But let me clear up one thing first. Is just not kosher to say 'West Indian' and 'West Indies,' and so on. The right name is 'Caribbean.' 'West Indies' was from the outset a mistake. A mistake made by a confused sailorman lost out he desperate way. So I say abandon it. Abandon it, together with all them other European mistakes—"

Punctuating with fleet smiles to full-lipped pout, he prattled on, his mobile mouth expressive of unsayable meanings.

"What sign are you?" she asked.

"Oh! A Gemini." He laughed. "Although with me,

that don't really matter. My destiny is cast by different gods, with different dice . . ."

His certainty amused her.

". . . sign are you?" he was asking.

"I'm Gemini, too," with broad, bold smile she lied. She didn't have the gumption to ask his age; figured from his verbal bio twenty-one, twenty-two. "So, are you on campus?" she changed the subject.

And right away realized she had poked a fragile boundary, as ever so slightly, his manner cooled, his smile dimmed. "Most of the time. But the old people say, 'You sleep in the bed you make, wherever that might be,'" he answered. Then eyeing her meaningfully, he asked, "That guy Harry, the other night. Your husband?"

"Nah," she calmly disinformed, "close friend."

"Great!" he said, smile powering up once more.

And despite her strangled conscience, Sassela again basked in the glow of his regard.

They got along; time slipped away, swift as day-dreams, ending as it had to. She held his eye, said, "I had a great time—" giving pause to let him ask:

"Some other time? I mean if you could get away, and all—?"

"It'll be a treat," she said, in tones suggesting more than ordinary availability.

Complications unaddressed, Sassela agreed to a rerun the next Tuesday, last school day before vacation.

The following week she arrived on time, got a table and a menu, and waited through an anxious decaf. All in vain, though. He never showed.

Since Harry's accusation, they had shared maybe a dozen sentences. Then a merciful break: Harry was invited to his brother's for the holidays. It made Sassela's intention to hibernate during the break easy, and she spent the time rearranging cupboards and closets, separating, replacing, and labeling everything "Harry's" and "Mine." Then, with a "Harry" label prominent on the pillow, she set up the futon in the spare bedroom. As a bed, it was narrow, thin, and, she hoped for him, temporary. It was her apartment, after all, and all she wanted was that he got the hint. She wished to be alone.

Cowardly, but this way of saying it to him was easier for her. Because, inexplicably, despite the fact that *he* was the incompetent at managing their life together, it seemed as though an odd-minded other self within her assumed guilt about this, and wheedled her common sense to excuse and accommodate his haplessness, as compensation, as penance. But this latest desertion— based on such an unjust assumption—was the limit. It provided Sassela distance to think, read her diary, compound his affronts; and like a lump in the lower guts of all her accounting she found one turgid constant: that Harry had grown lazy at appreciating her. That he could abandon her so cruelly rated his report card poor in the extreme.

Christmas week she turned off the phone's ringer, put the answering machine to work, then for the next two weeks went incommunicado. Aimless as a ship in a bottle, she did nothing in particular.

Without picking up she listened to Harry's Christmas message, all bluff and false-sounding cheer, then repeated it only to ascertain his intended return date. She remembered to call her father on his birthday, though, and swore to herself not to mention Harry. She saluted Pa with the usual birthday cheer: "Congrats, Pa, on getting to the best age there is!" Chatted a bit.

Off from a tangent, he asked, "That's a frog I'm a-hearing in your mind?" Their private code since she was in pigtails for, Was there something she wanted to talk about?

"Nah, just moods," Sassela said. It was his birthday, after all.

Wasn't long he got to updating her on family affairs. Pa was soft to anyone who could claim bloodline, but solidarity with immediate family quickened his heart— immediate as in his four brothers and three sisters, and their brood of two dozen plus offspring, each and every one afflicted with a devotedness to visiting.

Pa had moved up north with a salable skill, and opened up the first bakery on his block. Poor or not, people afforded themselves fresh bread and pastry, especially from as generous a merchant as Pa was. Custom was so steady, in short time he had bought himself the brownstone he rented space from—

A commotion on Pa's end of the phone. A thud, then silence. Half-laughing, Pa returned, explained, "Red Cyril and his gang of six, they want to take me bowling. More like kidnap, I say. Big man like that trying to snatch away the phone and hang it up. But be that as it may, sweetheart, still have to go."

"Sure, Pa. And take care, you hear."

"Sure you okay, girl?"

"Sure, Pa. I'm fine. Till next time. Say hi to them for me. Love you, Pa," said Sassela. She returned the phone to its cradle, sighed, "You are the best, Pa."

And meant it profoundly. She could count on him being there, but as she preferred, Pa had always left her to pull her own reins, clean her own spoil. He never bothered her about holiday visiting; seemed to admire her solitary bent so different from his own. Maybe he understood her attitude. Her family was strong and varied. She loved them well enough. It was just that most times she couldn't stand being around them.

Only child that she was, Sassela could hardly remember an unshared room in their three-storied brownstone. With a partitioned basement and two floors—the upper a railcar of three large bedrooms and a guest room, downstairs a kitchen, dining and living room—with all that, you'd think it would have been big enough. But it wasn't. Except for one vast, cobwebby basement space where stored stuff filled creepy nooks with looming flashlight shadows, there was never privacy. This became Sassela's favorite place, where she hid out to find herself.

Were there any system to Pa's generosity, the house might've been roomy. But it was completely arbitrary when whosoever would show up. The one certainty being that, once they could claim family ties, Pa would put them up.

And, from both sides, there were any number of blood relatives at the ready. In Pa's clan each of his brothers had at least three children. One had eight, another five. Pa's sisters bore three kids apiece. Sassela's mother had just one brother but three sisters. They were better off, of tonier class. Like proper folks, each had two offspring, hardly visited, and hardly stayed if they did. Sassela liked their style.

Then there were those far-reaching claims for which Pa was just a softy. Standing quietly behind him, Mams'd listen to them and roll private eyes to heaven, then be courteous as the folks trooped in. So forever, tons of people would be dropping by, staying, just plain mooching around. But Pa remained a man believed in bloodlines. His boast: He'd never close his door on a relative.

Sassela looked around at her neat, high-ceilinged apartment, crisply lit by the bright day outside broad, uncurtained windows. She sighed, heart gladdened by her room, her well-suiting space. She knew a tiny tremble of anticipation at the thought of Harry permanently gone, of freedom from his intrusion, of reclaiming herself alone.

6

Four days into the new year, Cathy left a message: She wondered if Sassela would consider having the limo pick her up second. She wanted to spare Paul the chore of taking her to the airport.

Sassela called back and played straight woman while, obviously for other ears a-listening, Cathy spoke long and enthusiastically of their anticipated school excursion to sunny, exotic Greece. "Eleven more days we'll be soaking up fifteen of Mr. Celsius's degrees! Can you believe? It's better than any shuttle countdown," she crowed with excited duplicity.

Which infected and aroused Sassela from her downtime, reminded that she, too, had a trick up her sleeve, and that there was serious shopping to do: here in the middle of a New York winter, she needed sunshine supplies. For the skin, unguents and suntan lotion with high numbers; for the bod, loose, light garments—sundresses, cotton pants, walking shorts, slip-on sandals, T-shirts, a sarong skirt with matching tank top; then towels and flip-flops for the beach; not to forget protection for the hair, and reading materials for the sunny, lazy afternoons under a beach umbrella . . .

The list lengthened fancifully as her mood lightened.

By nine o'clock Wednesday evening, Sassela had everything set and ready. The Bug was safe in her neighbor's vacant parking spot in the building's underground garage. Her mailbox key was with the super. Her house was in order, with every plant optimally watered and her well-planned suitcase sensibly packed. She called the car service, confirmed for 5 P.M. tomorrow. Ten o'clock she was in bed as usual—although it took a while before she fell asleep.

Thursday dawned and ticked routinely along until nearing three-thirty when, all of a sudden, time slowed down to a mudflow of anxiety as Sassela developed a sweaty premonition that Harry would show up prematurely. Before she got away, he would appear and spew ridicule on every label, note, and gesture of her left messages. Unable to sit with the tension of the thought, she paced the apartment, mangling many nerves.

Her skittish mind had no truck with facts: like commonsense information of Harry's phone message saying he'd return on the nineteenth, meaning she was free by three whole days. What her anxiety recalled were Harry's capabilities—his probables for returning early: like he might've felt sorry and missed her (unlikely); or he was lonely for some important basketball game on TV; or he needed certain textbooks to prepare for the next semester. The possibilities kept her twitchy. A hundred times she peered at the hallway through the door's peephole, and checked the plane tickets in her pocketbook, then worked the peephole again. At four-thirty sharp, she called to remind the car service.

"We downstairs in ten minutes, señora," a heavy Latino accent assured.

Sassela hung up the phone, once again checked the hallway through the peephole, made another skittish survey around her rooms.

The intercom buzzed, making her jump. "Taxi down here for you, ma'am," said the doorman. Sounded like Louis.

Sassela ran down a rapid final checklist: passport, tickets, traveler's checks, credit cards, suitcase. Then she took a deep breath, worked the peephole again before hoisting the suitcase. Slowly, she opened the door, sneaked out, clacked each lock solidly.

She pressed the button, waited for the elevator with breathy trepidation, and when it came, absolutely expected him to emerge. But it was empty, and took her safely down.

The driver, chatting with Louis while he'd waited, took her suitcase, bore it to the trunk. He opened the door for her. "Which airline?" he asked.

Sassela told him, slipped into her rented sanctuary. And only as the car drove off could she relax, away from her spoiling premonitions, rejoicing that her intentions would prevail: that Harry would get home and be forced to confront her unmistakable messages.

After all her tension, the rush-hour drive to Kennedy was a toast to leather-smelling luxury.

7

An eight-hour flight to Frankfurt with a one-hour stopover before going on to Mineros. Sassela welcomed her left-side window seat just aft of the wing. In this cozy spot, intending to write Harry, she would use the time well. She turned from staring at departure activities outside to watch a woman approach down the aisle. Fair-skinned white, late forties, vigorous, and barely on the negative side of portly, she was peering at seat numbers, until she stopped and confirmed that the one on her boarding pass corresponded with the aisle seat of Sassela's row. Here, with a final sigh, she handily lifted an expensive leather shoulder bag up into the overhead bin, snapped that shut, sat down.

Sassela returned to gazing out the porthole. The woman, though, had made an impression: straight-shouldered she sat, as if modeling her stylishly short salt-and-pepper hair, every strand perfectly placed. Her unwrinkled neck poised just so in a cream rayon shirt, a fresh red carnation in the top buttonhole. Even the seat belt, by not leaving creases across her light-gray wool skirt, seemed trying for elegance. Sassela figured her a businesswoman, perhaps high-level management on a routine perk.

After a while Sassela realized that, despite her regal manner, the well-dressed woman had turned and was steadily regarding her. Just as Sassela faced her, her seatmate low-voiced a pointed, unsmiling, "Yo!" Somehow the deep matching creases firmly downside her narrow nose contrived the street jargon into a barbed challenge.

Startled and abashed, Sassela shifted her look else-where and, as if the greeting never happened, busied herself at adjusting comfortably in her seat. Although she couldn't resist sneaking a sideways glance at her suddenly peculiar companion.

The plane jerked, recalled her attention outside: yes, they were backing from the terminal, heading for the runway. So at last! Here she was, taking off. The fact of it commanded: What from? What for, and why? Though she felt like an escapee, she couldn't properly define her prison. This found vacation, she mused, offered more than adventure. It was about making space; about being alone to consider her life at her own pace; about finding mental room to swing and swirl her thoughts, and let them spin to whatever rhythms. And if she were to be unbalanced by alone-ness, then she didn't mind falling and bawling on the floor before she rose back up strengthened by the tem-porary grovel. Her victory'd be that she had conquered her demons by herself, without the teetering shoulder of her not-so-stalwart helpmeet and too-constant com-panion: Harrod Marron, the major live-in threat to her independence. Harry— But no! She must avoid think-ing about him. Part purpose and point of this trip was just that: as a habit of thought, to cut him out alto-gether.

*   *   *

Moist-palmed apprehension of liftoff had been sucked into the air-conditioning. The canned music was receding in the rising hum of passenger conversation. In the aisle seat, the woman undid her seat belt and slipped over into the vacant center spot. Sassela's heart sank—she'd been thanking Luck for the buffer of space between them.

The woman asked, "First time over the big A?" Her pleasant, husky voice continued before Sassela could answer: "Don't mind telling it's mine. And don't mind telling I'm a trifle nervous about planes. I say boats or trains anytime. I do. Or walk, even. Nothing's wrong with walking. It won't make you nervous. Good for the buns." She chuckled lightly, confident sound belying her suggestion of anxiety.

Compelled into camaraderie, Sassela lied, "I can assure you one thing, not to worry about air travel. I do this every spring and it's never hurt me yet. Plus, according to statistics, compared to cars and stray-shot city bullets, chances up here are better than a million to one."

"Well, even if it's the worst, it's quicker, I'll give you that. A final thrill and outahere. A final comedown?" She eyed Sassela with untoward familiarity. "Though as I see it, may as well try stuff now 'fore I'm too old to ever summon up the gumption." Her airy chuckle again. "Call me Meeri, as in Janet Meeri Panney," she added, "from Kansas, and you?"

And easy as that, although wanting escape into aloneness, Sassela found herself stewarded into travel conversation. "Sassela Jack," she answered, "from Harlem. This spring I'm doing graduate work in Greece on changing, modernizing agricultural systems." She lied automatically, a habit she'd developed of presenting herself differently to strangers, nosy or not. A safe game—nothing to do with reality, it was a life created spontaneously from conversational context; she might be anyone. She hardly ever told the precious truth: that she enjoyed teaching fourth grade, felt she was making a positive difference. This life of hers was private business. Intimate.

"Which school?" her seatmate wanted to know.

"Columbia. I have a sociology scholarship. Y'know, qualified, minority, female."

"Good for you! Very good," exclaimed the woman. "Nice to see young people grab opportunity. Myself? I guess you can say I'm self-employed. More unemployed artist really, sculptress. Soft metals and hardwood. Some sandstone, too—it's subtler, closer to flesh. I do the human form. Some semi-erotic. Actually, most. Try to make 'em come alive. At it now fifteen-plus years."

"You live off it?"

"Oh, I manage. Now I do. At the beginning I was a housewife, and my husband supported a hobby, then came his passing, and this and that, and in the meantime my hobby became my art, and then his insurance payments supported that. You know how it goes. The usual woman's story. Raised three children through to college, careers. Our second boy found work as a plumber. The first and his sister are academics. Poor and proud. Yup! Married for twenty-one years, then the man, as they say, rolled on home and left me alone. And, bless his prudent soul, free of financial worry. So now I'm artist enough to live off my work. And more important, enough to try getting away once or twice a year, at least. Best thing I ever do. With nothing to keep me home, travel could be most irresponsibly exciting. Don't you think so?"

"Well, it does get me out of the family rut," said Sassela, composing her impromptu persona to sharing the plaints of Women's Burdens.

Hoarse voice lowered confidentially, the woman responded, "That's the least of it, girl. Lemme tell you, nothing's recharged my life so. Yu'see, I got married at eighteen, moved to backwoods country and within five years I'd borne three children, and bless 'em that they all survived. But all my life, before my Donny passed, I'd only had two, maybe three sexual episodes. And that's counting one attempted rape—an uncle. After Donny went that way, raising the children kept me busy. Well, at last they've flown the coop, and I'm independent of them, and what I have is my art and my traveling life, and believe me, girl, my energies and sexual statistics've roundabout changed. It's spring-alive time again. The men are biding out there, their sap rising, and I'm running for them readier than any teenage tart. Spring sap running, I call it. Heh heh heh!" she chortled like a dirty old man.

"'Sthat so!" Sassela exclaimed, taken aback at the woman's salacious turn. Her mind shied away as the woman's voice droned on in cadence with the faint roar of the rushing jets outside. What was she supposed to say? she wondered uncomfortably. Her seatmate's revelations didn't seem to need response, though.

Refocusing, Sassela listened in to hear a bit of daring sexual encounter with a train conductor: ". . . twenty-six, even twenty-three, he might've been— still had pimples—and he didn't want to leave, placed a sign on the compartment door, I think, and we weren't ever disturbed. Kept calling out, 'Lady, oh lady, this is so good.' Had to keep my hands over his mouth, I'll tell you. That alone made it good for me . . ."

Sassela hedged from the older woman's confidential eyes, avoiding their trap, let her glance range about the cabin. Near left a wrist raised to smother a yawn revealed a watch: six and a half hours to the stopover at Frankfurt before continuing on to Greece—possibly six and a half hours of this sex talk. Sassela sighed morosely at the prospect, and tuned in to the woman for a moment.

"—and who should appear at the cottage door out of the rain but this blind guy with his Seeing Eye dog. Of course I welcomed them in. The mood I was in, who wouldn't? That dog was one of the smartest—"

Sassela shivered as suddenly an image flared out of her memory: an old yellow hound dog, El Gringo, with his rheumy eyes and the sly surety he could outsmart people.

Since he was an excellent watchdog, Aunt May let him rule the yard. He kept chickens out of the flower gardens front and side of the house, and nothing made him happier than to rush a bold pullet and grab her in his slavering jaws, scaring her to the brink as she squawked and screeched to any scrambled safety at hand, since he wouldn't dare actually hurt one. Although Aunt May swore that once he had scared a fat, old hen to sudden death by heart attack.

The very first moment they met, he and Sassela didn't hit it off. She'd just jumped out of the cramped car and, rubbing her eyes from tiredness and wonder, was meandering through a garden bursting with brilliant roses and pastel blue hyacinths and sprigs of tulips beginning to sprout into combinations of reds and salmons and yellows. Aunt May came down from the porch and, three steps to Sassela, stopped and patted her lap and opened her arms and smiled broad. "Come here, Sass. Look how big you're growing."

But guess what! Here comes Mr. El Gringo bounding in and stumbling up everything with his big slimy tongue lolling about, throwing his heavy hairy paws all over Sassela. Frightening her and dirtying her, and making her have to scream and scrunch down right there on the ground, looking like a crybaby city girl.

That had set the stage for them, Sassela only despising him more as she discovered what a lazy bully he was. And it would have pleased her no end if she ever could beat him up. But he was such a big dog. She never could forget how, when he'd pawed her that first time, his feet were up on her shoulders and his sloppy toothy grin was slurping right in her face. And comfortably. So Sassela never did pay back El Gringo; neither did she admit being afraid of him.

Evenings when the men went hunting, down among the other dogs El Gringo'd be frisky and howling as if anxious and anticipating getting on with chase and excitement. But off he'd tug his handler—usually some novice the hunters didn't want along—tug him into the dark evening forest, promising everything. Half hour wouldn't pass, though, before El Gringo'd lope into the yard, or those left at home would hear his panting pass the window as he headed to his favorite night spot in the straw under the chicken coop.

With him Sass kept her distance. Whenever he'd quiet up and set his cold nose prodding and probing her, she'd cuff him away, always trying for extra *oomph!* in the blow. But it was short-shrift satisfaction. For although El Gringo'd slink off with head hung and wet eyes fallen falsely humble, he never went without a growl, a grumbled threat that vibrated long afterward like a tremble in her heartbeats.

Then came a perfect Saturday, clear, dry, warm, with a wavery breeze all day. The air rustled, alive with shed leaves afloat, and milkweed, and dandelions, and a multitude of colorful butterflies. Gave Sassela a yen to catch a large golden one leisurely flapping the air as if ready to drop out. So slowly flopping, several tries she made to clap hands around it. Misses so close, they changed her tactics, directed her inside searching for a net.

Aunt May's everyday cloth shopping bag presented

itself. Then the jumbo swizzle stick volunteered as handle. And shortly thereafter, Sassela emerged from the kitchen somewhat better equipped to conquer golden butterflies. And, oh! was it ever a great contesting! These fat golden prizes had tricks up their wings. Their slothful manner was all fake, deception to lull the opponent, to provide a surprise burst of tactics. As when a trajectory seemed set and her net well cast exactly where one should be, how it just dropped straight down and eluded that try. And then it'd fly suddenly high, juking on slack breeze, dancing as if following steps boxed on an elaborate air plan it alone could read.

Trying to follow that evasive dance soon led Sassela into the brush, then into a stumbling log that felled her facedown in the scratchy scrub, inflicting a stinging cut and a quarter-sized bruise just below her left knee.

She hopped up quickly, anxiously searching around. Then, finding no witness, allowed brief tears as she examined the raw flesh and, with gentle fingernails, picked from the wound bits of half-rotted bark and scraped away the seeping, beading blood. Then with many sniffles and a pronounced limp, she set off for home.

A limp that disappeared once in sight of the house, and that returned as, without adult attention, she achieved the safety of the workshed. She sat on the nail bin to properly indulge in her misery; and while she was inspecting her wounds, who should slouch into the shed, tail between his legs and looking mournful as could be?

Head bowed, nose close to the ground, he slunk over and sniffed the bruise, glancing at Sassela with wet, begging eyes. A tentative, sympathetic sniff, with surprising tenderness. Then he licked the bruise, too keen for permission, his long wet tongue also tender, and so unexpectedly gentle that Sassela resisted pulling away.

Again he licked, and again Sassela let him, despite a momentary qualm as the dog settled down more comfortably on his haunches, as if readying for a good long meal. Then he became absorbed with the bruise, licking the blood away, cleaning it, his slurping tongue illicit and soothing. And gradually a strange feeling began creeping over her—an electric tickle that crawled and crinkled the skin all the way up her thighs even to her crotch, which strangeness so powerfully alarmed her, she knew right away she should stop it.

Except that El Gringo was too into his pleasure, as fresh red kept trickling from the wound, and when she tried to pull her knee away he gave a low menacing growl. And right away the latent fear she always felt for him bubbled up, and she kept her foot perfectly still as he licked; awaiting the bloody droplets as they slowly sprang forth, lapping them up with his rough tongue, its raspiness now growing slightly painful, and whatever pleasure she had felt was absolutely gone. She couldn't look away from the dog, just tried to maintain an accommodating stillness while she stared, chicken at a snake, as El Gringo's long, pink tongue flicked and slid and folded up her blood's flow into his maw.

And, well trapped between sharp fear and panicking guilt, there was nothing she could do but let him. She was at a total loss for a way out of the contretemps until came Aunt May's call: "Sassela? Are you about, child?"

At which El Gringo started guiltily and stopped his assault; upon which she promptly answered, "I'm in the workshed, Auntie."

And a minute later, as the big yellow dog slunk out of the shed, Aunt May entered with wrinkled nose, asking suspiciously, "What you doing holed up in here with that smelly dog?"

"Just picking his fleas, Auntie, and petting him," she lied, puzzled as she did.

8

Something! She awoke from a doze as, three, four rows up the aisle, some young men were cutting up boisterously. A dozen or so college students—a sports team, maybe, judging from their logoed clothes and spendthrift energy. His back to her, one stood up, began treating the cabin to his rendition of the hostess's emergency procedures presentation.

A squareness about the stance, a cast to his shoulders hooked her attention. And slowly, reluctantly, Sassela recognized Ciam—Ciam Turrin—who'd helped dig her Bug out of the snowbank, and with whom, a few weeks ago, she was supposed to have dinner. Their first meeting came to mind: his smile up close, the rush in her heart he'd caused. She squirmed as she recalled, too, how he'd stood her up.

Funny mimic now, as someone threw him the flight attendant's demonstration kit, and making slapstick of each instruction, he had the cabin rollicking. Tall in loose, black jeans, mischievous of eye, he deadpanned the routine speech in a ridiculous falsetto, stopping off and on to crack his terrific grin. Uncomfortably, Sassela wondered if he had noticed her.

His chums and he were having a hilarious time, until the flight attendant—herself laughing—ended the entertainment by herding him into his seat. A minute again, though, and he was up—pushed by the others— to take a final bow. As a few derisive cheers promptly set him back down, Sassela caught his shiny eyes beaming at her. Despite herself, she smiled easily.

He clutched at his heart, winked at her, and collapsed on his seat in bogus faint. Sassela felt herself flush like a silly schoolgirl.

A moment later, twisting round and catching her eyes, he was up again, coming down the aisle, to lean across her seatmate and bend close to her ear, loudly stage-whispering, "When shall we be alone, my Snowed-in Queen Sassela?"

Sassela blushed deeply. "Hi, helpful stranger," she said.

"You forgot my name, didn't you?" he said with mock severity. "And, ma'am, you won't be told again."

"No, I didn't, Mr. Ciam Turrin," she said.

He grabbed his heart, fell to his knees. "To be so honored. Mea culpa. I am your dog."

To her utter embarrassment, he crawled the four rows back to his seat. Such a schoolboy—

". . . lapping you, huh?" she heard only this ending of the seatmate's suggestion.

"'Scuse me?" said Sassela.

"Well, yu'know, I see him and dreams of tropic sun and chocolate warmth begin lapping at my mind. And other points south, I'll admit in a minute. Company like him I wouldn't mind at all. He's all of one handsome promise, he is," said the woman, leering again.

A nice recovery, though not at all what Sassela had halfway heard first time. The lady, slick and slippery, seemed talking two-ways at her. Sassela set to put it to her right then and there. "Lady," she began, which only called to mind the woman's previously related episode about the praise-mongering train conductor, and intimidated her response into a less committal, "Lady, for your age, you're something else. But right now, I think I've got to stretch my legs a bit."

"And I pretty well know where you're aiming them," said the woman, casting eyes in the direction of her guy up front with the beautiful smile.

"No, ma'am. It's not like that," protested Sassela, fed up with the vice-track-minded older woman. She rose clasping her pocketbook, and pointedly walked to the bathroom at the rear of the plane.

An airline after Sassela's most prudent of pockets, everything came with the ticket's price: earphones, dinner, wine, and quite comfortable seats. Back in hers, Sassela decided to use the earphones for protection against the woman's persistently lewd conversation. But just as she'd plugged her ears into the piped stereo fare, dinner service began; which sort of licensed chat, which the woman began.

"Listen, Sassela. Don't judge me by my cover, okay? I'm not here trying to offend you. I'm just passing time, you know, eight hours up here in the air, nearer to God than I want to be. I've gotta distract myself from all this dangerous living. But you're young. You've got reason to be careful, conservative. When to leap, when to lie. You know, female canny. You have a lot of life to you. You got looks, probably a partner, maybe child or children. But don't tell me your business, I'll tell you mine. I'm free, you see. Don't have anything, anymore, to worry about. I've done the female thing, paid my dues completely. Raised my children. Made my career. Nurtured my husband till dead and gone. And now I'm done with all that. Now however I choose, my life's mine alone to mind. And that's all the point I want to make. To my thinking, I've earned my freedom to use my time anyhow. I hope I'm not offending you, but do you appreciate my point?"

"Well, sort of, I hear you, er . . ." Sassela searched for the woman's name without success. "And really, I don't hold any gripe about how you choose to use your life. And I don't want you to think I'm offended by what you were saying. But, well, it's just that I'm kinda embarrassed talking stuff like that. Always was. Sex to me is sort of private, personal, yu'know? My early girlfriends called me Princess Prim of Prudisha." Sassela laughed. Long time she hadn't thought of the nickname. "Maybe I'm just more old-fashioned than you," she finished.

"Well, I like you, child. I mean, I'm like you, too. Generally, I guess, my sex life is private and personal. For that matter, almost everything I do. We don't have any argument there."

"But how can you talk about it so boldly? And to a stranger?"

"Talking about it doesn't make it less private. I'm still a stranger to you. You don't know me. We met on this plane, and probably we're never going to meet again. So, you're the best person I can talk to if I want to share my private business. See my thinking?"

The logic was reasonable. "Guess so," admitted Sassela.

"Listen to Meeri. I'll tell you something. Your age, I had just that same manner. But now I realize everybody does the nasty. It's natural. Nothing illicit about it. I say anything so naturally available that can make tired blood run hot, well, it must be good for you. And there's no reason for people to hide and sneak and create this shy attitude. That's what I realized as I got freedom, got my version of womanhood. That's why I can talk so plain to you."

"Well, I guess you're right. But I can't help it, Meeri. I mean, you're a stranger to me, and talking stuff I'd close my bedroom door to read. Not that I might not think it. Maybe thinking it is okay, while talking it out so bold is what's illicit, huh?"

"Talk can't ever be illicit. Action perhaps, but not thoughts and not speaking out. To my thinking, speech gives dreams living color."

Struck by the thought, Sassela glanced sharply at Meeri, and found the intent face molding an amicable smile.

As she had planned, Sassela waited for the movie to come on, the cabin to fall into after-dinner drowsiness. Then she flicked on the overhead light, began writing the letter.

> *Dear Harry,*
> *I know this is a hell of a time to tell you this, you just coming back home and all, but when I return from this trip I don't want you to be in my apartment. I better say it clearly, plainly. I mean we will not be together anymore. Neither living together nor being together, I mean. We can't make it. I know for sure I can't. For the last three or four months, all we've been having for excitement is arguments. We've hardly gone out for dinner, or to a movie, or even to the goddamn grocery store for godsake—*

Aware that she was losing it, straying from her plan to filter out anger, Sassela stopped writing. She closed her eyes, leaned back in the seat. It occurred to her that tourist-class travel, like live-in relationships, was a trap of compromise, and always the victim was you. It had to do with trying to buy luxury one couldn't afford, and the other with security craved too much to be enjoyed.

Too tired for philosophy, she found the right button, depressed it to incline the seat backward, and stretched her tight neck, loosened the tension some. Immediately, though, a recent argument rushed to recall: Eight-thirty a windy, bitter night, she had returned from school to find him watching TV, crunching potato chips, drinking stout. First thing out of his mouth: "What's for dinner?" then braying "Ha-ha-ha, just joking" like a jackass. He in his dressing gown, the new one she'd got him for his birthday because of a growing disgust at the sight of his favorite threadbare other. Then when, with hands dry and burning from cold gloves, she'd got to the kitchen, all that was left of his dinner was washed pots and pans drip-drying in their racks beside the sink. Not a scrap. Not even a cup of warm coffee left for her.

So she went and turned off the TV, snatched away his potato chips, crushed them in their crispy bag and stuffed it all in the garbage can. She slammed into the bathroom and took a hot hour-long shower. Afterward they went at it.

Though, as usual, it was no win, no decision. Except she abandoning her broad bed to sleep uncomfortably on the couch.

This memory now prompted composition of her letter's next line:

Harry,
*   I am tired of lying down to sleep in tears*
and anger and frustration and feeling denied
and not wanting to touch you. This is not how
companionship should be. This is a road to
depression and a sad senior citizenship. And I
want to be happy, especially when growing old.

You will probably be surprised by the foreign stamps and so on. Well, don't get the feeling that I've sneaked off. You know that I hate confrontations, and with you, I cannot ever get to say what I'm thinking. You out-talk and out-think me, Harry. But you're cruel. You're clever with words. You may know ideas. As you always say, you're a natural-born teacher, and you practice with swift, clever minds every day. I can't compare and contest with you. I can't talk fast enough to let you know, in your terms, how I feel helpless and irrelevant in our relationship. So this is my way, my action. Remember how you say ideas are verbs in motion. Well, when I get off this plane, I'm going to post this letter, and that's how I'm telling you I'm making my moves.

I never wished or wanted it to end this way. I still feel for you. But right now, I don't feel I'm loving me enough. Maybe I'm part of your life, but affection trumped up by jealousy is not my scene. I don't feel comfortable with the role. I guess I feel taken for granted, arranged there like a fish in your bowl, dependent on your fancy, subject to your possessive whims. Not to say that I'm blaming you for any or all this, probably it's my fault. Isn't that usually the case? But with you crowding my space, I'll never find out for certain. And I want to. I want to find out a lot about myself. At least more than the cliché of thirty-eight anxious unhappy years restless to know I don't know what.

But as usual, I'm rambling. See how it's as you say, I can't keep my mind on a matter. So, I'll stop now.

So long, Harry.

P.S. I took your good shirts to the laundry, and your wool pants, too. The ticket's under the bread-pan. Take it with you.

Good-bye.

P.P.S. I'll be back on the eighth of February, and I don't expect to meet you. Put my keys in the mailbox. Thanks. Sassela.

Sassela imagined his confusion finding this letter in the mailbox, reading it and feeling betrayed, then moping endlessly without eating. For he was self-indulgent even to punishment. But she also knew that he'd get past it, survive. Harry had that talent as well. So with a resolute sigh, she sealed and addressed the letter.

Just two hours to go, the movie was done; Meeri was asleep and, as Sassela privately assessed from the smirk to her slightly parted lips, most likely dreaming of daring sexual encounters.

She had to admit, though, that a nap was a good idea. She shoved her seat back to its limit, settled herself to best comfort. Not too long she was dozing. . . .

. . . a low-slung rakish car, silver as light, flashing down an endless roadway . . . an owl sweeps swift, snatches her bonnet, laughing hoo-hoo wisps away . . . Sassela way ahead of the pack, and track is rolling away under her flying feet, smiling easy she's wearing Zy's light-as-feather spikes! . . .

She woke with a start. Zy! She hadn't thought of her cousin for years. But, a glance at her travel companion, she could see why, now. Looking back on it, her first real seducer had been her cousin Zy. First cousin, her aunt's youngest son—mother's side—he did it without trying, probably never knew. Country simple from Virginia, he only spent summers in the Apple. But he was a lover, direct and charming, and girls gobbled up his chat like gumbo. At eleven, for her he was the prince of masculinity. His life was a poem. He trod above the common ground. Brilliant suns rose with his smile. He ran high school track, and two years straight for the annual Harlem track competition he let her carry his spikes. She'd have done anything for him, dry his feet with her mane of black hair. For just like in the poetry in which she lost herself, the totality of her being belonged to him.

A ripe tomato flung against a wall, this illicit, unspoken first love crushed her. She could not cope, was overwhelmed. Innocence was a lot of it, ignorance some more. Not to mention the perceived competition. Case in point that first summer: he was seventeen or so, said easily that she was cute. He was interning at a newspaper, and through some hookup brought her M&Ms every evening. "You're my M&M, sweet chocolate," he'd say, hugging and hoisting her up tall as he was as he nuzzled her neck, and tickled and thrilled her to the very limit of her composure.

And later, or even next day, touching herself in the cool, private darkness of the basement, she'd remember the swelling thrills he set off, and redeem them for the warm, delicious confusion they powered.

Her feelings had focused somewhat after Zy came early from work one midafternoon, bringing a heavyset girlfriend with him. Sassela was in the kitchen when Zy burst in through the backyard door pulling the half-resisting girl by a hand. Zy was bright-eyed, intense as Sassela hadn't seen him before. No M&Ms, no nuzzling. Grinning for no reason, he low-voiced of Sassela, "Uncle Sam's home?"

Piqued, but shy in front of the girl she intuitively knew was responsible for Zy's slight, Sassela mumbled, "Uh-uhh."

"That's good, Sass," said Zy, too happily. "Now, go along and play, huh. I have to show Tina something upstairs."

He patted her shoulder, same time directing her toward the door they'd just come through, all the while grinning wild as if they'd made a joke together. And by the time Sassela was turning the doorknob, Zy had pushed the girl past him and, with his hands familiar on her heavy rump, was guiding her up the stairs.

No fool, it wasn't long before Sassela crept up the stairs after them. Crouched in the hallway outside the guest room, she could hear their noises. Murmurings and scuffings and moans and creaks and sighs and grunts—all suppressed and sounding surrendered to some grand excitement.

Sassela was transfixed at listening, wanting more. Ridden by the beguiling excitement of suggestion, she wanted to *see*, but there was no keyhole. For a mad, daunting moment, as their thrilling sounds kept on, she considered cracking the door an inch. The girl was groaning as if in torment, though off and on, she'd grunt emphatically, "Yeah! Gimme! Gimme hard!" and "Yeah! I want it good!" And every time she said it, Sassela knew within her sinews a swell of indescribable sensation, that made her hop-about antsy, fretful at the barring door. Itchy and tense with frustrated desire. And mad, so mad for relief—especially there in that discovered sweet spot persisting among the fresh sprouting hairs at her crotch.

A furor within set her off. Silent and furtive for no clear reason, she crept back down the stairs, into the kitchen for the flashlight. Then, trembling with tension, she stole into the close melancholy darkness of the basement where, misty eyes closed, she relieved some part of her heartbreak . . .

*   *   *

Having slept through the flight's breakfast, Sassela woke up to the PA's announcement that it was twenty minutes to Frankfurt, and that the crew should make necessary arrangements. In her seat, Meeri awoke from napping perky and talkative. "Well, I'll say for certain I'm glad I met you," she enthused. "Sassela. What a beautiful name. I won't forget it."

She had secreted two miniatures of Grand Marnier liqueur, now handed one to Sassela and bubbling humor, started expressing ridiculous examples of toasts for a farewell shot: "Here's to adventuresses!" "Here's wishing us lust!" "She who's last laid is a goose egg!"

Then as the plane began its descent, Meeri became quiet. Her damp hand covered Sassela's on the intervening handrest. Sighing dramatically, she met Sassela's eyes, began rambling: "Yes, I know I get anxious. Told you I prefer land or sea. But it's those blooming statistics, yu'see. Planes are safe, they say, safer than driving. And maybe it's true. But then they say that most aircraft accidents occur during takeoff and landing. I mean t'say, if you're going to believe one, you gotta believe the other, right? So you wonder I'm squirmy? Hey! All of these sixty-one years I've lived close to the earth. This air-flight thing is a first. I feel like a baby cut loose from mama earth's womb, floating on my own, high-rolling against tricky statistics."

Sassela grinned sympathetically, although astonishment had stopped her hearing when Meeri spoke her age. Sixty-one! And yet that bounce. And vim, and verve. Not to mention her insouciant sexuality, an altogether attitude suggesting not a minute more than— maybe fortysomething? Sassela couldn't believe it. Maybe there was something to the senior bohemian lifestyle, after all.

They landed without incident, got into the bustle of deplaning. Sassela briefly caught sight of Ciam grouping with his cronies. She wondered if he would be going on, and where. But then her queue started moving, and she joined the shuffle into the reception area. There, hugging Meeri a warm though awkward good-bye, she couldn't ignore the strength and yield of the older woman's body. Then Sassela was off in total concentration about gates and flight numbers of her transfer to Mineros.

9

No way a frequent traveler, in all her years Sassela had visited—including New Jersey—but a dozen or so of the United States, and three foreign cities: Montreal, London, Paris. And each trip away was marked by tension at the Customs and Immigration juncture. The cavernous hangar-type buildings miniaturized a thousand travelers into anxious antlines forced into tolerance of indifferent routines by indifferent functionaries. Boredom crassly unmasked, everyone plodded along to the time of completion.

Mineros wasn't like that. Tourism was for sale here, the authorities merchants. They offered no excessive smiles, but were energetic at providing service. Arrivals were corralled into six or so steadily moving queues— one for Greek citizens. Visitors were mostly European tourists who'd joined the flight's American travelers in Frankfurt. With a wry smile, Sassela soon realized that the visitors' lines moved considerably faster than the citizens'. She'd soon be at the immigration kiosk.

Obviously the merchant authorities knew where the profit—

"Yo! Sassela," she heard her name called.

Her stomach fluttered. It was Ciam! Strolling up with a large gunnysack hung over his shoulder.

"Hi," she said carefully, as he stopped and unslung his sack heavily to the ground.

"Thanks for holding my place," he said, and bussed her familiarly on the cheek. Before she could respond, he had turned to the couple next in line. "Sister," he said, casually hitching a thumb at her, "held my place while I needed to do something." He did his smile at them, finished with a grateful "Thanks!" and turned back to Sassela, his eyes a-twinkle.

What else to do? "I'm not your servant, you know," Sassela said in a halfway upbraiding tone, and smiled apology at the couple.

The man said, "No problem at all." A grating, Kissinger accent. Husbandlike, fiftyish, an ugly brown smoker's smile briefly lodging in his pleasant, pasty face.

"Let me carry along this handbag," said Ciam. "Told you that suitcase was too much for a week." And with conspirator's triumph in his look, reached for the straps of her shoulder bag.

Amused at his boldness, she let him have the bag. Freed her somewhat for the heavy job dragging and shoving her very loaded suitcase.

No problem at the kiosk. The officer flipped open her American passport, thoroughly inked his rubber stamp, and firmly pressed the welcome mark in it.

With Ciam, who had entered with her, it took a minute more. He had to locate for the officer his student visa to the United States. The fellow asked, "Where are you staying?"

"With her, my cousin," Ciam answered. "We're on the same tour."

It was "sister" a moment ago, Sassela corrected in her mind, smiling.

The officer glanced up at Ciam, at Sassela. Curiously, it seemed. But he stamped the passport and handed it to Ciam.

"Enjoy your stay," he said.

They passed on, Ciam now taking Sassela's heavy suitcase and her shoulder bag, while she dragged along his much lighter gunnysack. Must be only a few clothes in it, she thought.

They tramped a few steps to the customs area, where, next to every examining agent, a soldier armed with an Uzi semiautomatic stood posted. No smiles for tourists, these guys looked at arrivals with hard, cold eyes. Would probably march smugglers to a wall and waste them as target practice. Ciam lifted the suitcase onto the examining table.

"Anything to declare?" asked the agent. He had dark hair parted down the middle, which gave him a schoolmaster's aspect. Pale blue, serious eyes bored into her own as if daring her to try something.

"Nothing," she said, and unclicked the nearer clasp of the suitcase.

"Don't bother," said the agent. "What about that one?" he asked, indicating Ciam's gunnysack.

At which Ciam stepped forward. "All I gotta declare is two changes," he said, and deftly upturned the bag, emptying pieces of rolled-up clothing: a pair of blue jeans, T-shirts, rolled-up sweat socks, a dirty white dress shirt. And more than a whiff of funkiness.

The soldier was alert to it. A quick involuntary move, he brought his left hand to his unshaven face, flicked at and pinched the nostrils of his narrow, thin-slitted nose. His deep-set eyes stabbed disgust at Ciam.

As if intent on baring all, Ciam was shaking out the depths of the sack.

"That's fine." The agent stopped him, marked a yellow "X" on the bags. Waved them by.

Ciam restuffed his gunnysack, handed it to her, relatched her suitcase and gripped it up firmly. Together they walked through officialdom's boundaries with everything smelling roses and set ready for holiday time.

Through out-swinging doors into blazing brightness! A blast of discomfort to her eyes. On top of that, clothes right for the plane were immediately too warm for this relentless sunshine. First sight of the Mediterranean sky, Sassela found nothing beautiful about the heat and light; just too much of it, and shocking. The brightness demanded protection: with a clarity of air, a glare of increased sight, it heightened vision uncomfortably.

The heat was like nothing she'd ever known, certainly nothing like New York. Crisply out of the sky, it shed a wicked sting, a sharpness on the skin suggesting toast burnt black. As if it goaded, "You like? You came for sunshine? Well, here y'are. Take it with a vengeance!"

It was, in truth, a wickedly brilliant weather that hurt her eyes to watering. Even as, squint focusing hindsight, she realized the one thing not on her list: sunglasses. First chance, though, she was certain to get some.

On automatic about getting to her transport, Sassela reviewed instructions written on the back of her itinerary, and bore left to an area in which about thirty buses were parked. Ciam in tow dragging the suitcase, she began down the line looking for the logo describing the contracted tour buses to her resort. Not a minute of that before sweat was trickling from her armpits, down between her breasts, and she had only walked past three buses. So she stopped, ranged her eyes. An American-looking group heading to the far wall caught her attention. On a hunch, she followed their heading, and there were the correct tour buses: two of them, the drivers sitting together in one front seat, nonchalantly smoking and eyeing the gathering folks.

Finally, having decided that the assembly was complete, the smaller, mustached fellow marched down the door's three steps, coughed his throat clear. He raised his hand for attention. "I have sad news," he said gravely.

Sassela, near enough, gave full ear.

The driver coughed again, spoke up: "We have a breakdown. There is one bus only. The other bus will be, maybe, three hours."

The announcement like a signal, for the next few minutes folks, some already wearing various degrees of lobster tans, crowded into the available bus, claiming and trying to hold seats for their companions. But size or numbers didn't change; two buses were required. It took a scrambling ten minutes before the lucky settled down, and the excess hopefuls sullenly trooped back out. Resignedly Sassela stood watching the antics, conscious of Ciam nearby, lounging unconcernedly as if he had no plans. She stepped closer to him. "Are you with the ecology group, too? You don't seem anxious," she asked.

"No, no, no! I'm not with them. I'm with the soccer team." He smiled as if he'd cleared up everything.

"So, don't you have to go find them?"

"Well, not exactly. I'm on my own. As assistant team manager, they don't need me much." He performed various evasive hand movements, and again, lots of grin bright with the glitter of deceit.

"School paid, huh?" asked Sassela with Harlem-trained directness.

"Yeah, sort of," he said, glossy grimace still on his face. Although, as if everywhere else were uncomfortable, he still wouldn't look at her.

Sassela said, "Well, some folks have all the luck." Letting him off the hook of his not-so-aimless hanging around, and choosing to keep her suspicions unspoken.

A few minutes passed; then, noses wrinkled in distaste, two people came out of the bus. Their seats were rearmost, near the toilet. They couldn't stand the stink, they complained. Immediately, there was a little rush as one or two couples started for the rejected seats. But each, one step into the bus, changed their minds, and chose to stand, humbled to the three-hour wait for the replacement.

Never was a decision for Sassela, though. First moment the wrinkled-nosed couple exited, an emphatic glance to Ciam, and they were of one mind: a backseat by the latrine could never be an option.

As they mulled around, a rumor came whispering that someone who understood Greek had heard the driver say there was really only one bus. And that the plan was that this working bus would make two trips, returning later for the remnant group. And that this trip, in fact, would take at least three hours each way, plus a half-hour break for the bus to be serviced, necessary since this same bus company had got into trouble for undermaintaining their equipment and had paid—

Sassela met the query in Ciam's eyes, shrugged. "Who knows? We'll give it a bit," she said.

"Cool with me," he said, still readily adopting her itinerary.

By and by, the smaller driver rose and stretched to his full extent. He climbed down the bus steps, adjusted the mirror, straightened and pulled up his skinny black tie, arranged his canvas hat fastidiously. He readjusted the mirror, turned to the assembly now that he had their full attention. "We are to leave now," he announced carefully. Held up two fingers. "Two seats still we have. Please."

The leftover band stood unmoved by his muted eloquence; there were no takers. The driver sighed, elaborately content that he had done his best. He mounted his stairs like a captain, climbed into his cockpit seat. The doors swung shut with finality, and with a purr of restrained power, the bus slowly maneuvered into an adequate lane before setting off with a confident roar, a mechanical certainty that it held all sunburned destiny behind its gray-shaded windows.

Didn't dent Sassela's good mood at all. Since she'd got to the island, everything bordered mania: the heat, this hustle, the tourists' intentness. Having given herself no agenda, watching the folks around being so seriously busy about vacationing was funny enough for a quirky giggle. A spectacle of departure as high drama, she thought, furthering her amusement another nuance. She turned to clue in Ciam. Met his grin brilliant, his eyes merry with sympathy.

"And there goeth thy bus hustling away with your Hellenic vacation," he said. "Beautiful, ain't it?"

That close to her sentiments, it struck. And they burst out laughing, he stepping a fast little jig to help him be happy. "Quit clowning, Ciam," said Sassela, grabbing his arm, conscious of all the eyes turning their way. "Let's wait back in the building," she suggested. "It's cooler in there, anyhow."

"Bet," agreed Ciam, pulled away from her. Then up with the suitcase, he led the way to shade.

10

They weren't the only ones who had thought of lockers, and it turned out there were barely sufficient: ten files of twenty-five double tiers. Ciam lugging her heavy suitcase, she with her shoulder bag and his gunnysack, it was the middle of the tenth before they found success. Then he had to go change money to appropriate drachma value.

She perched on the suitcase and considered how to manage all his handy helpfulness. While his attention was flattering—and useful—she needn't feel over-obligated to a hanger-on. After all, whatever the reason for his deception, she hadn't blown his cover at the immigration kiosk. Then again, perhaps his solicitude was a thank-you gesture for that—although his constantly charged manner toward her did belie that notion.

Then he was back with proper coins and high-spirited muscles, and the bags were quickly and securely lockered. He turned to her bright-eyed, rubbed his palms vigorously in what's-next manner.

"Look, Ciam," Sassela said, "I, I can't thank you enough for all this, this—"

"—'portering' the word you seeking?" He grinned.

"Well, if *you* prefer." She grinned back, knowing 'nuff was said; appreciating, too, that he'd made it so easy to abort her get-lost plan for him.

His head cocked aside as if thinking a moment, smiling the Galahad, he said, "Listen to this. You heard the rumor, you know this could be a six-hour wait. So hear the plan. Now our stuff in the lockers, let's take a walk. I've got to go see a man about a house. And doing that, I could show you a better way to waste the time."

A walk in the ancient city—the perfect diversion, and opportunity to check out his company without risk, as car fare would cover the worst situation. Sassela sidled a look at him—there grinning fat, daring excitement—and knew she couldn't refuse, and be honest about the intrigue she felt for him. "Sure," she said.

On their way out through the airport lounge, they stopped at a kiosk to browse the reading material. While Ciam zeroed in on the sports section, Sassela was surreptitiously ogling a postcard showing a frontal view of some Greek god—Pan, perhaps? Whoever. Eye-catching was this god, black and hairy, and wearing nothing but a wicked goat's grin and a stupendously outsized erection.

She turned to amaze with Ciam and comment on the image getting by censors, but found him nodding solemnly with his lips pursed as he gazed at the magazine he held. This was a welcome tamp to her impulse, though, for she didn't yet know him that way. Then, more to himself, he murmured, "Yeah, everybody's getting hip."

She glanced at the magazine's cover: some French tennis star in dreadlocks. "Say what?"

"Nothing. Just thinking how dreads growing, yu' know. Solidarity, and so on."

As they sauntered on past a rack of picture post-cards, Ciam said, "Hey, got to send some cards. Need anything in the post office?"

About to take Harry's letter from her pocketbook, she was suddenly shy at the possibility of Ciam seeing her address and the name "Harrod" and perchance remembering the snowed-in incident and assuming whatever, which wouldn't be the current truth. And would misrepresent the fact of her accepting his—Ciam's—attentions. Because she wasn't leading anybody on. He was merely a fun fellow-passenger, and they were on an innocent outing. That was all there was to it. She was neither disloyal nor a flirting chum-fucker, loose or thirsty. She was a woman alone, out for a holi-day of rest and reflection, and the fact that she was being friendly indicated nothing else.

And in any case, it wasn't necessary to post the letter right then. She could do it later at the resort. "No," she replied.

Now set off on the jaunt, a light, cool breeze made walking pleasant, and they fell into a relaxed, comfort-able pace. Ciam, whistling under his breath, seemed content in his world, a glance of his beaming delight catching her unawares, tripping her heartbeat again. She tried sorting out the situation. Getting away from the resignedness of that waiting throng certainly was appropriate. But she had to admit there was another side to it: the fact that this boy's energy put yeast in her smile, and that felt good. Despite its danger as a carrot: without effort pulling a strong jackass. That she had to watch for. Be careful. "If it that good, it costly," was always her father's advice. And in her current distancing-Harry mode, emotional outlay was just not affordable.

Thoughts of her father reminding, Sassela broke their walking silence. "You know something," she said.

"What you said earlier, about the house? When I was a kid, that's exactly what my father used to say whenever I asked him where he was heading out. 'Going to see a man about a dog,' then touch his nose solemn as a burial preacher. Took me forever—I mean, I was a *teenager* before I got his message." She snorted at the memory.

Ciam chuckled. "Your father was a country boy, huh?"

"Guess he was that. As much as Cullen County was country. Still swears he never saw a car until he was past twenty. He's such a smoothie."

"You like him, though," Ciam said, grinning at her.

Sassela held his eye. "Yes sirree, sure I do," she said. "Who could resist a charmer? And I had to live with him."

"And your ma?"

"Oh, she's passed. Some eleven years now."

"I'm sorry. Didn't mean—"

"No!" Sassela patted his arm. "It's not a problem with me."

Silent again, well beyond the highway, just into the town, they walked the suddenly narrow streets, taking in the newness. Not much to look at, though. On one street she saw kids wearing caps turned around backward or sideways, raising their bicycles on back wheels and unicycling for long stretches; all just as home in Harlem, and it made her proud.

Suddenly reminded, she asked, "So, what happened to our dinner date?"

He halted, screwed up his face, and guiltily looked at his feet. "I was dreading you'd ask me that," he said.

"Dreading—?"

"Yeah. Is like that."

"So, tell me."

"It's sort of embarrassing—"

"I could handle it."

"Well, I was sort of financially strapped, yu'know."

"So? Come on, I'm a working woman. You stood me up because you were afraid I'd stick you with the bill?"

"Nah. It's not like that—" He raised his glistening eyes, met hers. "It's just that you're so fine and beautiful. And I wanted to spend on you, and I couldn't—"

Her heart raced to the ardor in his gaze. She had to look away, lighten the moment. "Yeah, pull my other," she sallied. But then, waggling a finger at him, finished, "Well, whatever, don't you let it happen again."

"Not ever, ma'am," he said, the grin in effect again.

The houses, the aromas, the miens of the faces they encountered—but for the street signs in funny alphabet—continually reminded her of Brooklyn. They turned up a short block and saw, about halfway along, a group of loungers. Five, six men crowding the tiny sidewalk, whiling away the afternoon heat, a well-eyed bottle passing hand to hand as if with measures of boredom. Well away from them, Sassela felt their challenge. Knew they would not yield the sidewalk, so she nudged Ciam into the narrow sunlit street. She approached, flashed a swift glance to take them in, then turned her eyes away from the men's assessment, the surly, suspicious, disdainful stares they cast.

Didn't catch any classic Greek looks, though. The men carried a sameness—like relatives with black hair, coarse pale skin, chunky to chubby stature. And then there was their shitty attitude. To the likes of them, Ciam was matchlessly handsome. And here he was, close at her side. Sassela grabbed his arm like an owner with a sudden winner, hugged it as she fell in with his stride.

He looked at her, eyebrows dancing as he smiled happily. "I've been good?"

"Not really. I'm just generous."

"I'll take it," Ciam said. A few steps along, he nudged her. "Notice how they watch our shoes?"

"No. Are they really? Why?"

"Why?" His voice rose in querulous Caribbean lilt. "Why you suppose?"

Sassela shrugged. "Don't know."

"'Cause we got good shoes. My sneaks're Nike Airs. What you got on? Whatever. Bet they're a thousand percent superior to what they wearing. Bet my Nikes're a month's wages here. At least a month. And you know what Nike means? It's Greek for 'victory.'"

Out of the mouths of babes! The answer spoken, the why she'd found so difficult to articulate. She looked at him, her mind flexing to his sagacity, reframing him with new respect. Just like that he'd put a name to the elusive stuff. Never the tourist data, what she wanted was insights, rationales, and perspectives of people's lives in a foreign place. That was giddily exciting, and in the fancy, Sassela imagined herself returned home loaded with genuine experiences, daydreaming with a good scotch, maybe after a Discovery documentary. Then she would've known firsthand the legitimate explorer's rush—like an Alan Shepard, or a Crusoe. Then she'd have adventured as they'd dared, to see strangeness first, to delve into other cultures—

"Listen to this," interrupted Ciam. "I've been thinking."

"Well, should we applaud a first-time effort here?" Sassela bantered.

"No, no. This is serious. My future, my fortune, my everything." He sang the last to the Barry White tune.

"Sounds important. Tell me. But speak."

"Well, if your waiting for that bus means what I think it means, well, to be honest, it's hard for me to see you spending the rest of your life with that bunch of environmentalists."

She passed on the impulse to defend ecology— despite not having intended to hang with the group—

said instead, "Nineteen days is not a life. Eighteen, really. When you count travel da—"

"You don't believe that. Eighteen days of ecology touring *is* a life. An ugly, boring life. Especially in a place like this and in company like that. Jeez, who knows? Could be the sort of miserable existence a beautiful woman might desperately want out of—" Hands spread in broad possibilities, he furrowed his brow at her, rolled eyes to the heavens.

"So?" said Sassela, smiling slow encouragement, waiting. His using as threat the prospect of being herded about in an ecology group was inspired strategy. Sassela would've never tested that boredom. Wasn't why she came. But beyond that dropping out, her plans were deliberately indefinite, depending on whatever options came her way.

And here was Ciam presenting: "What you say to this? True, this is not mih native one, but I am an islander. Natural born, Caribbean-style. But an island is an island, and I know them as only a nativeman can. You really want to see this place? Is not the first time I here, and I could show you things nobody else would even think about. So what you say? Whatever days you want, I meet you up wherever, and I be your personal guide. Huh? I have experience as a guide. Back home, a few years back, I used to work the reef summertime. Your summers, I mean. . . ." He stopped uncertainly, as her skeptic's smile and cool, cool gaze had never wavered from his face. First hint she got that his gall could be pinched.

Sassela eased the squeeze. "Sounds attractive," she murmured. "What're your rates?" The coyness added for tease, as truth was, in her mind she had reluctantly admitted to wanting more of this boy's company. Of the attention he lavished on her. Of the sensual turmoil he provoked.

Quick on the uptake, he cocked his head playfully, though still half-serious. "Well, you know my means. You'd have to be the purse, in charge of finances. Anything beyond bikes, you'll pay for. Other than that, I'll work for food and affection."

"Doesn't sound at all bad. But tempting me might be dangerous. I just might take you up on it."

"Well, I serious as sunburn. And if you don't, you lose a bargain slave. Remember, in my pack you're thief of hearts." And in broad Grecian daylight and screechy tenor, he burst into some blues ballad combining chains and love.

Despite her embarrassed look around, she chuckled. No one seemed to be taking notice. Still, it was a perfect example of her dilemma with him: this extraordinary lack of self-consciousness versus his effortlessly sharp wits and attention. A pleasure to be around, true. But should she afford herself his constant boost to her ego and spirits? Attractive as he was, good times with him could come easy. Same attractiveness, though, might provide the downside. She attractive, he attractive, singly or a private twosome, was fine. But both of them in public, together, crossed the line into ostentatiousness. Display that invited tough scrutiny, which might wrongly conclude an embarrassing May/December cliché. For as a couple they would certainly challenge hard attention from probing eyes that'd make them a spectacle. And there was nothing she despised more.

All of that was her cautious, everyday head on its soapbox.

Then Sassela thought of his ravenous, adoring glances, the suggestions they spawned, and a ripple of gooseflesh rushed from haunch to navel and spun a twist into the situation. So she let the unspoken tangle remain in abeyance, awaiting incident that might supply a casting vote.

11

They were passing through a poor section. Edge of the city, familiarly unglamorous to Sassela's bleak view, all it needed was some broken-down brownstones to make it a passable New York ghetto. Everything else was there, in spirit at least: with the youth—a dozen or more scrawny young men ferociously kicking at a soccer ball, antic at aping their particular hero, invoking his name as they practiced his latest miracle, wastefully showing off to each other and their scraggle of skinny girlfriends standing supportive on the sidelines. Just like any girlfriends anywhere. Like herself, one half-life ago. Here was a soccer version of inner-city hoops, complete with future losers misspending energy in a frustrating mime of ambition.

They turned into the major crosstown street, a slow incline wide enough for two-way traffic. Across the way, on the sunny side, a swarthy chunk of a man was struggling to push a car back up the long hill. A basic vehicle: straight-up windscreen, four thin wheels, and an engine under a patch-colored umbrella. Like an old aluminum pot, it had a battered homemade look. The man was working hard, sweating freely, grunting and bellowing explosively what had to be swear words. His effort was compounded because, at the driver's door, he was splitting force by steering the jalopy rear first up the hill.. Sassela thought of Sisyphus, noticed three draped older women watching. She couldn't be certain of their grimaces, but they seemed to be enjoying the show.

"Keep on in the shade. I'll catch up with you," she heard Ciam say, and like an eager puppy, he trotted off across the street. His back to the front of the jalopy, he set to pushing backward with the power of his thighs. To considerable effect as, at once, the car proceeded faster and under better control. Also, the man stopped swearing.

They were so fast, Sassela couldn't keep up the two long blocks to the top of the incline. Ciam had crossed to the shady side and was fanning himself with his T-shirt tails when she caught up. His flat hard belly glistened as he turned a grandly self-satisfied grin to the man, who got into the car and tooted the horn. Then the car was off—a coasting crawl slowly picking up speed all the way through the first long block. Well into the second it began violently wheezing and shuddering, back-piping a plume of heavy, black smoke.

Exactly Ciam's recommendation, it seemed: "That's it, man," he shouted. "Work the clutch."

Then, with a tremendous roar and a volley of backfires, the engine caught, the trailing smoke changed to clear blue as the car slowed and careened around the natural curve of the long street.

Ciam punched his fist in the air, shouted, "Yes!" as if he'd hit a winning three-pointer.

Sassela couldn't restrain her grin. "So, mission accomplished. Now shall we go on?"

They did.

Two further blocks, the car returned at full blast, throttled down to keep pace. The horn honked, and the man was gesturing a ride wherever.

"Go on! We're okay!" shouted Ciam.

But there was no denying the grateful man. They got in, Ciam in the front seat, trying to give directions. Sassela—in the back—was more comfortable than the car's appearance suggested. Above the rattle and din, they screamed names at each other. His was Dimitri Takadopoulos, or something close-sounding. Despite right away shouting, "No 'ave de Engleesh," he spoke to them all the way. All Greek, of course.

First stop was a saloon, where he showed them off to much cheering, and beer for the patrons. Ciam had a bottle. Sassela had water and a spot by the window with a breeze. Eventually some linguist among them translated Ciam's directions, and they recognized the party—another Papadopoulos-like name. Of course he knew the house, insisted their slightly drunk mechanic man. No choice but to accept his invitation, and back into the car—left running throughout the bar-time— they were driven to the doorstep of their destination.

A balding, middle-aged man with a thick brush of a mustache came smiling out the front door. "Hallo, hallo," he greeted Ciam, hugging him, kissing his cheeks. "You are the boy, Ciam. Of course, of course. And this is—?" He bowed graciously to Sassela.

"This is my friend, Sassela," supplied Ciam.

"Ahh!" the man exclaimed as if privileged. "Sassela, I am truly honored to meet you. My name is Yiorgis, and I am at your wishes. My house is your house. Come and meet my family." And he led them in.

In a neat, small front room, the women of the house awaited them. Yiorgis introduced his wife, Maria, his daughter-in-law, Marianna, her toddler, and a cousin, whose name Sassela didn't catch. Then they all went into a larger back room, a dining room maybe, judging from the family table centered by a bright-colored bouquet in a sky blue porcelain vase.

Ciam and Yiorgis got to talking, Ciam mainly updating the older man about his son, Nikos, who seemed to be Ciam's close friend, and living with Ciam's folks back in the Caribbean. None of the women spoke English, so Sassela, left to herself, grew reflective.

The Greek family, so generous, made her think of home, of Pa unable to refuse shelter because of that hospitality typical of black folks—probably poor folks everywhere—of offering their best to strangers. This family seated them to an improbably sumptuous combination: a salad of unpeeled cucumbers thick-sliced the same way as its fat juicy tomatoes, quartered radishes, and the luscious leafy greens of a bitter-tasting lettuce. No dressing but a sprinkle of oregano-flavored vinegar. Then meat, lamb maybe, but strongly flavored of garlic and spices. And balls of a different meat, at least in consistency, then pasta and rice. No couscous, which Sassela somehow expected, but an offer of hot thin soup with floating strips of shallot. Coarse bread and a chunk of cheese on the side.

Not until well into putting away the meal, after a discreet belch, did Sassela realize how hungry she had been.

She was relaxing on the couch when the child toddled over to her. Chubby, with round black, black eyes, looking ever surprised, she reached a stumpy hand, jerkily stroked Sassela's hair. Caught by the child's openness, and further roused by the absorbed zealot's gaze with which the mother watched her baby, some challenge stirred within Sassela, made her uneasily admit curiosity about a maternal urge that'd permit such fierce and full surrender to another. Impulsively, she took up the baby, gave it a big sloppy kiss. Maybe just to show she could. Maybe plain old-fashioned jealousy?

Uncomfortable with her broody turn of mind, Sassela looked for distraction out the nearby window: in a gently rocking hammock in the garage shed, his mouth slightly open, was Ciam catching a nap. It reminded her how drowsy she felt, and how her eyelids were heavy as blankets.

Maybe so much, the lady of the house noticed. *"Siesta ahora?"* she suggested, and smiled *sympatico.*

Sassela demurred with a slow shrug.

"We shut eye, *ne?"* Maria urged in fractured English. And it didn't take any more persuasion for Sassela to be led into the lady's proud bedroom, and her beckoning bed. Hardly had her head touched the cedar-scented pillow, when Sassela was fast asleep. . . .

. . . *a forest of abandoned flower gardens, glorious and magical, the trees gone wild, gigantic . . . she toddles out of her carriage wearing very light blue cotton pajamas . . . she hates blue, must find a particular flower that will change her pajamas to pink . . . pushy leaves protect this flower, threaten to grab her . . . she spies the smiling flower, reaches for it, though not carefully enough, as the big warm leaf brushes her shoulder, threatening . . .*

Heart racing, mouth dry, Sassela awoke groggily. Ciam's hand was on her shoulder, shaking gently. "Hey, Sassela," he whispered, "wake up. I think you might've missed the bus."

She sat up, worked her tongue about her mouth, swabbing away the sour of her dream's leftover alarm. "Damn!" she said. "You're sure?" She reached for her pocketbook.

"Looks like it," he said. "Yiorgis thinks so."

Indeed, it was so. The watch said she had napped more than an hour. Yet it turned out all wasn't lost. Yiorgis—he owned a taxicab—intended driving Ciam to a beachhouse where he'd stay. And Ciam had explained the situation, asked the old man, who happily agreed to take her to her hotel in the resort town Praxsonios. He found a map and spread it to show them her destination: quite farther along than Ciam's intended drop-off.

"What are hours but a chance to help my good friends? Don't think of it again," said Yiorgis.

About to offer payment, she felt Ciam's nudge, caught his warning eye. "Taken care of," he whispered privately.

Another time, my hero, Sassela couldn't help but thinking as she smiled her gratitude at him.

Then they said good-byes to the family, and piled into Yiorgis's car—a proper taxi, roomy as a New York checkered with a turned-off meter—and they were off to the terminal for their stored bags.

12

In the backseat, Sassela watched the scenery glaze by, the car chugging along. Idly wondering who the billionaire was who'd cornered the franchise for whitewash, she felt relaxed equal to that lucky fellow's financial ease. Soon she'd get to her resort and vacation would begin, and was she ever ready for creature comforts. Kilometers went quietly by, until gradually she realized Ciam was sitting on the edge of his seat, turned all eyes at her. Unaccountably, her heart tripped.

He burst out earnestly, "Listen, Sassela! I am not a boy, you know. You mustn't misread me. You shouldn't. I could take care—"

"That never crossed my mind, Ciam. I don't think of you in—" She paused, aware of graying boundaries.

"—of you," he'd continued. "Of everything, really, I can."

She swallowed, spoke slowly, soft despite the tom-tom in her heart. "Have I suggested differently?"

"No. But you think I'm kinda young. Not so? Young for a full woman like you, I mean. Right?"

"I never—"

"You don't have to. I know your mind. But what you not saying, too, is that I can make you laugh. And you like to laugh. Full-woman you longing to laugh. And that is all that I want. Just to do it for you. Make you laugh." Gently, very gently, he grasped her arm, searched her face. Breathily, cardamom-scented, he said, "Why don't you let me, huh? Sassela, please. Why don't you just come stay with me at my beachhouse, and let me be good to you? I think you're so fine."

She turned away, looked through the car window at the streaking glaze. Momentarily into her mind swam the memory of them close in the snowed-in Bug, the warmth, his coarse smell. Then that was swept away, too fast for figuring, same as her thoughts, as her blood, as her heartbeats.

This was inevitable, she admitted. Everything had been building toward the moment, this question. And she was yet unprepared, had no answer. One self was more than tempted. Fed up—dissatisfied—as she was with status quo, and order, and propriety, Ciam could be just the needed boost. He radiated an irrepressible humor at living, the sort she yearned for. But then her proper self demurred. How could she let herself go with him? Wouldn't she seem easy—and to a pretty boy? Certainly a queasy prospect. And then her pouting, needful self returned to primaries: given her current anonymity, who and where better to test chance with?

Ciam touched her shoulder, supplicant for attention. "Hear me, Sassela," he whispered. "I'll be decent to you, I say. A gentleman. Give me a chance to show you."

Her shoulder tingled where his fingers rested. She wanted to, but couldn't turn back and face him. So ardent he was being, her belly felt his tension. Seduction is a mutual act! flashed through her mind, the tingly thought evoking Meeri, her sip-the-flowing-sap promotion. And yes, indeed! this fine young man was a-wooing, and in truth, she loved the rush. She only now realized how sorely she had missed it.

Cool smooth fingers caressed her neck. Sassela wondered if he could feel her flush. "Don't put me down because I'm beautiful," he whispered.

Listen to him! Outrageous, and fresh, and promising. Gooseflesh followed wherever he touched.

"Sassela," he said, "I'll treat you like a princess. Promise. With castle and kingdom by the sea. Come stay with me."

Eyes out the window, she began, "I—"

"Look at me," he said, covering her lips with his cool fingers.

Sassela held her breath, closed her eyes ready—

"Here we rest now," Yiorgis's voice interrupted, as he braked the car, snapping the spell. "I will show you my special treat."

Sassela opened her eyes, caught Ciam's complicated look, and shied away to where Yiorgis was gesturing to see a roadside inn up on a rise. "My friend's place," he said. "Here we get the best coffee in the world." He kissed into his fingers, flung it to the breezes, then got out and led the way up.

Yiorgis's old friend, the proprietor, greeted them with effusive friendliness, and showed Sassela and Ciam to a small table out in the open. In no time they were sipping sweet coffee, and watching clouds and countryside, and the afternoon age. Lax in the soporific heat, except for a pending tension poised between them, edging the mellowness.

A sudden waft of rankness made Sassela wrinkle her nose, look about. A ragged old woman was cringing beside a tall sculpted bush; they hadn't noticed her at all. Though now, eyes caught, she hesitantly approached close enough for them to suffer her stench. Subway tactics, Sassela reached into her purse, handed the woman drachma.

The crone didn't go away, though. She took the money, said, "One more, I read your coffee, please. Maybe your life in the grounds. *Ne*."

"Sure," said Ciam, as if his nostrils were stuffed up. "Here, do mine." He paid up. Maybe directly to the gods, as a breeze freed the stifling air.

Sassela took a deep and careful breath, watched the crone study the dregs in Ciam's cup, then reach gnarled, trembly fingers to her own cup and study again. Then the crone grinned a brown vacant space.

"Most lucky, you," she declared to Sassela. "You soon time is best fortune. You long time? Ahh! Only the gods." She shrugged elaborately, then addressed Ciam, "*Ne, ne. Palicari*, lovely-boy. Ahh! You watch for *mekré* much bad—"

Ciam winked at Sassela. "See? I'm a bad *palicari*." He turned back to the crone. "What's a *palicari*? What's *mekré*?"

"#@!%*#&@!!" A burst of Greek from nowhere made Sassela jump. Scolding, the proprietor had rushed up, gesturing at the gamy crone, clearly telling her to be off. And, casting the man a poisonous look, she scuttled away, muttering.

"I am most sorry after her," the proprietor apologized. "But forever she is no more bother."

"It was quite all right," Sassela assured the man. And to her relief, he went away. For he had interrupted a flow of shining charm, an exciting moment when the crone, with her fortune fakery, had almost intersected with Sassela's tentative willingness to believe, to succumb to intuition. Seduction is a wheel a-rolling; fit into the spin. Armpits dripping beads, she wondered, was Ciam filled with fancies as daring?

Elbows on the table, face shiny, close, he gazed

raptly into her eyes. "You see that. Even the witching forces say you will be okay if you come with me."

Sassela blinked, gulped consternation. Was he reading her mind? Or were they actually in such close sympathy? He certainly seemed nervous. His right hand fidgeted distractedly, folding the paper napkin, drumming on the saucer's rim, on the metal table.

Sassela's eyes moved up, from his fiddling hand to the smooth brown of his forearm, the veins defined like roadways leading up, elbowing into his moss-green short sleeve, armpit sweat-darkened. Then her eyes sprang ahead, met his—alive with supplication he was again about to speak. Truth without smiles. Without teeth, or glitter.

"It's okay. Don't talk," she said gently, decided. Then reached out her hand and covered his anxious fingers, stilled them with a touch saying "Yes."

And the afternoon's ease just flowed along so much more generously.

A daze after, Sassela said, "Let's go now."

And, him humble at her heels, down the narrow path they went and into the car.

Ciam leaned over the front seat, spoke quietly to Yiorgis, who drove off without remark. Then Ciam reclined cuddle-close, took her hand and fondled and petted and laid it against his face and smooth, smooth skin all the rest of the way to his cottage by the sea.

13

First laying eyes on it, to Sassela the place cunningly combined surprise and disaster. Gingerly she walked through the wooden structure risen on three-foot posts well planted in the gravelly sand: two rooms—the bedroom with a window to the mountains, and a living/dining/kitchen space boasting two windows viewing the glazed sea on one side, scrubby hills on the other. Furniture was a big low-slung, homemade bed, one chair, a low three-legged stool, a plastic beer crate for optional seating, an unsturdy wooden table centering the common utility space. Next to the window on a sooty, waist-high shelf, an ancient, blackened, one-burner kerosene stove evoked Robinson Crusoe expeditions. A rusty faucet plunked steadily into a battered aluminum sink hung outside the hill-view window.

As she eyed the primitive circumstances mouth agape, Ciam appeared bearing a five-gallon petrol can in his hand. Grinning satisfaction, he sounded its side with a firm knuckle, declared: "More than enough."

Not comprehending his delight, Sassela looked her

apprehension out the mountain window. Adjacent to the kitchen was an attached shower stall. On a rise some fifty feet away was what had to be an outhouse latrine. Made her swallow a new flutter. "I'll take a look around," she said, tottering to the door, down the rickety steps.

As she started off, a brisk breeze shifted her loose mane into her face. Automatically, she handed the hair back, unconscious fingers swiftly braiding a thick ponytail. A few steps farther, she stopped, looked about the bare, undulate cove crescenting a flat, indifferent sea, took in the hut, the scrubby hills behind, the latrine in between. Her bleak assessment: not at all the accommodations pictured from Ciam's presentation. Misgivings nudging, she forced herself to remember: This is adventure. I can't be a wuss. I'm going to have a good time. And with doughty heart, explorer Sassela set out to test the underfoot crunch of the gray sand beach.

When she got back to the shack, he'd pulled some bushes and set them to burn in a picturesque fire lit in the front yard, which scented the area with an invigorating anise aroma. He was retrieving the bedsheets from where he'd spread them over rocks and brush, warbling unconcernedly to himself.

He broke off when he saw her and grinned. "Ridded them of mustiness," he explained, bundling the sheets up the steps and into the hut. As Sassela followed him in—he'd dusted, she noticed—he launched into an energetic but flawed variation of the gospel song "Bringing in the sheaves," a tune she'd always loved, and hadn't sung in ages. Through an awkward moment, she forced herself to join in, and after an effort finding voice and key, it became easy—especially with his bright-eyed smile so welcoming.

"Let me do that," she offered, taking over the bed-making.

"Sure you want to? Remember, you're the fine lady

here. I'm the native man. I do all the hard work."

"What makes you think the fine lady wouldn't want
to—" For no reason, she balked at "help." "Anyhow,
seems to me like you're having all the fun."

"Well, you wish to enjoy, enjoy." He laughed invit-
ingly.

And in a moment she was flogging the bed with a
towel from her suitcase, raising dust clouds.

At the window for clear air, she said, "All that stuff
you did. So quick. The fire and all. Think I want to stay
close and learn to work like that."

"That's not work. That's setting up house. Easy. Stuff
I like."

"Ciam—" She waited until he looked. "I want to
thank you for all of this. The countryside, everything,
it's beautiful."

"Thank their gods, not me. Not yet," he cracked.
Although his eyes went soft. "Tell me one thing, honestly. You comfortable that you came?"

Like pleasure penned, roistering to get out, when
she said "Yes" the cage was sprung, and he grinned,
reached and hugged her, hard. Through her breasts
crushed into his chest, she could feel his thumping
heart.

She closed her eyes as he took her face in his hands.
Warm breath on her cheeks, she felt his lips gentle on
hers, the sweaty rush of her flush.

"Thanks for coming and staying at Hut with me," he
murmured.

"Anytime at all," she said, trying through her fluster
for cool she didn't feel.

"We'll have a good time, Sass," he said, releasing her.

She lingered her hold of his hand. "I'm sure we will,
Ci."

Then, ice broken, they set to making home, she
busying with the oversize bed while they chatted about

inconsequential stuff—sights on the road, the overall brightness—getting comfortable, striking up a subtle camaraderie.

She was impressed, even challenged, by his deftness at transforming the ramshackle shanty into a tolerable living space. From a found toolbox, he had hammer in hand, and with precise blows was firming up the legs of the table. Clever like a country doctor, he remedied and rigged, his sensible competence and spirit swelling a twisty wave within her; made her sigh heavily, from a sweetness edging melancholy. Then wryly, she admitted to her whimsy that, yes! the setting was romantic, the leading man charming as could be, and all in all, it was an ideal setting for a great adventure.

While, very far in the back of her mind, there peeped a wistful admission that, dependent on whatevers, she'd not resist a seduction.

They had arranged for Yiorgis to bring them weekly supplies, but he wouldn't deliver until the morrow. So they settled for a rude first-night dinner of bread and cheese washed down with warmed packaged milk—Ciam didn't want retsina. Then, casually, he said, "Oh, Sassela, pass me your pocketbook for a moment. Something I put in it."

Unhesitating, she reached under her chair, handed him the pocketbook.

He flipped open the flap, groped in deeply, and removed a bag of dark green stuff Sassela immediately recognized as pot.

"And what have we here?" he voiced in mock official tones.

A cramp in her heart struck home as Sassela realized she had unwittingly dodged a smuggling charge. On the plane, reading the customs declaration form, seeing herself safe from actual experience, she had considered the penalties un-American, monstrously oppres-

sive: ten years for grams of hashish, life imprisonment
for heroin. Now her righteousness quivered at finding
she had been duped into just that same risk!

Incensed, she began, "You mean to say—"
Expectantly, with a smile you'd sell by the yard, he
turned to her. She swallowed her harshest protest, said
instead, "—I mean, how could you, Ciam? That was so
irresponsible. So dangerous. How could you smuggle
contraband? I mean, I could've been—"

"No way, Josita," he came back gaily, "there was
never a danger."

"Wha—!!!"

"You only hindsighting, Sassela," he pointed out. "In
fact, what in mih hand here is the same contraband you
anxious about. Look at it. It here in mih hand. And I
not arresting you. So what you talking?"

She just had to contradict his sanguine attitude:
"Look, Ciam, let's get this clear. You cannot treat this so
lightly. But for the favor of chance, I might be in jail
right now. Let's not dismiss that. And I'm telling you
that putting me in such danger was cruel and irresponsible and—"

"What you so anxious about? Here we are, totally
home free, and all you can think about is what didn't
happen. Listen, Miss Lady," he ended leadenly, "if I
were you, I'd lighten up and act as if I'm on a vacation
with everything going fine."

Then he gathered his smoke apparatus and bluntly
strode out to his pretty, scented fire halfway down Hut's
beach side.

Evening crept stealthily in, silhouetting him lonely
by the fire. Oppressed by an awkward mood, Sassela
watched from Hut's beach window. The seascape darkened with unnatural quiet; not a civilized sound to be
heard. After a bit, Sassela came to wondering: Why, in
truth, was she fussing? Squarely faced, what outraged

her most was the idea of him rummaging among her sanitary napkins. Especially when combined with him standing there with that grand, yellow-feathered grin all over his face. And when she gave thought to the situation, every logical extension became weighted by misgivings. Right off she had to face that she was here stuck with a twentysomething egomaniac of menacing confidence and intention to impress. And for all her coulda-shoulda-wouldas, there was nothing to do. She honestly had never discouraged Ciam, had squandered every opportunity to do so. Clearly, to back away now would be stupid, schoolgirlish. Still, did that disqualify her hesitation? Was her trepidation righteous nervousness, commonplace fear, or plain hypocrisy? Did she, in her innermost self, truly want to discontinue this intrigue? Was she serious about managing the romantic possibilities all the way to their purple end? And if that came to be, could she handle it?

It was not just a question about chasteness: Nobody begrudges a slice from a loaf that knows the knife. And, in coming here with him at all, her willingness was implicit. Anyhow, beyond that, she was more than warmly intrigued. The kid stirred juices at her core, dizzied her blood—gave her an electric giddy of anticipation for his voice, his zest, his glances weak for her.

Yet the simple bother of it was that—if the sex happened—she just wasn't sure how to actually do it with him. What moves might he fancy? What kind of response would engage and excite? Would he be savvy to working her fat, engorged nipples to advantage? Suppose he didn't take to the wiggling excitement that slipped into her hips? And then the special difficulty of his age. These times, with the mores so always changing, he might be aware of a different, younger way of doing it. Maybe a rap line to get it on with. Maybe even a special handhold. She'd been home so long, such a better way might've evolved. Bottom-line qualm was, could she fuck to suitably impress a twenty-year-old? She had been won by his charming confidence when she took on his dare. But deep in the cool of his eyes, had that gleam been part smirk? What had she given up, in truth, when she accepted his challenge?

Startled, she admitted to being anxious, even scared about what was to come. This was no first date. This was a straightforward sexual assignation. She and a pretty young man were scandalously shacking up in the wilds—in Greece, cradle of civilization—with bare amenities and each other for hedonistic amusement. Sassela, the cradle robber. Sidetracked momentarily, she envisioned herself in a loose white toga, reclining on a sofa, indifferent to the luscious grapes she munched as, her legs tossed obscenely, lusty men went wild for her. Smile grown to snigger at the picture, a rapscallion sense lightened her mood. After all was said and done, she was *supposed* to be on an adventurous vacation, having a good time. So why then was she acting the schoolmarm?

Still in a slough of indecision, she started toward the door.

A cheeky breeze kissed, the breakers murmured and chuckled. Take it easy, vacation-time rules are elastic, they seemed to suggest, and she'd helped to make it so. She should chill, her kids would say. The gravel, smooth to her bare soles, seemed bottomless black to her disappearing feet. It put her steps off, stumbling her, until she realized not looking was the better way.

As she came and squatted opposite him, she watched his eyes. Neutral as fire, then he looked away, into the busily fluttering flames, yellow against the darkness, gilding his skin. She wanted to tell him how beautiful he was, said instead, "Ciam, how can I say I'm sorry?"

Behind cool fences, slow eyes slid her way. "Anyhow you want, ma'am."

"Stop it, Ciam. I mean this. I want us to start a new beginning now. We're just arrived and I'm having a great time. Okay? I was wrong just now. Guess I was being automatic. So let's make it finished and done. From this moment we go back to fun, okay? Now, I don't want to have to *beg* forgiveness." Halfway playful, she roughed her tone as she finished.

He was softened, though, and smiled. "Okay, okay. You wouldn't look so good begging. Say three amens and go in peace."

A deep breath; pointedly she asked, "Now can I have a drag?"

"You brought it in, remember." He grinned like a wolf. "This kinda drag was what I always had in mind."

She had not smoked pot in a dozen years, but she toked smoothly as ever. No misinhaling. No embarrassing coughs. In no time she was stoned.

The action within the fire was not nice anymore. The little gossiping breeze blowing in from the sea had grown into a boastful bully, whipping about the pretty flames, stripping them off charred sticks and brambles, leaving behind wispy smoking ruins. Maybe it was her head, but this breeze was being far too strident to maintain its title; squall seemed better warranted. To make the point, she raised swimmy eyes, found Ciam looking suggestion at her. This squall, said his concerned regard, shouldn't we go inside?

"Sure, my gallant," Sassela agreed. Although she might have merely nodded.

Reaching hands, they helped each other up—she, with decidedly more stagger, the more needful. He steadied her, then kicked sand on the fire. Vaguely, Sassela noted he was barefoot also, and promised her own poked soles slip-ons on the morrow, and tried kicking sand at the fire. Muffed it by plowing her big toe into a sandy mound. Ciam had done the job, though. The fire died in silence and the breeze. Then his tentative arm passed around her waist, clasped, let go, clasped again, but less a stranglehold. Sassela slipped her arm around his waist, felt him quiver, wondered if he was ticklish. She started to ask, but dismissed the curiosity to a private chuckle.

He chuckled right then, too, laughed outright. "This is great. The night of my life," he shouted to the busy breeze.

Her close ear got most of it. "Not so loud," she protested, guffawing as she saw the birth of a joke. "Not so loud," she repeated, "the children might hear."

And found that so uproariously amusing, they laughed themselves staggering up to Hut.

Silent again, they paused at the steps, unhooked embraces. Her eyes snatched at every way but his. The wind swished about prissily. She felt where his hands had been, thought she might want to pee, decided it wasn't that urgent. With a sigh that might've been hers, she had to look at him.

Found his eyes rapt on her as, at that moment, the shifty wind suddenly stilled. She read true want in his nightstruck gaze and, quaking, led the way up the three wobbly stairs. With each step, she thought of thresholds. Then she pushed open the door, entered, him crowding right behind.

With his Swiss army knife, he cut a candle in half, lit the wick, slid it flickering down a cracked, clear bottle. The flame faltered a moment, then burnt steadily, albeit less brightly.

"Is okay," he explained the dimness. "Less oxygen, but it out the wind." Then, a flash of white jockeys in shadow, he stripped off his jeans and was through the bedroom doorway scrambling into the oversize bed, where he pulled the cover sheet completely over his head. Though not before she sighted the shorts' tent-poled front.

Thankful for his modesty offer, from her suitcase she searched out an extra-large T-shirt, undressed to panties, then pulled it on.

Softly, she stepped to the other side of the big bed, pinched up the corner of the cover sheet, slipped in under it. Into a pillow of ease, the foam mattress yielding just so much, sucking her in comfortably. The tightness of jet lag, the walking, the travel; she wanted extravagantly to stretch it all away. But his close, tense quiet challenging intimacy, she held off.

Concentrating past her own pitter-patter heartbeats, straining to hear his, she suddenly felt his damp hand on her thigh. Shit! she thought, more disappointed than annoyed. She'd expected smoother moves. She pushed his hand away. "Not yet, Ciam."

His hand again, sweaty, immature, it never left off . . . shoving and gouging between her clamped thighs . . .

"No, no, no! Ciam. Take it easy. Stop."

. . . with hardly the energy to shift away . . . grabby hands reaching her breasts, then one again down there, fingers strong, scrabbling, pinching hairs . . .

"Ciam, stop it! You're spoiling everything."

. . . twisting away . . . she stopped, panting for breath . . . he was stronger, insistent . . . was partway atop now, straddled over her, forcing her thighs open with his bruising, bony knee . . .

"Ciam!" she screamed. "What're you doing? You said you wouldn't. You promised."

He was breathing hard, too, holding her arms pinned to the bed, pinching the strength out of her, using his knees, forcing apart, yet, eyebrows fierced together, he still had a grin in him. "Lied," he panted.

That did it—the answer in his wicked, competitive grin, as if he were playing a game with tricky rules. The old conquering-male game. Shit and hell! Sassela cursed mentally, I don't have energy for this. Why am I fighting? Why should I? I am here in fact, tired and stoned and travel-sore in his bed. In his rustic cabin by the sea and, I'm sure in his eyes, I should be playing the appropriate female role. Instead of igging the spirit of the game and acting as if ignorant that Necessity's other child, the girl, was Compromise.

All of it—the presumption, the boorishness—was ridiculous. But, exhausted by the fighting, she gasped, "Okay, okay. Stop. If that's how you want it."

Took him off guard. She could have slipped away in his disconcerted pause, but where to. Instead she remained accommodatingly limp as he tugged and tossed away the sheet and her T-shirt. Then when he set to pulling down her panties, she shifted up her backsides, lent a hand. He moaned at that, stroked her belly with cold fingers.

The panties stripping past her ankles, she shut her eyes, averted her face in the dim, flickering light as he clambered between her thighs, moaned again. A desperate tone that forced her eyes back, to see him crouched there, humbled like a penitent.

Contrarily, the sight stirred her desire, unexpectedly melting her ready. So that, swallowing restraint, she arched her back and raised her knees up, opened scarlet for him.

He was fumbling down there, creeping nearer, thrusting forward. Expecting entry, instead there gushed ejaculate all over her belly and thighs as, flopping onto her, he cried, "Oh, gosh. Oh, gosh—" crushing his head to her breasts, tears dripping steadily, tracking down her shoulder.

Everywhere was slick: her pussy still squirming

ready, belly to belly gooey where he lay, the tracks of his slinky tears, their slippery sweatiness. She held him coolly, without chagrin at his failure, wryly in control. His body's heat was nice, gratifying. And he fit her embrace just right, his weight a soothing massage. Languorous, soon she drifted off. . . .

. . . he's rummaging through her sanitary napkins, his hands and face becoming stained with dirty blood: he looks at her helpless and accusingly . . . she laughs at him, and taunts in childish singsong, "Y'own fault told on you. Y'own fault told on you. Y'own fault told . . ."

She awoke from black empty sleep needing to go to the bathroom, and was almost from under the covers when, with a start, she remembered and a rush of anxiety whisked away the urgency to pee.

Some of her disquiet relaxed when she saw Ciam scrunched up fetal, a corner of the sheet clenched at his face as if he were suckling sleep from it. By the candle in the glass still dimly flickering, an innocent bundle of shadows he made. She realized she was naked, skimmed the floor and found her big T-shirt. She got quietly out of bed, the boards cool underfoot as she put on the shirt. Only then did she feel the chill in the room, and her bladder reminded of why she'd woken.

Just then, fast asleep, Ciam resettled himself, muttered something. Sounded satisfied, intimate. A noisy snoozer, huh! Sassela thought, and tiptoed to her slip-ons.

The track to the privy showed quite plainly; convenient, since even with hurrying her last few steps, she barely made it in time. More relaxed on the way back, she could now notice east vaguely clearing for dawn, and the soothing susurrus of the close-by sea, and the tentative caw-cawing bird calls. A sense of timelessness, and ease. She heaved in a deep breath, released it as a long sigh. Although right now her chilly goose bumps pointed inside, yes! she admitted, she could like it here.

He was just as she'd left him when Sassela as quietly got back into bed. She lay for a bit thinking, knew a sort of relief after last evening: it seemed the worst was done with. She wondered how he'd manage his failure, and how she could help. It hadn't been her first encounter with haste laying waste. For though he'd behaved like a lout, she felt Ciam was a nice guy at the core, just clumsily trying to impress. Look how he'd fixed up the shack, christened it "Hut." Yes, he promised fun, and stirred sympathetic, Sassela gently embraced his shoulder with one arm, and spooned her belly into his spine. Unawakened, he wiggled back reflexively, his naked skin very warm, very nice. And yes! she admitted as well, she liked his being there.

Close to dozing off, she nagged herself to remember: When they went to town, she needed to buy birth control.

14

Around midmorning, Ciam nowhere to be found, Sassela walked the fifty or so yards up the track to where it met the graveled roadway, and there at the arranged spot was their bag of supplies. Her heart did a stutter-step for marveling at the folks' simple, honest reliability. And so close to a tourist town! Baby could get used to this, Sassela decided, lips twisting down in a smirk.

Then she opened the plastic-lined brown bag, poked around inside. Packets of whole-wheat flour, red beans and lentils, rice. A small tub of margarine. Garlic— maybe in excess, as she recalled seeing several aban- doned-looking cloves on the shelf back in Hut. A small bag of cherry tomatoes, another of golden apricots. Three bottles of retsina, two of white wine. A box of those convenient three-inch-long matches. And, stacked together like green barbed swords, two fat and thought- ful aloe leaves. A welcome surprise, since she'd not mentioned them when she sponsored and helped com- pose their weekly shopping list with Yiorgis. She thought of the older man, by design or chance, certainly Ciam's co-conspirator. For it was that stop at the coffee-house that had bewitched the moment, beguiling her to how Ciam was charming, and made her hold his hands and admit in her guts that she felt beautiful with him, and would stay with him at his beach shack.

She hoisted the bag to her bosom and, in pleasant reverie, started back.

The day continued with perfect weather as if con-cerned about promises in the tourist brochure. When Ciam returned—Sassela surmised shyness, though he said just roaming—the early part they spent easy, indulging to wants of bellies and bodies for the sunny beach. Using a page at the back of a travel notebook, Sassela briefly attended to a makeshift diary until she could unpack the original.

Hi Di.

Excuse the inattention. Busy having fun without measure. The trip's guide recommends: we have to put away watches so that "BusyMan can't turn daily rhythms into a timeclock." Can I fight that philosophy? NB: Should mention that I've remembered how to dream in full chapters. Not the usual phrases and paragraphs. Am I glad? Guess.

Bfn. Sss.

Mission accomplished, reading over and thinking of her promise to Cathy, she decided—two birds with one lazy stone—to make her diary do as a journal. Then she snapped the notebook shut, returned it to her pocketbook.

Midafternoon, they decided on a stroll into town, the plan to rent bicycles. It was a three-kilometer trek over a low goat-cropped hill, through olive and grain fields. From just a bit down from the crest, the bustling seaside town looked picturesque as a postcard: pervasive whitewashed walls, reddish-brown rooftops, here and there a plume of chimney smoke, a punctuation of church spires, crucifixes imploring the sky. Sassela breathed deeply, held in the clear sweet air as if to keep it, make its zest part of her. Sensitive of the cliché it suggested, still she couldn't resist feeling she had happened onto the much-storied and elusive undiscovered paradise.

The business district was some six or so blocks along a main road midway down a peninsula of beach. Interspersed among the expected merchandise storefronts along the way were a post office, a modern pharmacy (with contraceptive sponges, she found out), two banks, several eating places, guesthouses. Not much selling was going on, both tourists and locals mostly using the store awnings for shade. Ciam went into a handbag store, returned with directions to a bike rental.

It was a block back the way they'd come, and down a side street. They were to look for a blue door, ask for Gregori. Ciam knocked on a blue door, pushed it open. They entered a tiny storefront office divided by a low plywood partition topped by a shiny counter bare but for a bell. In charge again, Ciam rang the bell.

In the small space, the resounding clangor was startling. No other apparent effect, though. Time lingered like an echo; amused, they exchanged looks. Sassela eyed the bell, gave a face and shrugged. His thoughts exactly, Ciam took the bell and began clanging like it came from Poe's poem.

Behind the counter, a door burst open and a man rushed through shouting exasperatedly, "*Ti, ti* . . . What!" A burly, mustachioed, black-haired man with glaring slits of black eyes. A busy man wearing a checkered tan sport-

jacket a size too small, who obviously had been interrupted from matters of import.

Ciam slammed down the bell as if it were guilty and
he a dumb audience. He nodded sheepishly in Sassela's
direction.

The man's glare turned her way and held, the glower
slowly fading, the salesman coming back.

"How I help you?" he said in a professional manner,
hairy left hand elaborately spinning the air. "Tell me
now I hear again." Baritone chuckle forgiving from his
throat, black slits disappearing in the crinkles of a
much-practiced smile.

Sunrise to sunrise, Sassela matched him as falsely.

Bursting through the artificial glow, Ciam said, "We
looking for Gregori."

"You are here then. Gregori, I am," the salesman
said. "John I can be, too. And maybe sometimes, Takis.
It all depends on who is sender. You see? Huh?" He
leaned across the formica counter, looked from one to
the other.

Sassela shrugged indifference, shook her head.

Ciam started a slow "Nooo—" then said tri-
umphantly, "Yeah, I got it. Bet you know who sent us.
Right?"

"You bet," boomed Gregori. "The leather man. No?
With his bags and purses, no?"

"Right first time," declared Ciam, smiling. "And
from now on, I call you 'Mr. Slick.'"

Sham all the way, but as if it were the praise Gregori
always dreamed to hear, he reached for Ciam's hand,
shook it vigorously. "You a good man," he exclaimed.
"Whatever you want for? I take care of everything."

"Bikes," said Ciam.

"No problem." Gregori held up two fingers. "A great
price, and you get the best. When you want for?"

"We want to ride back home. Keep them a few days."

"No problem," repeated Gregori.

"How much per day?"

"One thousand drachmas. Only four American dollars."

"Great," said Ciam. "That's for the two bikes, right?"

"A good man." Gregori laughed heartily. "What a good man. But no, no. For one bike. Look, I make it six hundred each since you take two. No profit, but you a good man."

Halfway listening to their haggle, Sassela wandered to the door, looked out at the scene on this side road. Fronts of low houses crowding the bitty sidewalk; a toddler naked but for the diaper, playing where the sidewalk had risen to a one-foot drop; a shrouded woman well inside a window: baby-sitting from a casual distance?

Ciam's suddenly risen voice caught her attention. No problem, though. Just that their talk had turned to soccer—La Cupa Mundial, World Cup qualifications. And as if he would score the goals, Ciam was crowing, "Is Brazil all the way!"

Gregori, unshaven face caricaturing incredulity with a scoffing chuckle, began pointing out Ciam's naïveté—

Sassela disengaged. It was a discussion she had witnessed all her life, whenever her menfolk got together. Never arriving at a point or resolution, she found these debates ultimately boring.

So back to the street scene her eyes drifted: the snotty-faced toddler still exploring the pavement; the low doorways' quaintness closing near to dilapidation; the stolid, still-life quality so close to the bustling sounds around the corner just a few feet away. Her mind drifted from seeking a point to the peculiarity, shunted back to men in general.

It was funny how similar they were in their interests, in what jerked their strings. She remembered herself—a child in Harlem—every summer Sunday morning, asking, "Where's Pa, Ma?"

"As ever's gone fishin', child."

Yes! Pa, rain or shine, a fishing fan. Still was, as was every man of one sport or other. And Pa, like them all, certainly had the treasury of facts and stats, remote and superior to any. Had to be a man thing. Same as they had lunatic affinity for philosophies and political persuasions. Same as they lived close to pride, and wished to leave a grand mark on earth. Men were patriots, and universally felt a right to pass judgment on women's choice of lovers, claiming earnestly, "She's mine!"

Beyond her thoughts, in her glazed vision, the toddler on the pavement ventured closer to the foot-high edge, no one seeming to notice . . . no problem, though: handily, bottom first, he swung down . . . diaper wobbling loose, he crept farther into the street, intent on tiny life-forms.

Somewhere, Sassela had read that men's hearing and smell, the most emotionally significant physical and chemical senses, were inferior to women's. Some languages derived the word for man from lesser roots, as if defensively lowering expectations. As if readying the world for men's squander of time and energy.

Caught up to his quarry, the toddler plopped his bare bottom on the gravelly asphalt . . . with grimy hand and stubby fingers, he reached and captured something, brought it to his dribbly mouth . . . absently apprehensive, Sassela's gaze ranged about her view of the quiet street, her mind still preoccupied.

Men focused, believed in targets, knew the sum of one and one. Then they missed the point. Even with matters as basic as lovemaking, men were preoccupied about esteem and dimensions. Must be men's dreams were of themselves. They wished for the moon, their image in it as dreamscape. No blood, no cramps. They lived in worlds of their own mind-set, sweated at making maybes. This made them poets, inventors, maniacs. Made them interesting sometimes, and even fun.

Draped completely in black, an angular woman with a strangely equine face—although a horse is a beautiful animal—came out the blue door and swooped up the toddler, who immediately set to piercing screams of protest.

A louder outburst of whooping amusement drew her back to the men. To find Gregori sweating, manic face shouting, "*Ne, ne, ne!* They are crazy—" He couldn't go on for hooting, and slapping the counter, and clapping his hands as Ciam waddled to a near corner and vigorously wiggled his hips at it, somehow further sweetening the joke. Succeeding perfectly, as Gregori exploded into laughing fits once again.

At last, hilarity subsiding, Gregori led them out of the shop and showed them the bikes, then bowed himself away with a flourish and his fistful of drachmas. They decided to leave the bikes be, and walk about the winding, narrow backstreets. But it was dreary there with few native folks except an occasional shrouded one, even forbidding eye contact. So they hit the main thoroughfare for the shops. Sporting partial tans, designer clothes, and various ready monies, a few easily identifiable tourists strolled about. Sassela went into one or two stores, found the offerings of cheap quality, the scene too much a bazaar act.

Because it boasted a back room with a window on the sea and smelled of cardamom, they chose a tiny restaurant, asked the waiter for a typical Greek snack. "I know what you wish," he said confidently, and was off. Soon enough, he was serving them *dolmades*, and smoked octopus with whole-grain bread dipped in olive oil. Ciam had plain milk, she had strong tea. All of the repast delicious, and they chowed down to muted sounds of traffic noises, riffs on a tuned guitar, bursts of some man's delighted laughter, cicadas, waves. Beautiful.

On their way back to pick up the bikes, Sassela noticed a young girl at a street-level window with an older woman who might've been a chaperone. Noticed because the girl sported an enormous pile of black hair pulled up high on her head, precociously adult. Gauche. As they approached, the girl beckoned. Ciam hesitated, glancing questioningly at Sassela, then stepped forward. But instead of speaking, the girl simpered, reached her hand through the window and caressed his face.

The chaperone roughly tugged the girl back in and admonished her as, hand to the surprised cheek, Ciam flinched away, returned to Sassela's side. "Saw that?" he asked as they walked on.

"Did I!" said Sassela. "What brought it on?"

"Surprise to me." His tone supported the slow-spoken words. "She did wave when we passed before, from a higher window. Must be my magnetism."

"Whatever. For a little girl, she needs to learn where to keep her hands," said Sassela, and glanced back. The child was leaning out the window, gazing intently after them.

Sassela flashed her a stern look, took Ciam's arm possessively, smiled at the half-questioning grin he gave her. She didn't let go until they were around the corner heading toward Gregori, ready to collect the bikes.

15

Back at Hut they sat at the table chatting amiably. Sassela was sipping her second cup of the local retsina Yiorgis had selected for them. An acrid, though sweet-ish, pine flavor.

A rising wind whistled in through cracks between the wall boards. "We might've to accustom weselves to this, yu'know. It might be a pattern," observed Ciam with scientific seriousness. "You know, like night breezes in the Caribbean."

"You might be right, Ci," Sassela agreed absently, side-minded by his fingers crumbling the ganja fine enough for joints. "Not sweating it, but what I'd like to know is when did you put, er, hide the ganja in my pocketbook," she said.

"You don't want to know 'bout island breezes, lee-ward and windward, and so on?" Ciam teased.

"No, not really. Come on, Ci. Tell me how you did it."

"Does the magicman reveal his gimmick?" Smile half-playful.

"S'not right," she pouted, sucked her teeth frothily.

"Weeeell!" he sighed like it was the fate of the world. "Only to get back the shine in your smile again. I'll tell you. Was first thing when we met in the customs line. When I put down my bag with yours and took your shoulder bag—"

Pricked by a pang of hindsight consternation, she said, "But, but what if—?"

"You were never in danger, my Beautiful One. Not ever, at all. I had the old divertissement ploy going." He smiled madly, the confidence quavering her heart. "Here's how we do it. The pretty female is the obvious number-one suspect. Right? So the idea is to make myself the better suspect, by overtalking, overdoing, being overquick to offer help."

He paused to lick the joint and seal it. Then he lit up, toked deeply, eyes closed. Then, exhaling like a chimney, he passed her the joint, continued: "Then comes the old stinking underwear bit. Yup, now he's really covering up something, speculates the watchful guardian. Meantime you, suspect number one, is so surprised and embarrassed by the whole proceedings, you honestly behave—the honest reaction is impor-tant—like you're wanting to get out of there, and estab-lish that you are *definitely* unacquainted with yours truly in any way, shape, or reincarnation. So if it'd come to that, they'd've stopped me, but they'd've let you through. Just so to clear decks and better investigate moi. Dig? And easy so, is mission accomplished. The pretty cover-lady gets through with the stuff." He clapped satisfied hands as period, reached for the joint from her listening fingers, filled his lungs again.

Details of the flaws in his thinking fought forward for her asking. Details like, Why wouldn't the authori-ties associate them together? And, How many times might they have encountered his trick? And, What if there were dogs? And a muchness of other stuff. But the ganja aroma had recalled a flash of attitude long forgotten: of riding wild wind, while letting the Devil take hindmost. Impatient and excited, that remembered self asked, What difference does it make? Isn't the smoke working? As ballsy as it was brought in, it had to be a worthwhile move.

More than halfway there, getting higher, she watched his silhouette cast on the walls from the flaring of their rude flambeau—the light source hinting of a Molotov cocktail under controlled explosion. His image, its color, shade, and shape, kept changing on the wall, forming surreal impressions. The light on him, his cinnamon brown melding with the gray-worn board walls, making him briefly indistinguishable, except where he was limned by the black gaps of outside night where the wood slabs casually met. And with every sway of the wind on the half-naked flame, his shape made adjustment. It became a leonine profile, his baby dreads an exact mane. Then more like a leopard—with a smooth, stalking slope from neck down to back, a slope suggesting grace and the lethal swiftness of a strike. Then the flare'd change him again, accenting the pout of his mouth to a snout and his brow to an apelike overhang. Ceaselessly, the jerky impressions kept changing, alarming, unsettling, spinning her mind. She decided she should get up, take a little walk, a breath of fresh air to clear her head. She stood up. Tried to, at least. But her knees misbehaved, acted unfamiliar with the task of bending yet supporting. She sagged in her attempt, and suddenly on the wall, noticed her shadow swaying like a junkie. Unexpectedly amused, she grinned, then guffawed out loud. She looked at him, found Ciam grinning at her.

"Feeling good, huh," he said. "It hitting you?"

"Something is," answered Sassela. "Want to take a walk?"

He took her hand firmly, helped her up. "Sure. If you will, madame, we shall now view the grounds." With his accent, the delivery was a ridiculous mockery of English nobility.

She lurched to her feet in laughter. They staggered down the steps, went up a bluff at the western end of the crescent-shaped cove.

The wind awaited them, busy but not hostile. They could stand cuddled against a rock high above the dark sea, and watch Night hold court. Warm and safe with him, Sassela saw big waves violent against the rocks below, splashing relentlessly, flicking up white foam to be caught and shredded by the foraging wind. Even in the cozy nook, Sassela tickled to a cool sprinkle of sea mist. Somehow, the barrage down there energized her spirits. Here was a *real* holiday. In this natural place, held in Ciam's fierce embrace, she was truly away from it all. Yes! Perfection would be a long, warm, relaxing bath. But remembering Hut's spare shower, she sighed.

"Hmnmn?" murmured Ciam.

"Was wishing a nice warm show—bath, I mean."

"If you shower now, the tapwater will be warm. The pipes're close under the sand exposed to sunshine."

"Really?" said Sassela.

"Radiant energy. Yiorgis bragged about it. And it's true. Checked last night."

They returned to Hut. She opened her suitcase, took out some necessaries and a towel, went outside to the ramshackle shower stall. Out of the chill wind, the tapwater was indeed body-warm and balmy. She had an efficient, unexpectedly relaxing shower.

Finished, and crossing the darkness to the three steps up to Hut's door, she warmed to a good feeling. Here she was, vacationing with her picked-up pretty youth, and everything copacetic, proceeding A-okay.

And why not? She grinned to herself, mentally toasted Meeri's philosophy of romantic getaways.

Last night had played out his way. Tonight, her mind unconsciously set for it, she intended a queen's gambit. The wind whistled musically, a seductive melody. The low light of the candle flickering like boudoir shades, in unbuttoned long sleeves and panties, she stopped his bolt under the bedcovers, put a finger to his abashed lips. "Hush!" she bade. "Just sit, watch."

She caught his eyes, round, black in the dimness, entranced. She led them with her own to her hair, deliberately pulling down the panties. Revealing slowly all of the curly pelt, thick and black down from her navel and growing even blacker as her plot thickened. Empowered and amused by his staring, compliant eyes, she then revealed her undersides: spread and slowly crabbed a vulgar striptease, let him see her naked as she'd have never recognized. And when she had him trembling, she went to where he sat, knelt and pulled off his bulging jockey shorts. Then she stood him up, and drew him close to her in full-length embrace, his bone-hard cock a throbbing racer against her tremulous belly.

A while—then without breaking embrace, Sassela laid them down on the bed. But so ardent he was, so quivering, he couldn't hold off, and swiftly was poised lithe between her welcoming thighs.

She gasped as his cock slid in—smaller than her custom, but rock hard. Too hard. He jammed it in, she not minding the roughness, his smacking hips down so fast. But it was too fast. And even as Sassela thought how to slow him, he gave in, collapsing onto her, throwing his head back and shuddering as he spurted. Oddly thrilled by his quick surrender, with legs and arms, Sassela held close, and took him all.

His cock half-stiff and giving pleasantly inside her, after a bit she set to roll them over, careful to keep him in, so she could straddle. It wasn't hard; she almost as big as he, and he with his muscular suppleness. But as soon as she bent forward for a congratulatory taste of his brow's beading sweat, his cock slipped out, smacking thickly against her leg.

He made a move to put it back in. But the solid smack had spawned a vague suggestion, and Sassela shrugged her hip away, said instead, "Just stay there quiet."

As the idea took form, she caught his quick halfway-up look before it fluttered to hide under trembling eyelids. A tiny tear peeped bright against his cheekbone. How shy and vulnerable he looked. So pregnable, it stirred and set her wet, and she began hip-rocking atop him, slowly, wanting to torture although still teasing her control and herself to the squishy slick sounds of their meshing juices.

"Stay there. Can't you?" she goaded. "Just right there."

But he couldn't stand it, and committed a little wiggle, made her lose the spot.

Fierce again, "Stay quiet," Sassela said hoarsely. "Let me do it all." She shifted on their slickness, trying to get it right again. But he was getting harder, and with all the wet, any little nudge went farther, and once or twice, just as it was getting close to as before, he fell to a spasm of wiggles.

"Oh, it so sweet," he moaned.

It raced her blood to hear him succumb to the ride. "You like that, huh?" she panted, and held onto his arms to brace him, while with her feet she hobbled down his ankles. Then, teeth gritted, and eyes hard into his, she grunted, "You just stay put. Hear me?"

And, going slack, he complied. So then she could settle down and trap his rigid cock between his belly and her electric spot, and ride their slick gently and just right. Until all at once, the delicate rush was there, blooming power, taking over and charging her with a surging breathlessness that crashed her, gasping, onto him.

Lying there, face in his neck's sweat, smelling him, the thrills of her climax combined unexpectedly with his man-scent, flavoring the moment with illicitness, and gratitude, and conquest. A potion that almost immediately revitalized, and squatting up, she set to a sweet trot up to the brink. Until soon, so soon, she was caught in the vacuum of another orgasm—this one truly a swoon.

His breath close on her cheek, she opened reluctant eyes.

"You crying. Why?" he whispered, smoothing a tear-track down into her left ear.

She passed a listless hand down his slick, hard back. "It's okay," she murmured. "Happiness."

Drowsier than could come to mind, she tried smiling to the concern in his earnest face. Their cheeks touched, and in a sudden fancy, his soft new hair, more down than beard, seemed representative of his tenderness. A softness Sassela hardly admitted craving, and which now, so ardently given, swelled her heart. To hide her teary rush, she pulled him closer, sniffled in his dusky aroma as she cleared her nose and stifled the queer emotion.

16

She awoke first; it wasn't even dawn. Ciam slept on. Despite jet lag, her body was keeping strict rhythms. Back home, it would've been at a more sensible hour, but here it was time to squat. Careful of the quiet, she pulled her big T-shirt overhead, tiptoed to her slip-ons by the door. One tiny squeak, and she was out in open night-light, on the path to the latrine nooked against the black hill.

She had been holding in, queasy about the bare facilities. But though spartan, the outhouse did not smell at all, and the cool seat was smooth and clean and comfortable. Fresh toilet paper rolled from a rope hung at easy reach, and the whistle through the cracks reminded of her down-South aunt's rustic latrine. She got to thinking comparison stories for when she got back home, and eventually left the outhouse well relieved.

On the track back to Hut, buoyant from a good one gone south, she heard a splattering that didn't take long to identify. Swift to Hut's mountainface side, she looked around the corner: saw her confirmed suspicions arching sparkly to the sand. "Hugghh!" she cried, moral disgust intermixed with civic propriety. "That's cheating, Ciam."

Startled at discovery, the graceful flow fractured momentarily, then continued to its sputtering conclusion. Then, grin in his tone, he called back, "You wrong there, Bubulups. Is just another way I-man make his man behave, another control womankind can only crave. Advantage male."

"That so? As if nasty and cheating wasn't enough, you're turning male chauvinist on me. Well, we'll soon see about all this male advantage you're claiming."

Tone of fun set for the day, one tease to another, they were back to the bed, to explore the virtue of a certain early morning pursuit involving raw flesh, salty and slippery.

"Is a delicate trait of any true Caribbean man," Ciam claimed as he shifted himself for good vantage.

Taken aback at his frank and single-minded pursuit, pro forma, Sassela indulged him. While relaxed into the easy pleasure, back of her mind she toyed with setting ideal rhythms for their lovers' vacation.

A doze later on, true morning come, Ciam lit the kerosene stove and, all done in one battered skillet, made them a breakfast of feta cheese, whole-wheat bread, and eggs. He dropped tea bags into two mugs of boiling-hot milk, let it steep for two minutes. No sugar. Turned out steamingly delicious. Eyes sparkling with braggadocio, he knew it was, too. She toasted his boast, her smile crumbly with bread and cheese.

Sassela anointed herself in industrial-strength sunscreen against the afternoon's glowering UV rays, and they set out to explore the crescent-shaped cove. Strolled from end to rocky end, noting that at high tide turning, the beach had narrowed to near impassable around the points. With the tide well out though, within the cove's curving belly, sandbars would trap pools. Already there were a few. Ciam waded in and squatted knees to chest, testing. "It's great! Warm, really warm. I can see my toes. This'll be great."

Expert opinion enough for her. Intending herself a full-bodied tan, Sassela scouted for the most private patches; ones out of eyes' reach, and modestly away from the public approach to Hut. One likely spot Ciam wanted to test was a shady berth, beside a rock large enough, the gravelly sand smooth, dry, lewdly inviting. "Why not?" she agreed.

They stripped, and then and there determined the location perfectly suitable.

Content, faraway nearing a doze, Sassela was snatched back by an out-of-place sound. Slitting her eyes open, she itched up a frown. A breathy snigger? A titter? But that just didn't make sense. She turned, murmuring, "Did y—?"

Ciam was on his back, lips slackly hissing sleep. No help. But she was so close to certain. If that wasn't a human something, she had to find out what it was. Carefully, risen by her curiosity, she stalked naked toward the dusky gullies of boulders.

It happened again as she prowled closer. This time she was certain. A snigger, all right; a carnal urging, close followed by a deep, slow sigh of pleasure, all distinctly female.

The sounds fleshed up images of herself and Ciam earlier, and, squeamish in her voyeur's role, Sassela stopped. About to return, she heard a splash of footsteps approaching through the tide pools. Solid, certain splashing—something odd about it. Quickly she crouched behind an interposing boulder as the footsteps passed on the other side. She waited, jammed against the warm boulder, until the footsteps squelched to safe earshot. Then, rising cautiously, she turned to retrace her path to her towels, and Ciam. She cast a glance over her shoulder and stopped short: the couple was plainly silhouetted against the dark, violet sky.

Right off the oddness was identified and explained: the single footsteps she had heard! For the departing figures seemed to be a burly man with a very small woman astride his shoulders, riding him. Something about their picture, a strangeness seized her, nagged her mind for identity. But she just couldn't pinpoint it, except for a discomfort she felt at seeing such a pairing, an intrigue awry with the kinky lovers' sounds she'd heard.

Unsettled, she stood in the shadow of the sheltering boulder, watched them disappear around the crescent tip of the cove's shoreline. Sassela shook her head, gave up. Had she only been dressed, she definitely would have been on that trail.

At his request, Sassela took a walk while Ciam made dinner: "Chef gotta figure out his kitchen lonesome. Is a matter of professionalism," he declared with his paunchy laugh.

So she took her diary, went strolling their matchless cove. Went high on the rocky bluff, lit crimson by the cooling sun. She tried for a serious effort at her journal:

Do you address an alternative journal as a person?
A personal entity? A person-ally T? What to say to
a deputy diary? Well anyhow, I've been dreaming
like a baby. The strangest stuff. Fell off after first
ride with the Guide—

She couldn't resist caginess.

—and saw Time as a stone flung, directed from an elsewhere, and immensely powered, the drive based in what's past, and forwarded or pushed by the hands of what's going on, creating what is to be. All of it, very weirdly, going on simultaneously. Still, despite that, I understood Time was all about water and trees and sky, gray or bright blue. And somehow many stars were involved, from a sky softly brilliant, although it was night. But that wasn't what the dream was really about. All that was more of a setting for what the dream was proposing—to me, primarily, although other people were somewhere in the background. Although I'm not certain about the other people. Not 100 percent. Y'know dreams. Anyhow, the dream was meaning for me to realize the essence behind the things happening around me. Like why schools are always behind the times. Why toothpaste is white and green, but never black or yellow. And all sorts of other ordinary, absolutely unimportant things. Unnecessary, even. Except for somehow illustrating the flow of Time. That was what the dream was mainly about: flow of Time, and what I should know from it. I woke from it remembering every detail, feeling very strange. I mean, since I came here on this outing, I've been dreaming every time I close my eyes. Even if I can't remember it, every night I dream something or the other. That's not me at all. Was never much of a dreamer. But whatever's happening, I like it. It's a good time. Having an exciting existence even in my sleep. Might've even come upon a weird mystery on the beach. But more to come on that. So overall? Well, I think this trip and everything else has been a good idea. Am enjoying.

Seeyalata, Sss.

* * *

Content with her journal entry, and pulled by hunger, she returned to Hut and met aromas of another one-pot marvel: tantalizing garlicky rice, corned beef hash. A bottle of pale yellow retsina. Enough to make her a believer that Ciam was a genuine poor man's gourmet.

They ate like starvelings, went to sleep fulfilled, she never remembering to speak her intrigue about the odd couple.

17

The third day, on the bikes, they ventured farther away from the commercial side of town. A wealthy section: paved road and a grocery with shopping-mart ambitions, both serving pricey pastel house-palaces, most with enormous pools. These millionaire country hideaways were, every one, well fenced and locked away and, despite their striking architecture, seemed aloof and longing for homey folks.

Around a hill, away from the superior sea views, the roadway became commonplace and gravelly again. Alongside it, spiny, gnarled shrubs with tiny flowers—purple, pink, gold—survived audacious. Farther away, white-tipped mountains slant-sided sparse brown vegetation among plateaus of forbidding gray rock. All of it stony ground, defiant to mankind's plows, or will. Off and on, the stark, yearning landscape displayed slivers of white-walled villages which, Sassela could imagine, with soft evening light might resemble bones on black velvet.

Green was a rare promise, stood out like oases and

made Sassela thirsty. So the first meager shade they came upon—a copse of olive trees—they parked the bikes to have a snack, quaff some wine to spur their mood. Which was just what it did. With the isolation and the concealing grass, Ciam recalled a promise to himself. Huggy and kissy like a teenager, he wanted her breasts. To suck and lick and watch the nipples gorge into sweet blackberries. After which, bear to the honey, he followed the pelt starting at her navel.

"God, it so, so much," he mumbled, thick-tongued. "And musky."

Sassela lay back, let him.

Since she reached puberty, every bathing suit she'd owned had been long-legged; primarily because of an abundantly hairy crotch from high around her navel to sideburns down her inner thighs. A personal feature that changed her life around the time she hit ten or eleven, having discovered with her sweet and tender spot a weakness to caress it. From the romantic poetry she'd been reading, she was certain it *was* her heart. That innermost heart over which she flushed, embarrassed at the boldness, every time she heard a phrase suggesting "giving one's heart away."

Then rapidly—in a matter of months—the hair around her "heart" grew luxuriant, covering it somewhat, protecting it from the brushes with underwear, toilet paper, other ruffians. Although it might've been simply her softness growing tougher and more tolerant to touching—a habit now stolen for quick pleasure, or plain relaxation.

Puberty past, her practiced delight developed a leakage problem: a readily gushing slipperiness that quickly dripped down the long jet black hair of her inside thighs. Damp, wet, and uncomfortable it kept her. First solution she tried was shaving, and found out the essence of irritation as the hairs regrew in their natural bent, some short shafts curling back into the tender skin and growing there subdermally, creating painful yellowing pimples. After which came the torture of picking them out; the unreachable being left to her mother, to Sassela's absolute embarrassment.

The moral, why now she kept her hair. And to keep that hairiness in place and out of sight, she wore swim-suits almost with inseams. Although with time she had also learned kinkiness and valued her pelt, was person-ally vain about it, and wont to grooming it for pleasure, her fingers smoothly through the coarse curly hair, sen-sually soothing.

Harry was the first to go crazy about and in it, and truth said, he was the one who finally convinced her of its outstanding erotic quality. So whenever a decision arose about giving it up, or even trimming it some, her dominant reasoning remained that she didn't go to the sea nearly as much as to bed. And her hair stayed.

Now here was Ciam too, gone wild with fondling and petting. Content to lie with his head in her lap, sniffing extravagantly and sighing happiness at being close to "her honey," his moniker.

The downside to his slobbering fascination with the musk of her hairy pubes was a certain itch; a swollen tenderness that bespoke incipient yeast infection. Which, of course, had never entered her mind when she was packing. Set her wondering, though, about the strength of the local plain yogurt.

A bit later, mellow and soothed, they set off again. Only now the barren sameness discouraged. As did the dusty, hot road (plus prickling privately for Sassela, a sore butt), so they decided to head back most directly, by commuter main road, paved and bearing hard-core Grecian traffic: mopeds daring air-conditioned power cars whose sealed windows shielded dark-shaded daredevil drivers; laughing school-aged innocents antic on their fragile bikes; and smoky chuggers of dinosaur vehicles slowing down the chaos. Yet, adjacent to all this busy groan and hiss and swish, they rode past a field Sassela remembered from her map, asterisked as producing olives since Christ's time. Too much traffic to stop and stare, but she could believe it: along the face of one clifflike break in the landscape, a taproot system sought down no less than six or seven hundred feet!

Beyond the traffic, the evening fell pleasant—a cool breeze at their backs, and on seaside roads again, they enjoyed a leisurely ride. Along the way, the moonlight conjuring a humor, Ciam began reciting stanzas of "The Highwayman":

> *The wind was a torrent of darkness among the*
> *gusty trees,*
> *The moon was a ghostly galleon tossed upon cloudy*
> *seas,*
> *The road was a ribbon of moonlight over the purple*
> *moor,*
> *And the highwayman came riding, riding, riding*
> *The highwayman came riding, up to the old*
> *inn-door . . .*
> *He'd a French cocked-hat on his forehead, a bunch*
> *of lace at his chin,*
> *A coat of the claret velvet, and breeches of brown*
> *doe-skin:*
> *They fitted with never a wrinkle: his boots were up*
> *to the thigh!*
> *And he rode with a jeweled twinkle, his pistol butts*
> *a-twinkle,*
> *His rapier hilt a-twinkle, under the jeweled*
> *sky . . .*
> *Over the cobbles he clattered and clashed in the*
> *dark inn-yard,*

And he tapped with his whip on the shutters, but all
*   was locked and barred:*
He whistled a tune to the window, and who should
*   be waiting there,*
But the landlord's black-eyed daughter,
Bess, the landlord's daughter,
Plaiting a dark red love-knot into her long black
*   hair . . .*

A love poem, a poignant story of jealousy, passion, and death. He recited well, playing with different vocal timbres, his rendition perfectly suiting the incomparable Grecian evening.

The following day they decided on some shopping in town, just to check out the scene. Commercial indeed, Sassela found the market area: guesthouses, liquor stores, tourist traps with plastic mementos, and a phalanx of street vendors. They pushed their bikes through the throngs, stopping here and there, browsers more than buyers. After a while they withdrew to watch the action from a little café, while snacking on grainy bread with feta cheese and sweet red wine.

In the brightness outside the wooden shutters, the tourists, sporting self-assurance in their cameras and trendy outfits, crowded among the vendors, hobnobbing on the weight of foreign currency. The merchants, faces eager, accorded their transient customers a strange mix of aggressive obsequiousness. For Sassela, the business, the strident hustle of buying and selling, the bazaar bustle of it all, evoked past eras of repression. The only difference was that she could now play observer, brooding about the oppressed natives. For not much was changed from serf and slave times she'd read about. Here was the same ignorance in the groveling masses, dependent on bazaar economics. Here, too, was the mean abuse of women, ubiquitous in their dark shrouds. Most likely, Sassela guessed, drabbed so because their aggressive men went after and died for masculine notions of significance.

She cast reproachful eyes at the pervasive, most damning consequence of that silliness: like butterfly stages of adult grubs, the bands of beautiful children hovering everywhere, roaming, ownerless beggars learning to smile false and dance for coins rather than contentment. Their flawed childhoods so invulnerable, so precocious, these queer, sad children horrified Sassela. She cringed whenever, offering to amuse for money, they came close enough to touch her.

Out again walking, she and Ciam found that the usual buzz of the little town was compounded by religion. A feast day, it seemed, a fullness of faith with pious devotees everywhere. In the shops and sidewalk trade, business in worship was booming: various pendants, emblems, and charms in plastic, pewter, or precious metal—written pamphlets explaining each ceremony and trinket—all at bargain basement prices, every item an advertised steal.

A beautifully robed threesome swept by. High priests, Sassela guessed, from the reverent scrambling aside of the natives. Up to now, they were the best-dressed men she'd seen. Also, they sported in common a vigorous, no-nonsense bearing; seemed the privilege of devout duty had aged them well.

"Check out the threads, Sass. Ain't they fine?" Ciam said, too loudly and in taunting tones.

Sassela glanced at him. "If you have to, then keep it down, Ciam," she cautioned.

"They remind me of something," he said lightheartedly.

"What?"

He took her arm, paused them under an awning.

Then, eyes a-shine, he said, "Check this out. Two bulls on a hill, a young bull and an old bull. Both big strong guys, they looking down on a herd of cows grazing. Young bull looks at old bull. 'Yo!' he says. 'I got an idea.' Old bull looks at him. 'Mmhh-hhmm!' he says. 'Let's run down the hill and fuck a cow!' says young bull. Old bull considers for a moment, and his eyes brighten. 'I got a better idea,' he says. 'Let's *walk* down, and fuck all of them.'"

Sassela cracked up, and did again as Ciam threw out his chest and strode in a ponderous gait fairly mixing horny bulls and the clergymen just gone. Knocked over her cranky mood altogether.

But then Ciam's story reminded her in turn of something: the local merchants, another group seemingly with an incurable condition, an automatic reflex. Each time she'd walk into a store, ask to see something, the merchant'd come panting, overdressed, overeager, and overcharging. Eyelids half-mast with droopy suggestion, somehow he'd find cause to exclaim furtively, "Ah! So beautiful, for you a special bargain? Huh?"

Unless Ciam was with her. Then it was a whole different set of eyes for him. On the street she'd catch a widow's contemplative stare on him, always eyes on him, hardly ever her. At first, she felt a jealous spike at the attention he commanded. She was as exotic brown, as attractive. Age difference wagged its weirdkin head until she noticed that the older men watched him with a similar eye. Not at all sexual, but cool, gravely speculating. And with just a hint of hostility.

"Ci," said Sassela, "you notice anything about the men in this town?"

"Yup. They're a mightily macho sort 'round here. Keep their daughters indoors."

"Daughters indoors?"

"Look up to the second stories of the buildings.

Notice no curtains? Or they're drawn aside? And notice the vague movement of figures there in the spaces?"

Sassela followed his directions, and with unexpected apprehension exclaimed, "Ci, you're right. The things you notice. Well, check this item. Something else about this town. It's strange, but I don't remember seeing any young men about. I mean anyone about your age. Have you?"

"Come to think on it, not much. But what's up? You looking for young men?"

Sassela laughed at the concern in his frown. "Not with what I have. I just think my honey is in danger," she said, clasping him close around his waist. "Seems like fine young men are rare around here. I gotta keep close watch on you."

An explanation had occurred to her, though: military conscription. The country probably had a strict policy, she reasoned. Men of Ciam's age were called up to serve. Thus there were boys up to teen age, then there was a gap, then came men beyond thirty, though older-looking—hard life accounting for that. The gap was the country's army. So the locals could see Ciam as a potential soldier, or the one that got away. Maybe even saw him as a bitter reminder of their own kin's absence or commitment. The last consideration promoted her theory from plausible to smugly fitting, as it cleverly accounted for all those ever-present black and baleful widows.

"The lady see. Here. The lady see," an old sidewalk vendor accosted, breaking into Sassela's reverie. Her head skillfully wrapped with colored shawls, she grabbed Sassela's arm. "Here, here. Want cheap."

From under her humped shoulder, the vendor showed a gapped grin, raw and friendly. Sassela let herself be pulled aside, away from Ciam, and the woman drew her ear close to whisper of wares. Some charm she could have—Sassela hardly understood at first, so lewdly the vendor grinned, so slyly she winked, so mangled became her pitch. What she offered, it turned out, was a bracelet woven of ram's hair—a charm to help Sassela keep her "full-blood boy from harm," brazen leer at Ciam standing at an adjacent stall.

The vendor's rude friendliness suggested easy, intimate familiarity with Sassela's affairs. Her rough hand pushed the bracelet into Sassela's. "Take, take, take," she commanded. "Is value of strong blood."

Sassela searched her purse, and passed over drachmas. As she put the bracelet away, the vendor continued with winks and words, "In he clothes, you put. *Ne?*" Wink, leer. "He not know. You save, *ne?*" Wink.

"Thank you," said Sassela, starting away. She was in a foreign land, expected curious cultural difference, she mused skeptically. But charm bracelets were really pricking her limits. She caught up with Ciam, and not long afterward, they started for Hut.

Back there, sore all over, Sassela undressed and went to the cove for a sun-warmed soaking. She got no relief, though, and giving up, returned to try modern drugs: aspirin and sunburn salve. After which, with the help of a carafe of red wine, she was soothed enough to drop to sleep.

18

Morning on the fifth day, she awoke feeling tender as raw veal, decided to sleep in some. Ciam, gallant and concerned nurse, fed her breakfast on a tray. She reassured him it was soreness rather than sickness that bedded her. She'd stay around Hut taking it easy in the shade, wearing loose soft clothes. She'd be fine, she said, encouraging him not to wait around worrying, to go off and explore. Eventually, he went; she heard the bike scrabbling up the track to the roadway.

"Alone at last," Sassela murmured, and she felt better already, truth be told. Starved for her own space, she was relieved to be rid of him. Ciam was fun, but four days of constant company—even the best—was irksome to a woman who valued, even treasured her privacy. She dressed, and decided on a saunter.

She was lazing in her favorite sunset puddle when he returned. He stripped, splashed in. After a while he got to soothing her bruises and tender muscles in the sun-warmed pool. She handed him the oil she'd brought down. Quick to the suggestion, on the smooth slate pebbly beach, he began massaging her sore butt. What with the setting sun, and the cool breeze, and the sloshing waves, and his less tender, more meaningful touches, one thing led to another, and soon they set to most intimate and lusty contesting.

Fully taken with their special twilight tanning, riding her slippery peaks close beyond recall, Sassela was jolted by an unpleasantly familiar sound: a giggle or snigger, female again, and nearby. And, she felt certain, evoked from watching them.

It spoiled the plateau some, though the consternation was too late to stop her rush. Ciam, it seemed, had not noticed, and for some reason she felt constrained about mentioning it.

Later on, she maneuvered their stroll to the suspect area, but found no supporting clues from a surreptitious search. It was close to darkness anyhow, and the tide was coming up. So they went back to Hut and did another one-pot marvel of a dinner.

Midafternoon next day, they rode right through to the backsides of the town and headed for the hills. Pushed at their backs by the afternoon sea breeze, they made fair pace, the packed gravel crisp under the bicycles' whirring wheels. The road spiraled up by a series of rises and flats providing an easy ride, and in but twenty minutes they were at the top. And into a broad plateau of continuous grapevine country, cruising through field after field of trellised vines, many with fat bunches of cool grapes luminescent like froth under the bright shade.

"Thirsty?" asked Sassela, her gaze suggestive.

"You psychic, or what," said Ciam. He stopped, dropped the bike to the road, and vaulted a low wire fence into the field.

When Sassela thought of the fence, she immediately realized it was a live wire aimed at more natural foragers, like sheep, or goats. Ciam was squatting under a trellis, judging for prime choices. "Hon, look out for that wire, huh," she warned, thinking of both his hands occupied with juicy bunches as he returned. "I think it's hot."

He popped exaggerated eyes at the wire fence, shouted, "Demmit, ma'am! By Jove, you're right. Guess I owe you my life now. So you got it. Okay?"

At any time, he could so play the fool. "Okay, okay," she laughed. "Hurry up and get out of there."

Which he accomplished with elaborate caution, after which they dogged the juicy grapes.

Biking along, they came to the town that evidently tended the grapevines: a dry gray has-been of a town with narrow cobbled alleys bounded close by cramped, dun-colored sandbrick houses, each with one door, one window out of a gray, moldy world. Sassela rode along gingerly, keeping close behind Ciam through the desolate village, the rat-a-tat bounce promising, at the least, a persistence of saddle-soreness. She considered the bleak streets, postponed suggesting a break. Called instead, "Say, Ci, think you could use your magic and find us a candy store? With cold liter bottles of seltzer, maybe?"

"That, Sweet and Sassy, is why we're on this winding trail," he came back. "Figures we soon get to village central, and we in business. They must have a taverna, or something."

Several twists and corners later, they turned into an open area—a marketplace, maybe—and came upon some villagers. Draped as usual from head to foot, a dozen or so drab women stood in pairs or singly, staring gloom at them. Several dirty-looking youngsters lounged aimlessly. A drunkard squatted in a corner, suckling from a bottle. The whole scene was distasteful, made her uneasy. Then, from an alleyway, a hunched crone in dirty ragged black appeared, painfully dragging a flat four-wheeled wagon, like the ones in which children pull each other around. Wobble-wheeled and creaking, it carried an ancient figure with back so excruciatingly bent, his malcurved shoulders rested halfway down his painfully drawn-up thighs, his head drooping like a weight between his knees. Extreme osteoporosis! the ugliest example she'd ever seen.

"My God!" she gasped under her breath. "You seeing that?"

"Damn!" muttered Ciam.

"Never thought I'd—" Sassela stopped short as she plainly saw a youngster throw a stone at the crippled couple painfully inching across the square. "Hey!" she shouted, not stopping to think. "Hey, you!"

The kid—and several others—turned attention. The stoner began a saunter over. From all points of the arena, others joined him, until it was a gang of a dozen and more heading their way. Threateningly.

Trusting her instincts, Sassela hissed, "Let's get out of here."

"They're all around," Ciam whispered back. "But take it easy. I can handle. Back me up however."

The kids by now had grouped into a close semicircle, hemming them in. A smudged-faced, smelly lot, aged variously about ten to twelve-ish, with not a single smile among them. Sassela breathed faster at their wolfish menace.

The Stoner, a mean-looking ringleader, stuck his hand out to Sassela. "Drachmai," he coolly demanded.

Ciam straddle-walked his bike through the closest standees and got between the Stoner and her. "Can you dance or sing for it?" he said.

Stoner pointedly ignored him, began edging through the group, aiming for Sassela's other side where Ciam, trapped by the close circle, couldn't interpose.

Sassela saw his intent, sensed his mugger's moves right away. "Okay, children," she raised her in-charge teacher's voice. "We have some change for every one. You just await your turn, okay."

She pulled the pocketbook around to her belly, unbuttoned its flap and dug into it. As, with a chorused grunt, the pack of children surged hungrily.

"Lemme give it out," said Ciam, reaching for the pocketbook, actually snatching it and spilling some of the change she clutched.

Instantly, the children were scrabbling on the ground for the coins. Not all of them, though. Not the mean Stoner who, eye fast on the pocketbook, was shoving himself back to Ciam's side. Mowing through. Getting there with vicious elbows and cruel fists, smashing whoever barred his way.

Ciam meantime was tossing whatever coins he scooped from the pocketbook: to his own design, Sassela realized, as the children's frenetic scrapping for thrown money shifted farther and farther away.

And a clear path out of the pack was forming. Sassela joined the effort, threw her handful, and the path opened up some more. She caught Ciam's eye, balanced her foot on the pedal, ready to follow his drive out. But just as they were about to do it, Stoner snatched her pocketbook from Ciam's grasp. And off he raced.

"You l'il shit!" screamed Ciam, swift off his bike in pursuit.

"Ciam, forget—" Sassela began, but he had already disappeared into an alley, the pack of feral children following.

She clutched Ciam's bike, holding it upright, looking

around anxiously. Like dreary sculptures, the black-clad women stayed where they were. The drunkard, too. The crippled couple were out of sight. Seemed no one else moved, or ever would. Top of her voice, Sassela called into the eerie stillness, "Ciam! Ciam, come back."

Distraught for a long, long moment, she felt an empty confusion about what to do. Then, from well left of where he'd disappeared, came heart-rushing sounds of tumult. Clatters and shrieks. Crashes of missiled bottles. And clearly through it, Ciam's good-times cackle, jolly as ever, though somewhat labored, high-pitched, and huffy.

Then, arms pumping, knee-lift perfect, he galloped into the arena, shouting, "Sassy, we outa here—" although pausing to explode a guffaw as he swifted to her, waving her pocketbook, and something else of cloth.

Then he had snatched his bike, and they went pumping madly away.

When it was safe, they stopped for a rest—and refreshment: which Ciam provided with another careful jump into a nearby vineyard.

"What happened back there? How did you get it back?" Sassela asked.

"Oh, nothing. He thought he was fast. Didn't expect my kinda speed. And he was running right up my alley. I grow up in his same profession. Yu'know, the Grabbit and Runn practice. Different jungle, but same animal, him and I. I could follow his trail like it marked. I ketch him in no time, and take back the pocketbook. Then I started to cuff him up, but he so small, I decide to pants him."

"Pants him?"

"Yeah, yu'know. Upend him and pull his pants off, leave him bare-assed. But you know something," suppressing bubbles of laughter, "the l'il brute was so mad,

after the first shock of surprise at breeze on his back-
side, he was hardest after me." He chortled in surrender
to the amusing memory.

"Where's the pants?"

"Oh. I tossed 'em back there a bit ago. Dirty rags."

"Wonder if he'll get another pair."

"Maybe he still trailing us, and he'll find them," said
Ciam. "But I hope not. He's an evil little bully. I
should've broken him off."

A qualm crept over Sassela at how easily his face
shifted to that of a dangerous stranger.

19

Their seventh day on the island, and she had put it off too long. So habit compelling, she set aside midmorning time for her diary, a.k.a. journal. She got it out of her suitcase, sat down at the basic table and cast musing eyes out the window to the hills. She sought for a good first line suggesting the vacation's progress.

A flicker on the window ledge caught her eye, tripped her heart! Head cocked sideways, darting her a hooded eye, was a lizard stagnant on the wall. With oversize toe-pads, glue on gravity, it seemed stuck in time but for its translucent trunk, like bellows processing air, gulping as if each pulse was an important count of life.

Pale gray at the belly, gradually blacker near the top, it must be a gecko, Sassela figured. Then, abruptly its tail flicked, the visible eye blinking from drowsy to staring alertness as if it were a dime-sized, yellow-to-black traffic light.

Sassela glanced ahead of it for a clue, saw nothing. When she looked back, the lizard was gone.

Her impulse to record wiped away, she returned the

journal to rest. The indolent noontime beach was calling.

Later on, curious to popping about how her full tan without strap lines was progressing, Sassela realized that, for the first time in recall, she was without a mirror. Not a word from her, yet Ciam rode into town and brought back a six-by-four-incher, with the handle grip just right.

"For a queen," he said, when he gave it to her.

Evening fell cool and sombrous. Ciam fixed them a simple supper, ate, and as Sassela washed up, went down to the cove and lit his beach fire. When Sassela joined him, he was smoking a joint—pensively, it seemed. She squatted down, and not to interrupt, just reached the joint from his fingers, took a drag.

Time grew slow and gooseflesh tingly. The flames danced in rhythm with the slapping waves—

"You want to hear a story?" said Ciam, his dreary tone breaking the sultry flow.

"Sure. What?" said Sassela, and reached again for the joint.

"Is not a good story, or a bad story. But is a personal—"

"Hon, I want to hear it anyhow," she encouraged, returned him the joint.

He dragged in deeply, maybe of the ganja, then exhaled in synchrony with the flabby splash of a dying wave. "Is about how I come to be, mih beginnings—"

"Just go on and tell me, hon. I want to know."

He got into it: "First thing to know is that I grew up orphaned. My mother birthed me first full moon after her fourteenth birthday. Never telling who was my father, by next full moon she was gone. Dead and dumb as a gravestone. And no man ever claim me.

"My name is all I have from her. In crazy spells before she passed, she wouldn't stop chanting that she

was sailing to Siam. Is mih godmother who misspell it
with a 'C'. They say she tended to be chubby, mih
mother, I mean—"

Sassela glanced at his lean, muscled figure with surprise, unable to picture a chubby mother.

"—why she was a flirt," he continued. "Making up
for fat, trying to feel attractive. But she was in a difficult scene. Grandpa was both the baker and the candy-
maker in the village. And she was the full-time help. So
she probably sampled a lot. I know I would've.

"Since he's the sweetieman, everybody was
Grandpa's customer. Schoolchildren, street vendors, all
the little penny store-owners. He supplying everyone,
tout le monde. He'd sell in the front of the shop while
my mother worked in the back, blending flavors, mixing taffy and making molds, shaping the sweets into little hearts, or long canes, or balls. Up in the country yu'-
could find sweetie-shops still set up in this system—"

She knew it was foolish, but Sassela couldn't help
caricaturing a behind-the-scenes quality-controller
wearing a clean apron, a cap against falling hair. She
marshaled her attention back to Ciam's soft, serious
voice.

"—they say that defending against her sweet tooth,
Grandpa tried keeping her out of the front room where
the sweets were stored. But he used to get busy selling
across the counter, scooping up pounds at a time into
his customers' bags and baskets. So he really couldn't
keep constant eyes on her. And soon as he blink, she
fool him.

"Funny, eh. Heh heh heh!" Ciam did a harsh,
humorless version of his laugh, "he marking she so
sharp-sharp and never realizing she pregnant till
Grandma told him. All the time he thinking he daughter
growing fat from stealing his sweet candy.

"When they confront her, she refuse to tell who did

her. Stubborn she was, beyond threats and licks and everything. So in the end, they put her out, and she end up living with her godmother—a crazy lady making she own way all alone at the forest end of the village."

Ciam sighed and slumped his shoulders, stared abstractedly into the fire. His story sounded unfinished, though. So Sassela watched, quietly waiting.

Then he reached over, stoked the fire, provoked a spiraling rise of sparks. He drew back, still gazing at the flames. "How it happen we don't know," he started again, "but I came early. At a time when godmother was gone out on her crazywoman business. So, in delivering me, my mother had no help and no ideas but instinct.

"But, nature in charge, she managed anyhow and make the baby, me. Whatever courage that waste, though, is what probably turn her against me right off, and maybe why she decided to throw me away. She was never clear about it. What she did was bandage up she self and take a backtrack to the *labasse*, as that's the first place she figure to throw away her baby, me. Remember that all this happening eleven, twelve o'clock, bright-bright moonlight sheening the scene like was morning.

"From what they gather afterward, I was a bawling baby every step of that muddy backtrack. Later on, when she was dying crazy, that's all she could focus on: how the baby was crying all the shiny, slippery road to the *labasse*. Even right at the end, sweating from pep-per-hot fever, she was still cradling arms and rocking she self and making hush-hush sounds to the bawling baby she leave lying exposed to night scavengers in the *labasse*. Because she *did* get there. Must've picked her way up the hill of stinking garbage and left the baby, me, still birth-bloody, and wrapped up in a ragged skirt she'd used to clean and tamp her bleeding. In a card-board shoe box she'd found. In a nook among the refuse. She left me there, a wailing baby, and weak from all that went before, she deafened her ears and start back to her godmother's hovel.

"And that would've been it for baby me. Except that on the way back, she happened to look up and see the silhouette of a big corbeau perched low on a cedar tree. A sign. A threat from the ancestors. Story say that she see the corbeau looking straight at her, eyes like flambeaux in the clear night, beak hooked down greedy. And when the corbeau eyes make four with hers, and hold on sticky when she tried to slip away and walk on, she find it hard to finish the first step. And every other step she managed, all she could think was that corbeau with the hungry beak floating down to her baby and hooking its crying eyes out. Is how they do it, yu'know. First thing for a vulture is to pick the eyes out from their carcass. Is true!

"Then next thing my mother know is, she racing the devil back to where she throw away the baby, me. Running wild, feet looking for theyself, fighting to climb back up the slippery stinking garbage hill, thoughtless to everything but the corbeau-beak in her mind threatening her child.

"Then when she had struggled to the top, she realized all of a sudden that she couldn't hear the child at all. Well, you could imagine the panic! Yes? Had to be like searching for a needle in a dumpster, only worse. But nothing else to do, weary or not, it was the task she set to.

"Falls and slips and slides, it had to be more than many after the scratches and scrapes from scuffing through rotten filth and muck and mess and garbage. Had to be. She must have gotten slick and wet and stink through and through, head to toe, because her bandages had slipped askew or undone, and allowed all the *labasse* nastiness to enter into her. Maybe after she gave up to Hysteria for guidance, whatever the jumbie, it came through, and she stumble on to the little niche of cardboard shoe box where she'd safed her crying baby to die, and who was now so quiet; although merely asleep for her to take home to her cracked godmother, and life.

"Three days later the fever came, bringing its headaches, and diarrhea, and sweats, and chills. The whole team. Next three, four days—whenever she got sensible—they made her nurse her baby boy, and ramble through her story again. But they soon decided it wasn't proper; the mother was too sick. So that was that for my nursing days.

"Some folks say is why, up to now, I never had a sick day: yu'know, she suckle me from Death's rocking chair, they say. The jumbie milk I got from her set me up for good, make me immune. Because, back of everybody minds, they knew my mother wouldn't leave that bed walking. And they wasn't wrong. That soak in the *labasse* garbage had infected her beyond any medicine cure they knew. Nine days after my birthday, she was dead."

His lilting voice stopped in uncompromising silence. The pleasant high of the smoke gone, Sassela was at a loss for what to say, how to express her heart-wrenched sympathy. No comment, no punctuation statement, no summary, or cliché sprang to mind. Beyond the balmy sea sounds, a cumbrous quiet built. From her recline on the ground, furtively, she followed his profile's gaze into the fire. Watched the fire flare and frizzle the sticks, leisurely consuming them into indifferent yellow flames and heat.

Time after, she asked, "Want to go up?"

He nodded, stood up, and morosely kicked sand on the fire—as Sassela restrained herself from pointing out that, with nothing to feed on, it would've died anyhow.

20

As the pattern had developed lately, Ciam awoke with the dawn, and went out for his morning jaunt. He always came back buoyant around ten. "Doing nothing, looking about," he'd said with a shrug when she'd brought it up a couple of days earlier. Now, remembering a promise to note the observation, she got out her diary, wrote:

> *Nota bene: We have learned that using the horse is our option. We can ride whenever we desire or casually feel like. Whether the guide is surly or sad or glum or pouting does not matter. The animal is there for our use. A well-said word, a gentle touch can turn things around, regular as clockwork. Then, horse or bike, we can do as we will with the ride, use it as the landscape demands. Very pleasant, this casual control of saddled forces. More on this to come.*
>
> *Bfn. Sss.*

Sassela smiled like a fox as she replaced the note-book in her suitcase, then she sprawled on the bed and considered her options. Usually she preferred to laze until morning was well established. But today's edition seemed to have come with fresh wind briskly whistling through Hut's slats, rousing, insistently suggestive of vigorous activity. Feeling perky, she got up, had a yogurt, set out to hike the shoreline.

A sweaty trek it turned out, as, to avoid risking her sneakers to a doubtful fringe of dry beach, she was forced to trail over many rugged, stony rises gradually reaching higher and higher. After about an hour of huff-ing along—several times having to put hands to the ground to get by—on a high promontory overlooking what seemed to be a public beach, Sassela decided she'd had enough of roughing it. Choosing a nook out of the sharp breeze, she stopped to catch a breath, take in the vista.

The sea looked hungry, the crisscrossing waves cut-ting about, churning white, chomping and tripping over each other in their rush to gobble up the beach. Watching its appetite from her craggy point, Sassela shivered, contented with her distance. That sea was cold. The wind, brisk as salt and pepper, whisked by, leaving a frown on her face to match its sting in her eyes.

Then into her squint strayed five skinny strokes in a purple bathing suit: a girl. Dauntless in her youth, engaged at jumping breakers, three times straight she was undered, but seemed totaled with insane joy from the dunkings. Upturned yet again, she emerged gasping but afoot, unhurt, and over-thrilled by the great game with the big, rough sea. And screaming glee, she chal-lenged the breakers again.

On they came, fierce and frothy, unwary of her fun.

From her high vantage, Sassela studied the panorama.

Some distance from the playing child, faces to the rising sky, a couple in bathrobes and sunshades lay on deck chairs. But the little girl's scream commanded again: "Wee-oohh, wee-oohhh, weee-ooohhh!"

As her eyes turned to the irresistibly happy noise, halfway down among the looming boulders at the very edge of her vision Sassela glimpsed a shadowy figure, and suddenly frowned—the dark complexion, white slacks, white shirt—could it be—?

The little girl's cries quavering ecstasy snatched back attention, as her keening delight pierced the growlings of the hoary sea: "Aaiieeeee!!" Sassela heard the child scream. As, louder than all others, another breaker roared in.

Then her raucous celebration was suddenly drowned out. As maybe she forced her lips shut tight, and swelled her puny chest its fill, and dove into her game daring the busy sea.

Her timing seemed fine as she plunged under with confidence and air enough to hide until the graybeard's fury had waved past. But unexpectedly, a second fat swelling wave appeared, and right as she surfaced, it swamped her under again.

And she did not come up a second time!

With a guttural cry of total dismay, Sassela started up, eyes raking the beach from her impotent height. No one close seemed to have noticed the child's peril. Desperately she turned eyes to the remembered white flutter below—but, when she scanned the rocky shadows, the white-clad figure was gone.

She turned back to the sea, hope insisting: just as before, bloated, dirty white swells, frothy breakers, hungry-looking. No purple, nothing playful. A sudden, achy sob wrenched out of her, doubling her over from an agony in her stomach. A torment about guilt and helplessness that crouched her all-fours to the cold ground.

A pain about larger purpose that wracked her guts as if she were vomiting. And she let it empty her. Exhaust her. Until, snotty-nosed and drained, woeful as a penitent, Sassela staggered up, wiped at her face with her shirt sleeves, and turned heavy steps from the sea. And all the rough rocky trails back to Hut, she felt as if she were sneaking away.

Close approaching Hut, she heard Ciam whistling—a doleful pop tune whose name she couldn't quite bring to mind. She went up the steps softly. Bare-backed in his long white slacks, he was busy at the window fixing them brunch. She opened her mouth to greet him; a lyric sang sudden into her head: "and the sea rushes in to the shore—" And with a sickening chill she recognized "Ebbtide" as the tune he whistled.

Barely reaching the bed in time, she flopped heavily, trembling as the seaside scene she'd just fled swallowed her up all over again.

"How ya doin'?"

Behind closed lids, like an echo in her swimming head, Sassela heard him. In the pause before answering, she filtered his inquiry for subtlest clues. Was he baiting? Had he been there, too? Seen it all?

"I'm all right." Neutral as a flat line.

"Long walk?"

"Yeah, tiring." Carefully toned for fatigue.

"You could rest up a bit. We'll be eating in fifteen minutes," he said.

In the somber blackness behind her closed eyes, she considered each response, assessed and hefted it mentally for duplicity, and could detect no ill intent. Yet she still couldn't decide *how* to talk about the incident. How to bring up, explain her sense of abject guilt to naive him. Eventually, playing it tight for the time being, she set her mind to blanking out the disappeared child.

Later that melancholy day, lolling by the sea, his

head in her naked lap, Ciam asked out of the blue, "So what's your name for her?"

A stab ripped through Sassela's hazy forget-it-all cocoon. Starting up guiltily, she said, "Who?"

"Yu'know," he rolled his head back to snuggle his nose in her crotch, "yuh thang. Yuh sweet and nasty slippery sp—"

"Stop!" she said sharply, simultaneously relieved and discomforted by his detailed response.

"Calm down. You can tell me," he encouraged, misunderstanding. "Mih lips're sealed. What ya calls her?"

"I don't, don't call her anything."

"Yu'making joke," he said, sitting up himself, eyeing incredulous. "You don't have a name for your, your—?"

A trifle impatiently, she said, "The name for it is vagina, Ciam. Everyone knows that."

"But you can't call your personal, er, personal pleasure organ, you can't call it a textbook name." Reasonable tones couldn't camouflage his sincere puzzlement.

Sassela had to laugh. "'Course I can. Everybody does. And, for your macho information, this isn't, primarily, a pleasure spot."

"Well, have it your way. But if you want, I'll give it a personal name for you. An appropriate nickname. Something sweet like, like 'honey marsh.' Eh? What you think of 'honey marsh'?"

She shrugged, still grinning. "Why, thank you, Ciam. If you like it, but same difference to me. You have a name for yours? I mean, your—er, penis?" She couldn't get her mouth around "dick."

He palmed up his traffic-cop signal. "No, no, no! Don't ever use that word. Never penis. That's Latin for something or the other. The sobriquet for my here personals is none other than 'Mjolner.'"

A rush from her gut exploded into cackling laughter. "Mjolner? You call it Mjolner?"

Grin proud, nodding madly, he stood up, grasped his balls and penis, shook the slack bunch at her. "Yup!" he crowed, "Thor's hammer. Thor, that Scandinavian thunder-god guy."

All too much. His dick's limp threat, the notion of a Norse legend for its nickname, his posture ludicrous, him such an ass. All so much, her glad-bag broke, gave throat to her cackles and screams, and she could've died helpless to laughter's roar.

Later, she gave him his due plus a dollop; the lagniappe in gratitude of him lightening the oppressive day.

21

Late the next day, having smoked a joint down by the cove, they were idly watching a red sun die. Mellow, wrapped together in the rough bed blanket against the sea breeze, her fingers worrying his kinky tufts. She said, "Ci, hon, you know these are becoming knotty."

"Hmmnn," he grunted, his head shifting in her lap.

With her fingernails, she set to combing out a tuft. But he rose up and sharply slapped away her hands. "Don't do that!"

"Come on, Ciam. Aren't you going to comb out your hair?"

"No! And don't touch mih dreads."

His vehement naming of them recalled the tennis star's photo in the airport, and Sassela divined she had pricked some personal bruise. As decidedly more quiet and self-conscious, the sun slipped down its traveled, scarlet way.

Awesomely beautiful, the bruised-purple sunset sky soothed no more. The idea of his hair in dreads bothered her. She knew it was foolish, yet couldn't resist a nag of anxiety. Already they were such a conspicuous couple, and with his reggae hairstyle, she didn't want to imagine the attention.

She figured she'd register negative spin before his resolution firmed too far into practice. As if to herself, she began, "Guess they're sort of hip, huh? Like in the seventies. Everyone with Afros to reassure themselves of their proud African heritage. And meanwhile nobody in Africa with food enough to grow hair—"

"You could stop right away. They here to stay!" he said, voice stubborned, rising. Full face at her, he declared, "And don't you try to Africa me, okay? They have no good examples as I need. Don't you ever think I into African. Into blacker than thou—"

The ganja had made her tremendously aloof. Dispassionate as a rock to a squall, she considered his naive pronouncements, his passion and justifications. The tone of his delivery, the personality revealed. Seeing so much, so clearly, she aborted the urge to protest even a "Wait a minute."

Palm up like a traffic cop, willy-nilly challenging all and every, he was going on, ". . . say nothing. Look at me true, Miz African-American. Look at me. Hundred percent Caribbean mixture people, and proud about it. Is African in me, true. But is as true 'bout other bloods too. French, Taino. You ask any African, he say right off, you, I, we, not African. And I, for one, don't want to be. My Caribbean people make up from everybody. And my dreads promoting Pride for my mix-up place and people, and we culture. Africans don't wear dreads. Your kinda blacker-than-thou Africanism is something special 'bout allyou Americans. Allyou who always measuring your suffering, and higgling your hearts and pride to microphone and media—"

He was so upset, and ranting! In her state of cool analysis, the word "fulminate" came to mind. What exactly did it mean? she asked her contemplative self. Its sound somehow suggested fire. Was it then, possibly, fiery speech? Haphazardly, the buzz in her mind flexed from the query, and instead, "harangue" suggested itself for consideration. . . .

He had never stopped: "—yes! Is nothing noble in America that don't have black all in-between it. But who trying to be core for the country? Is certainly not them who looking back to Africa for future. Nah! They too comfortably vexed with history to take charge. So instead, they looking for some kinda African Camelot. Well, not so I see it. So don't you rile me, Miss Black American lady. I nice as lamb laying down once you don't simplemind me with Africa yearning—"

It made no difference to her. Whatever he said, she didn't care, had furthered herself beyond common argument. His was just naïveté spouting, insolent innocence compelled to speech, and turned hectoring.

". . . I-man not your kind. Never me to act like sun shining out mih asshole while I don't even know which country I belong!"

And abruptly, before she could digest his point—far less respond to it—he sprang up and strode off haughtily through the gloom toward Hut.

Her high soured, she frowned him on his way, puzzling. What had set him off like that? Bafflement tempering annoyance, their beach fire flaming out, she mulled on it.

When she got herself up there, for the first time of their vacation she lay down on the cool, silent bed, the pillow making a wall between them, the sheet more shroud than cover warm. Sleep came eventually. . . .

. . . *smack dab in a sugarcane field, a clearing for the family picnic . . . the whole sprawling rambunctious set of them, uncles, the cousins by dozens, aunts, in-laws, everyone in a harmony zone . . . checkered sheets spread square on the perfectly manicured grass . . . seltzer and soda and sparkly, lots of food, a yellow tennis ball, crisp bright sun, a radio blasting blues just right . . . but when Sassela looks harder at the field, the sugarcane stalks seem slowly closing: like stalwart soldiers, are fat stalks tightening a perimeter? and she is farthest out, nearest the advancing phalanx . . . the sun now not as bright, or warm . . . family laughter is hollow, drafty, swirling . . . a rustle close by her foot, and a smooth powerful tube of cool life nudges her bare leg as, enormous scales glittering malevolently, a great shiny black snake crushes by . . . a prickle of her total shudder, the foot jolts away, the rest of her vortexed, cringing terrified and smaller into herself . . . and the field is growing dark, the family laughter very much a ways off, the sugarcane stalks creeping closer . . . the obscenely outsized serpent slithers in among them, threatening her from its shelter . . .*

Teetering at the edge of the bed, still pulling away from his foot's cool touch, Sassela awoke. But he was sound asleep, only changing position.

As she rearranged the covers, he pooped a long whispery fart. A down and dirty "silent but deadly," the stinker chased her to the window for fresh air. There, she drew in deeply. Cool, damp, the close black sky was thick, electric as the disquiet her dream had left: a pulse of foreboding from a pause bridging future, mind, and body. Trouble was about, it warned.

22

As if compensating for forty days of floods, the sunny morning was cool, the sky Mediterranean colors—perfect blue, puffy white. Even better, Ciam was already gone when Sassela woke; the relief stretched her mood expansive now she wasn't confronted with salving the prickle of his pride. She rolled out of bed feeling good, the saddle-soreness completely gone. After a leisurely toilette, Sassela headed for the shower to let the brisk flow thoroughly wash the sea from her hair.

Snatches of thoughts fluttered hither-thither through the windows of her mind: what a tangled mass her hair had become, her first stop back home had to be an appointment at Julienne's for professional help . . . somehow, she was regaining control of her vacation, returning to first intentions . . . what surprising moods Ciam wore behind his flashing smile, the more she uncovered, the glossier his good looks became . . . although still, he could be boyish fun, and seemed mostly trying to show her a good time . . .

*   *   *

Sassela was perched on a rock seaside of Hut, her loose hair drying in the sun, when, nearing midday, Ciam returned from his usual morning jaunt. "How was it?" she asked.

"Nothing much," he said with a flat fish-eyed look.

Sassela caught his chill glance. "You okay?" she asked, ready to make up for her *dread*-ful blunder.

"Yeah, sure. Guess I'm just hungry," he said, his voice suddenly bright as if it'd slipped on a happy shirt.

Sassela bit her lip to contain the sting of his falseness. "Listen, Ciam, I—" she started, but already he was turning toward Hut, so she said instead, "I, I've eaten already."

"Fine," he said over his departing shoulder.

She was still reclining on her comfortable rock when, naked as usual, Ciam went down the cove toward the pools. He seemed to want solitude, so Sassela went inside. Did skin care, and some intimate hygiene requiring yogurt. Wrote in her journal, then opted for a decent nap on the inviting bed.

Late afternoon she woke, went down and sat in a warm pool. All at once Ciam came galloping in, splashing apart her peace, wetting her hair.

"How de lady feeling?" he yelled.

No doubts about his high spirits, Sassela answered, "Who wants to know? Not Mr. Caribbean Aloof and Alone, I believe."

Which provoked a barrage of belligerent splashes from him, and similarly aggressive response from her, until, clean hair as sacrifice, Sassela joyously tried to drown him.

Enormous fun, some bruises and dunkings later, she settled for a second (not as thorough) hair-washing shower. Then, evening coming close, she realized she was famished, needful of dining-out food. And wasn't indulgence the agenda?

"What about your butt?" asked Ciam.

"I can ride," she reassured him.

"I know, but what about a bike with a flat saddle instead of a slippery pole?" He came up behind her and held her to him, letting her feel his meaning.

Herself surprised at the immediate arousal, she turned face, pushed him to the bed, and in short order was jockey, tupping him. Afterward, they dressed and left for town. Wasn't long before she also adjusted to the bike's saddle.

"There's a place I saw the other day," said Ciam. "It seems really popular. Guitar music and so on. That's where we should go tonight."

He was so enthusiastic, she agreed right off, although a bit surprised, not having noticed the gala-man in him before. She rode on with him, curious about his table tastes. All too soon, her buttocks sore again, she was praying for the road to shorten, or at least smooth out some.

At the top of the gentle slope, they paused to rest and watch the little town. From this vantage, Ciam pointed out the restaurant: a prominent warehouselike structure right on the sea. The owners had painted the whole property white, then festooned it with ropes of tiny light bulbs strung on every beam and pole, every eave and rafter, every edge and plane. The result was that, with the dark sea as background, the building glowed like a lit-up circus tent—or an outstanding beacon for hungry tourists.

"God! It looks bizarre," Sassela exclaimed with a laugh.

"Damn *cosquel* in truth," agreed Ciam, "but don't blame me. Was daylight when I saw it. It couldn't look like this."

"*Cosquel?*"

"Yeah, yu'know? Too much, gaudy—"

"Maybe the lights were thrown into the deal," Sassela suggested.

"Maybe thrown away," Ciam amended. "So we try somewhere else?"

"No way, José," said Sassela, teasing his discomfort. "Now I really want to see the rest of your tastes."

They coasted down the road (smooth asphalt now) and parked their bikes near others outside the eatery. Then, with lightened demeanor, Sassela hooked arms with Ciam and strolled through the glowing doors, and into a brilliant joint designed for festive consumption. The walls were rose pink, with black-line classic murals, and the large main dining area was moderately filled, the tablecloths red, and long almost to the floor, every table with a tall lit candle. The dark wooden floor gleamed of wax and sweaty polishing. Several huge chandeliers—with many, many bulbs each—hung high. The lights bared everything: glittering faces, winking jewelry, heads bald and hairy, sheening grease. Every which way, mature waiters smoothly went about their deliberate business. Dressed in sashed black pantaloons and white shirts with red trim on the pockets and collars, they greeted with extravagant plastic smiles. Some of them wore black, wide-rimmed matador hats like senior Zorros. Others sported bandannas tied around their heads pirate-fashion. The whole lot of them, with their automatic simpers and bumpkins' eagerness, behaving like some absurd carnival.

As they gaped about, taking it in, a Zorro type glided up and took charge of them. "All at your service, please," he said, tipping his matador hat and bowing cursorily, then led them farther in.

Some way beyond the regular dining area were tables placed along wide, covered piers leading out into the sea. Large potted plants separated the tables for a semblance of privacy, and transformed the piers to romantic promenades, especially in the clear starry night. An ornamental picket fence established a safe edge to prevent the unwary starstruck from sudden submersion.

Sassela preferred this atmosphere right away. She said, "Let's go over there," indicating the farthest pier, imagining herself and Ciam dancing closer than was decent. The waiter guided them to a table near its end.

The sloshing sea as company, they were like balcony spectators to the manic activity of the main section: the strolling trio of guitar, fiddle, and castanets, entertaining patrons with melancholy songs; the bustle of the waiters bearing trays to and fro; the laughter and hubble-bubble of a night out. Sassela reached across the table, took Ciam's hand. Warm, firm. Entwined hers with his strong, long fingers.

His eyes a-shine, he raised her grasp to his lips. "Look—" he said softly, turning to the night's sea.

Rising out of its blackness, the moon was a golden egg pregnant with romance—

"Have a lovely time?"

Startled by the high-pitched voice, the interruption, Sassela's mind whisked back from pleasant reverie. Yes! it was a child who had spoken. Almost immediately, Sassela recognized the little girl from the window, the touchous one. She was addressing Ciam.

The lustrous black hair was piled up on her head, combed in an elaborate adult style. Someone had taken careful time to fashion it perfectly. Other than the astonishing hair, she was unremarkable. The expected black eyes, cream-colored skin, and high, thin nose bridge. About ten, eleven years old, she seemed trying to humor Ciam, leaning familiarly on his shoulder, whispering her broken English into his ear. He was grinning like silly.

Feeling left out, Sassela asked, "What's she saying?"

Before Ciam could answer, the child put her hand over his mouth.

And abruptly, Sassela wasn't amused anymore. For although he did look taken aback, Ciam's response was to put his arm around the rude child's waist, and remain mum.

Sassela parried annoyance by asking pointedly, "Do you know her?"

"Sort of. Remember at the window, when she called 'Hi' to me the other day."

"And that's knowing her this well?" queried Sassela, raising eyebrows for greater sarcasm.

"Well, I've seen her around since. Off and on. Yu'know." He grinned and turned his face to the bold child now caressing his cheek, murmuring, "Pretty brown, pretty brown—"

Close to stamping her foot in frustration, Sassela said sharply, "No, Ciam, I don't know. So you're this friendly that quickly. How many times've you met her?"

But caught up with each other, neither of them looked at her.

Sassela turned her face to the black sea, snarled silently, screwed up her eyes tight.

As she opened them again, a half-glimpsed movement turned her back; astonished, she saw that the girl had straddled Ciam's stable right leg, was hugging her face possessively to his, cheek to cheek, her belligerent eyes square on Sassela's.

And more incredible than all, Ciam was just letting her.

Partly to vent the gasp she had inhaled, Sassela asked, "What's your name?"

Without straightening up off Ciam, the girl answered, "Fifina." And stealthily set to a slow sliding motion on his leg. A motion Sassela, with quickened heart, immediately recognized from forbidden childhood sessions in her Harlem basement.

"Well, aren't you a bright little girl?" she said.

But so involved was she with riding Ciam, the girl missed or ignored her snide remark. Pale hand over his coarse dreads, cheek caressing his cheek, over and over she crooned, "Pretty brown strongboy—"

And unbelievably, like some charmed country yokel, quite at ease, Ciam sat like a dildo doing nothing but vacantly skinning teeth.

Speechless with outrage for a moment, Sassela then called sharply, "Ciam! What're you doing?"

As if popping awake from a dream, he gave a quick glance to her—but an instant later was caught back to the girl's adoration.

Then the girl turned her eyes to Sassela. "You old. He sister?" she said.

And in the closest, strongest victory of her life, Sassela didn't slap the little bitch. Instead, she said, "Shouldn't you be with your mother somewhere?"

Totally ignoring her, the brat began rocking herself again, unsubtly horsey-horseying on the saddle of Ciam's standing thigh.

Fury flashed through her, and Sassela scraped her chair back and started to her feet, thinking only of snatching the brat off her obscene ride.

"Fifina!" It was a heavyset waiter, arrived bearing the house wine. He directed a spate of angry words in their language to the child. At which she stopped her public diddling, and slowly, sullenly dismounted, standing by while Sassela sank back in her chair and Ciam contrived a foolish grin.

With a glare to Ciam, the waiter said pointedly to Sassela, in English, "My deepest apologies for the, ah, annoyance. May I take your order now? Of course, your dinner is now compliments of management."

"Maybe you just shouldn't allow—" Sassela started.

"He more pretty than she," the child remarked nastily, addressing no one in particular, before she skipped away down the pier.

Alone at last with Ciam, Sassela was uncertain how to broach the matter. One mind just wanted to destroy him for embarrassing her so. A whiny other had questions: Had he merely been childish? Was she judging too harshly from her own female experience? Struggling not to be accusative, she said, "Was that what I thought it was?" Her tones juggled suspicion and incredulity.

"Maybe I'm irresistible," he said lamely, his sick smile strongly suggesting her nastiest suspicions had been, in fact, his sleazy experience. Then he looked away over the bare, black sea. All the absolutely wrong answer.

Cool poise deserted; she snarled, "Playing smug won't get it, Ciam! What the hell's with you? Are you crazy or something?"

"I didn't do any—"

"No! Just stop, Ciam. You're not stupid, and don't play me stupid. And look at me. You know what that child was at."

A surly glance at her, he sucked his teeth, looked back to the sea.

Not representing her real concerns, she said, "You realize that man, the waiter, must be her father or something. You heard the tone in his voice? I'm sure he noticed something, too."

He mumbled coldly to the sea, "He wouldn't've offered the food free." He wouldn't look at her at all.

Chilled by his rejection, in softened tones Sassela asked, "Why didn't you stop her, Ciam? That child was being indecent on you. Right there in public. In front of my face. Why didn't you do something?"

And finally, cool as the distant moon, he turned his

look to her. Boredom in his eye like a high, halting wall, he declared, "Maybe it's all in your kinky imagination, Sass. You know, a fuck story for your fake comes."

A low, low belly cut, which would've crumpled her poise, but for waiters approaching pushing a trolley laden with large, brass-covered dishes.

Dinner was silent bedlam, her mind seething over the confusion. How could he be so nasty to her? Or was it she who was ugly-minded? Was what she saw what she thought she saw? And could he have stopped the dirty little brat and her rude remarks? Was it jealousy on her own part that had stirred the whole thing? Furtively, from her automatic forkwork on the plate, she glanced at him.

His lids lowered like window shutters, face closed like private property, he was indifferently busy with fork and food.

Finally they were done, and ready to get out of there. Ciam motioned to a convenient waiter, asked for the bill. The man sped away and returned with the heavyset waiter in tow. Smiling and bowing at both of them, this man said, "Everything compliments of the house, and management. Everything, everything."

"No, no—" Sassela protested halfheartedly; at the corner of her eye, she caught Ciam scowling her a sharp look.

The waiter raised his arms expansively, broad, smooth palms firmly pushing her offer away. "Not at all. We insist. Compliments of the management. Dessert, or anything else? Some more wine, maybe?"

"No, no, nothing. We're done," surrendered Sassela. "And many thanks about the bill."

"No problem," said the man, as he turned and left them.

Ciam looked at her and smiled teeth white like a new-painted fence; then, the perfect gentleman, he came around and held her chair, and helped with her sweater over her shoulders, and walked beside her to the garish exit door. All the while, in her mind, Sassela kept comparing his plastic manner with his searing look when she'd responded negatively to the complimentary bill.

Outside, she went like a freed bird straight for her bicycle. Ciam mumbled, unconvincingly, that she should go on ahead, as he had to pee, and he'd soon catch up with her. She couldn't have cared less. Only felt freer as she mounted her bike and set off for Hut.

She'd only gone fifty meters or so when, obliquely opposite, the front door of a large house suddenly opened, and a tall, oddly extended figure emerged and started up the road. As they came closer, Sassela stopped and stared, recognizing the stern waiter-man of just now, bearing on his shoulders the nasty little imp of her impossible evening: the black-haired Fifina. Up the other side of the street they came, as a thrill of goose bumps began up Sassela's abruptly sweating back. High on the robust man's shoulders, black dress up to her waist in straddling his neck, sat the childlike figure, and as they passed, the rider looked straight at Sassela and giggled unmistakably. Then they were past, she guiding the man striding like an automaton toward the shoreline.

An electric chill of recognition took over so completely that, weak bladder and all, Sassela wet herself.

All the way back to Hut she rode with the worry of how to broach the matter. Should she tell Ciam? Considering the pervading arctic shift in their relationship, would he believe it if she did? To and fro she vacillated, for and against. She hesitated at responding weakly to his all-around immature behavior with the forward Fifina. But what she had seen made the strange girl even more mysterious; it seemed that she and the man had spied on their private lovemaking, and that that stolen observation was no accident.

Some time after she had gone to bed—too long—Ciam came in. Seemed he had making-up on his mind. In the pitch black, rustic night, he climbed into bed and under the blanket. "Sorry about tonight," he said tentatively.

"It's okay," Sassela murmured.

A minute of quiet breathing. Then he turned and spooned his naked self into her back, casting his arm across, cupping her breasts. "You still like me?" he asked softly.

Her own trepidations predominant, Sassela was in a fix for how to respond. Though heart-wrought at how he'd turned on her, she still needed to satisfy her suspicions, get his reactions. Some insight, or angle that'd answer. For there was certainly something bizarre about that Fifina: her astride the waiter, how they matched the voyeurs on the beach. So to thaw the situation, she answered coolly, "'Course, Ciam. Don't be silly." Encouraged, he hugged tighter. "Maybe I was kinda overreacting," Sassela added, feeling his vigor throb against her.

"Nah," he said, still very softly. "I should've shoved her off."

She said nothing, just squirmed, and wiggled her ass to his quickening breaths on her shoulder.

Eventually, helpless to the hint, he climbed on top, slipped his eager hardness in, and began working his normally delicious wiggle. But she could put no heart into the business. Once he was finished and nodded off breathing as if scuffling with sleep, she got up quietly and, feeling nastied, washed with a rag and some water from the drinking goblet. Then, back under the covers, she succumbed to a spell of fidgets and unfocused thoughts about whether to tell him her suspicions of what she'd seen. Was still undecided, when eventually she dropped off. . . .

. . . into an endless desert shimmering unnaturally, a desert of sparkling diamonds filling the farthest extents of her eyes, in every size and brilliance, piles and dunes and drifts of glittering diamonds settled as nature has arranged them, shiny and sharp, blinding her eyes to cry protest as with every blundered step they take, her bare feet shred a little bit more, as behind closed eyes she keeps in mind that it is important to retain her liquids for already she is losing too much blood although ahead, at a certain moment coming close, there is harbor . . . from which, suddenly, she hears Ciam's gleeful snigger, and his snorting in sexual frenzy and somehow of cruel amusement at Sassela's personal distress . . .

She started awake: cold because the covers had been lost to Ciam's usual hogging. He slept scrunched up against her, as if she were his ride to dreamland. She leaned up, reached over to adjust the balance. But just as she did, in his sleep he laughed a vicey snigger, a Heh! Heh! Heh! echoing with all the sleaze of their restaurant experience.

And the terrible dream just now, with all its horrid details of blinding diamonds, and him and the forward child, and their wicked glee, all of it rushed back to her wakened consciousness. And in mid-reach over him, she froze, cringed at the thought of touching him. Then, or ever again.

She got out of bed and tiptoed like a thief to the bedclothes trunk in the far corner. Easing it open, she pulled out a coarse woolen oversheet, laid it on the bed, partitioning him away, and despite its itchiness at first, she fell asleep secure, and warmer, in truth.

23

She woke in the warm nest feeling well-slept and rested. A chatter of birds was bragging how the day was formed fine. As if to confirm it, shafts of radiant sunlight infiltrated past the cracks and crevasses of Hut's rude boards and tickled her lazing eyelids: forecasting blue skies, and high white clouds, and nonchalant breezes, and sultry sea-bathing, and sun-tanning. She rolled over to share the data with Ciam, was taken aback at her cocoon of rough blanket.

Last night's restaurant debacle and her dream resurfaced. Only briefly, though, as she let the beams of sunlight help deflect their threat. A nice one today! they insisted. Not too many more good days, they reminded; after all, she calculated, they'd been here, what? Eleven days already? It'd soon be ending. "Thaw every freezer," should be her motto, she decided. So she unwrapped her itchy cover, turned to find him lying on his back, eyes mischievously guiding to the peak of an erection on proud parade under the thin sheet. In a thought she realized it'd fit her resolve exactly.

*　　*　　*

Today's agenda, Ciam declared, was adventure. "Enough of tamed towns and civilization," he crowed with leers and body language where fitting. "Off to the wilds we shall go thrusting our way onto virgin regions, gaining inner sites."

Up to the jaunt, but cautious, Sassela asked, "How far are we going?"

"I know what you thinking," he announced. "The ride. Your round sore-muscled ass. The effort to combine. But worry no more. For this excursion we shall require most comfortable transport. A flying carpet—"

"A Pegasus," cried Sassela.

"For the goddess," said Ciam, with many bows.

Eventually they biked off into town to challenge Gregori's stables, found a suitable moped. Gregori and Ciam indulged a few in happy haggling, until their deal came down to so many drachmas, or a good joke.

"Come back me up on this, Sass," Ciam called. Then, with the wickedest smile, he began: "Bear and Rabbit went to shit in the woods. Bear look at Rabbit, asks him, "Does the shit stick to your fur?" Rabbit answer, "Nah. Not ever!" Bear sort of smiles and says, "That's good." Then he picks up Rabbit and wipes his asshole with him."

Laughter wiped out drachmas, and Ciam rode the free moped back to Hut, Sassela following on her bike.

Up through the hills they rode, shedding the pitched drone of the moped behind them. Grown comfy, arms easy embracing his hard belly, Sassela became absorbed with trying to exactly identify the smell of his neck. Foremost it was warm, though not sweet like roses or jasmine, but with a darkness, rich and edging unpleasant like West Village tobacco shops, or the fetid gasp of the fresh goat milk they'd been served since their arrival. Although Ciam's neck was milder, with a spicier sparkle suggestive of cloves, and something else. She snuggled her chin into his neck, closed her eyes and inhaled slowly, concentrating—

"There goes another one!" Ciam exclaimed.

Sassela straightened up, away from the subtleties of his scent. "Another what?" she said.

"I'll soon show you. They're every hard curve almost," he yelled over-shoulder.

They leaned gracefully into another curve; now that she'd learned the trick of surrendering her tension and being as one with him as they took the curves—now, riding was fun. Like giving in to a roller-coaster, she snuggled into his back, allowed him control—

"Here comes another!" Ciam announced.

"Let's look at it," said Sassela, and he slowed, stopped the moped.

It was a headstone: a memorial for a traffic accident victim, with a plaque and a photograph of a long-faced black-haired young man. Large somber eyes. Full, apprehensive lips upbraiding the camera: "Told you so!"

"They're shrines," said Ciam. "Seen them in Mexico, too, at dangerous spots on the road. Guess it's a Roman Catholic thing, huh?"

"No," said Sassela, recalling demographic data from her travel guide. "It's more likely Greek Orthodox." She skimmed over the Greek writing on the plaque, stopped at the Arabic numbers: birth and death dates, as she expected. The young fellow had died two years ago. "He was twenty," she said.

"You read Greek?"

"Uh-uh. The numbers are here on the stela—" the word "stela" springing from the subconscious of her Ivy League education. An old word, Sassela reflected, from an old language satisfying basic needs of a people that hadn't changed. A people primitive as—she rejected the automatic "Africans," and sought for a moment—Amazon tribes.

"I-man move we step most lightly from these haunts," said Ciam, starting for the parked moped.

"Hear, hear," Sassela agreed.

Following a meditative spell of atypically deliberate travel, the silence was at last broken by Ciam. "I-man just figured what it's all about," he said.

"What?"

"The shrines. Is a particular spell they carry, a charm against these mountains. Think of it. These hills must be haunted by a bunch of very neglected gods. Those long-ago fellas like Hercules and Circe and Zeus and such. Yu'know. They not getting attention anymore. Mortals igging them, and ghosts or not, they can't take the disrespect. They still want worship. They still crave sacrifice. So in spitefulness, they accidenting off these faster, braver moped riders as tithes. Is a typical colonial-power empire thing. These poor Greek fellas only dying because of celestial temper tantrums—" he stopped shouting his theory, gave completely to laughing self-congratulation at its perfect silliness.

Sassela chuckled at his humorous spin, and they leaned around another curve, passed another somber shrine.

The late afternoon sun glared fiercely down on fields of dryness shaded yellow straw to wrinkled, golden brown, and the fruit of the parched soils genuflected slavishly, like waves. The cowering sway of grass to wind won interest, and she sauntered from their moped's roadside pause into the middle of a field, where she stood and let the baking land reach out its plea to her.

From the faraway distance to close around her waist, the tall wheatlike grain rattled and rustled, as if wailing and whispering plaints for water; the creamish-yellow tassels bending low, faded Grace itself, ragged to the will of the rush-about wind.

Then she looked to the sea in the distance, and for a flick of suspended moment saw the shimmering as a reap by the wind of gemstones swept rattling from the jeweled fields.

A sudden urge to tell Ciam her vision, Sassela quickly retraced out of the field. But when she got to the roadway, he'd ridden a ways on, irking her from the impulse.

Her journal'd better welcome the notion, she decided instead.

Still along the pebbly coast road, dawdling the moped to Hut, they skirted a cliff from which they could see huge waves battering the shoreline. Such a ferocious battle, they stopped to view the violence. Great gravid waves lumbering to the coastline, crushing each other then fusing, gathering up then mightily crashing down against the adamant rock; trying to move the world. Unending force at an unyielding wall. Well-met foes, though sort of melancholy, too. Such waste at pointlessness.

Watching the struggle had quieted Ciam, and back on the moped, grim-lipped, he sped up, faster, faster, the swift gravel rattling vibration from the seat, the wind stinging her face, whistling tiny shrieks through the curls of his nappy hair, tearing her eyes, terrifying her grasp onto him; clinging tight she felt goose bumps rise and scurry all over her belly faster and faster, again and again, to a kind of orgasm of mad delight, which lassitude left her enjoying the dangerous speed.

24

A cloudy, drafty Saturday morning woke her up cold, and provided a shivery track to the early latrine and back to Hut. After which Sassela promptly huddled into the still warm bedclothes and, as usual, an almost febrile Ciam. She'd come to realize that his normal body temperature was in heavy-blankets range. Cashmere-soft, silky-smooth blankets. When they cuddled belly-to-back under night-covers, her belly burned. Sometimes she had to pull away. This morning, though, she welcomed every erg he gener-ated, embracing him close as she daydreamed, dozed.

Roused from a dream of eggs smelling sunny-side up and golden, vaguely Sassela knew Ciam was making breakfast. But then, background to the seething sizzle, from the roof came the gentle rattling of a drizzle, and just so, her appetite for food curled up slumbrous, and she returned differently sated into a fog of fulfilling warmth.

She awoke to a brightened midmorning, pulled on the big T-shirt and tiptoed the cool floor to the sea-view window. No longer raining. High white clouds scudding away. Blue appearing patchily. She searched the empty beach, called, "Ciam."

No answer.

She sighed; back of her mind a nag niggled, a wonder whether his unexplained absences had anything to do with his behavior to Fifina. She shrugged off the unpleasant half-thought, turned back inside. From the cupboard she took a chunk of feta, a sealed cup of yogurt, then went out seeking. The slate beach clammy underfoot, she trudged to the high bluff, called again.

No answer but the quiet sea; he was not there. Munching down the last of her high-calorie breakfast, she watched the wavelets lick the quivering shoreline. It tripped a threadbare memory of a purple bathsuit, a queasy tweak that didn't catch, fell back wherever. Although, strangely, it was enough to send a chill all up her back, and set her scooting back to Hut.

On her way up the steps, she noticed the moped gone; Ciam must've run into town and would soon be back. She changed into warmer slacks, went about her business, attended to the journal some.

Around midday, eager as the moped's buzzy engine, Ciam returned bent on touring.

"Think Hell's Angel gone native guide," he previewed his pantomime, then swiftly into a rude parody of local accents, suggested: "Yes, ma'am, today we have for you a magnificent trip. We go far into our island. Many kilometers away from the very much beaten and complaining tourist track. We display for viewing pleasure our little-seen treasures. All at special discount price. All especially for the pleasure of yon delight of tanned femaleness. Oh! my funky swamp of delight, please allow this lowly beast of a guide to take you along his paradise ride!" He fell to his knees groveling like some ridiculous puppy, pawing ticklish at her calves.

Laughing weakness hampering her frustration with him, she barely managed to escape up the steps, and sat with her knees hugged tightly away from his gamboling and clambering on all fours over the sand beneath her perch.

"Woof!" he barked, and crouched in an attitude of clumsy appeal.

What to do? Surrendering to her role, Sassela jumped to her feet, brandished her arm in forward salute. "Oh! Thou lowly peon dog of a guide," she improvised, "you got a bet. The gracious foreign lady allows permission. To your bike, and hie me, er, wherever!"

While he pranced about at bows and antics of servile character, she went inside for her pocketbook. Heard him call out, "Bring refreshments!"

So she unflapped the deep pocketbook, stuck in the half-empty bottle of retsina, a cup of yogurt, a handful of apricots.

Set as they wanted to be, off they went.

The day had brightened considerably and, without the shoreline's sea breezes, was even warm when they turned off the recommended-for-tourists, primary asphalt road into a native-traveled graveled secondary. Sassela's heart skittish at their pace, swiftly along the open road they went. The second curve along, loose gravel and speed admixing, the moped went into the skid she had feared. She screamed as Ciam shouted, "Hold on!" and they capsized into a dry roadside flood-drain three, four feet deep.

Thrill and thud done, her senses still shrill, Sassela tested herself for damage. An extensive numbness there reported a big bruise on her butt; a sharp sting in her left foot's little toe. Everywhere else in good order, though. Tentatively, she called, "Ciam?"

A shadow falling started her with confusion; she twisted her head and sought the source. A donkey's head was peering down. She scrambled upright, remaining crouched as far as possible away from the curious jackass, called more loudly, "Ciam?" Her growing concern, that he might be knocked out. Or worse.

Another presence: an old grizzled fellow, eyebrows up, mouth turned down, every line of his face deep-chiseled by hard life. "Ahh-humm! What on earth?" he enquired.

The jackass stretched its neck, opportunely nibbling brown scrub from the inner edge of the flood-drain.

Sassela nodded to indicate she was all right. The old man eyed her murkily, roughly pulled his donkey's busy jaws away from the forage.

Sassela stood up. Now, farther up the drain, she could see Ciam lying still. Heart quick-booming, she clambered toward him. "Ciam," she called, alarm rousing her voice to a higher register.

At which he moved a little, moaned.

She grasped his shoulder. "Honey! Ciam! Can you hear me? Ciam!"

He reached a floppy hand to his head, moaned again. Then groggily whispered, "Shit!"

"You okay?"

Touching his head gingerly, he answered, "Guess so. You? Was I out?"

Ignoring numbness and the smart in her sneaker, Sassela nodded. "I'm fine."

Tentatively fingering, he probed chest, arms, thighs. "Yeah, guess everything's still there," he finally said.

Above, the jackass sneezed. Sassela caught eyes with its owner, indicated Ciam, and pantomimed they needed help by clasping her hands as if in prayer. Then the bristly wizened face eyed her solemnly, turned abruptly apprehensive. The old man shook his head mysteriously, and pulled his jackass back onto the roadway. When she rose and looked, they were plodding on the way of their intended business.

"It's okay," said Ciam. "I'm reviving all right. Just knocked mih head on the way down. Feel it right here."

Sassela fingered the fleshy, new bump under his knotty dreads.

"Ouch! Hurts," he cried. .

She hugged his head to her belly, and trying to lighten the mood some, said mock-plaintively, "My poor baby. Nearly lost my personal guide."

He shoved her away brusquely. "Is not the movies, Sassela," he said, getting cautiously to his feet. "Just help me lift the bike back on the road, okay."

Quelling an answering flash of irritation, Sassela scrambled, and they managed without much difficulty.

Then, in the drain, she found her pocketbook— yogurt and wine bottle miraculously intact. "Isn't that something?" she exclaimed, showing Ciam.

"Right," he returned, dull as a dud.

She assumed his manner to be embarrassment about their spill. His surliness intimidated though, and she refrained from sounding her opinion: that they should abandon the outing, return to Hut for R&R—rest and repair. Instead, she remounted the moped, and they continued, although more cautiously around the bends.

Gradually, over the next few kilometers, Ciam became more assured with the moped's controls and power, riding them safely..

Her pinkie toe, meantime, had begun a painful throbbing. Working it around, shifting it however slightly, sharpened the sting. Sassela suspected the worst. She kept it to herself, though, as they buzzed through a pine-tree-lined mountain pass, heading up, the scenery close-ups of the spare vistas they'd seen afar from the bikes. The hardy plant life was a surprise, vigorously surviving despite the stingy duress of rocky, grudging soil.

Much else of the tour was being missed, though— the distraction being that through her loose cotton slacks, a chill was penetrating, and growing more intense the farther up they rode. Hugging him lightly, Sassela questioned herself: Was it her mindframe, or was it actually becoming windier, and cloudier?

She occupied herself estimating and converting temperature from Fahrenheit to Celsius the way she taught her class: F minus thirty-two, then divide by two. Her best figures, discounting wind chill, came to maybe 14°C, and falling. Put anyhow, far below comfortable.

Then she thought of his bare legs, their speed. "Ciam!" she shouted against the wind. "Think we should go back? I'm kinda cold."

The moped roared as they down-geared for yet another curve. "Hold on," he shouted back, "can't be too long now. Should be but a couple miles to topping it."

And the moped surged as they whined farther up.

It was what she'd expected him to say. So Sassela retightened her hug, wished her T-shirt was long-sleeved.

Same situation: many ruts, loose gravel on the road, and they going too sharply around an extreme curve, the moped skidded viciously. Sassela braced for another crash. But Ciam, by sticking down his foot, and performing other muscular miracles, regained balance and defeated disaster. Although the bike stalled.

Sassela got off and watched as he pumped and stamped and twisted thingamajigs and levers trying to restart the engine. No go! He squared his shoulders, repositioned the machine, tried again. Nothing doing. "Shit!" he said.

Four, five more times he tried. Then, mysteriously, he concluded: "Bet the carburetor's flooded." And determinedly set to pushing the moped uphill. He grimaced false cheer at her. "At least with this exercise, we'll sweat up some warmth," he said.

"If that's what you want, hon," said Sassela meaninglessly, tying her tongue against further comment. To her their most sensible course was obvious: simply coast back down the hill all the way, and return to Hut.

Instead, side by side, they crunched on up the gravelly road, him grim-faced pushing the transport. A couple hundred yards along, he got an idea: turning the moped around, he mounted to ride it in neutral back down some distance. "Trying a jump-start," he shouted over his shoulder.

First try, it worked perfectly. And racing the engine in successful whines, he returned to her, a small smile begrudging his lips. She mounted, and they resumed the climb, riding smoothly for perhaps a kilometer. Then he decelerated for a sharp curve and the wretched moped choked to a stall once again.

She dismounted to stand in the cold while he tried the coasting-down-the-hill trick again. Not this time, though. Back up the distance he pushed the machine, panting frustration and curses all the way.

While, becoming colder, Sassela began silent prayers for rescue: some sort of scheduled transport that would pick them up. And miraculously, just then, a vehicle chugged slowly around the curve ahead of them. Impossibly laden with bags, and boxes, and fowl and beast, and many a face a-bulge with curiosity, a crowded, covered truck came gingerly past. A jam-packed hope that never hesitated in its downgrade passage.

She was breathing very hard now, the push of every footstep goading unaccustomed muscles. One positive: well a-sweat, she wasn't too bothered by the high altitude cool. Ciam, too, was working up a steam, bare arms and spare-muscled legs glistening. Every fifty yards or so he'd stop for a breather, and she could see how almost right away the perspiration'd evaporate, and chill bumps would rise on his bare skin. Then, to ward away cold, they'd start off again, trudging and shoving up the hill.

Her muscles were protesting tired every step, and even through long slacks and socks and T-shirt and bra the coldness was creeping in bone-deep. And she couldn't but compare Ciam's mere sneakers and shorts and sleeveless T-shirt, and imagine his exhaustion and coldness. Turning back so near the top now seemed not to make much sense; their only option was to continue. Even talking wasted energy. So she put a resolute hand on the moped's seat—surprisingly cold—and straightarmed some force to it. Can't be much further now, she encouraged herself silently.

Then around yet another hairpin curve, they came into a splash of bright sunshine. Eyes meeting in concert unspoken, they headed toward it. More cheered than warmed, she watched Ciam push the moped off the roadway, perch it on its stand and, in the cool spotlight of sunshine, stand free for a moment. Then taking an extra-deep breath, he began a slow jogging in spot, clapping and rubbing his hands.

To the bravado in his eye, more consoling than query, Sassela asked, "Cold—?"

He smiled ruefully, nodded.

Scarcely she opened arms, he'd come to her: they hugging so tight and close, she realized his semicontrolled shivering.

"We can stay here and warm up a bit."

"How? With what?" he mumbled into her shoulder. "Mih hands feel big like breadfruits, I can hardly use them."

"Put them under my armpits," she said. "They'll warm up there."

She steeled herself to endure the icy stumps he placed.

"Boy! You're soft and warm," he muttered.

She shifted her pressing breasts further into him, and

with contrived humor said, "That feels like a boy to you?"

He managed a brief snigger, then, as if punishment for wasting the breath's heat, a spasm of shuddering.

Sassela sniffed back her alarm, hugged him tight as she flung a troubled look past the trembling hunch of his shoulder. The vista was queerly thrilling, for a moment unminding her of their peril. It was a reverse of the postcards—down from their gray heights, a checkerboard of mountains and hazy valleys fading to shimmering flat blue, a sheen of distant ocean sunshine. Beautiful, too, was how the intermittent clouds and drizzles softly graded the scene from spotlight of their chill perch, down the weathered mountainside into the brilliant promise of the sun—"Got an idea!" Ciam said, abruptly disengaging himself. "All this time the gas's been draining back. So the fuel line should be clear now." he concluded excitedly, fast to the moped.

He fisted his hands, flexed fingers, grabbed the handlebar. Then he positioned himself to stamp on the starter. "Cross your fingers, crimp yuh toes," he said, grinning.

And never looked so rakish as when he heeled down on the pedal, and the engine roared to life—

Above them came an awesome hollow whooshing sound; gaping upward, Sassela beheld a gigantic yellow and brown bird flapping monstrous wings into the silver misty sky; outside her focus, Ciam lay prostrate and straining on the ground where surprise had nearly dragged the whining moped from his grasp, had tugged it to the brink of the rocky ledge where they stood, he scrambling to keep the machine safe.

But she couldn't react, her vision mesmerized, absorbed after the swift-departing bird, which stroked the air with incomparable power and passed into a sunbeam that feathered the wings into an incandescent spectrum of golds, red-tinged, green-edged, brilliants . . .

"An angel!" she worshiped.

"Ahhhh! Sassela, yuh see that?" she heard Ciam's strangled call from the edge.

. . . as from overhead swooped another massive flapping sound, and a second enormous eagle whooshed away. Instantly diminishing, though not before, in its startled golden eye, Sassela caught its irritation at the moped's still roaring engine.

They were tiny in the distance before the spell broke, and she was released from their apparition and could rush to grab the moped's seat, and help Ciam pull the machine back to safety.

The engine adjusted to a steady *phut-phut-phut*, Ciam raised the moped on its safety-stand. Then from this and that vantage of their ledge, they searched the rockiness above. Saw bare cliffs—some with magnificent paisley striations down their facets; saw tufts of tiny, May-colored flowers, unaccountable here in the cold; saw a bush like gorse (did gorse grow this far up?), a hairy, lanky sprig that at its end sneaked out a wee green bud. Until cool began mattering again, they eyed about, but never saw signs of an aerie. So they mounted up and, with deliberate speed, rode on through a light mist to the mountaintop without further incident.

Up there in the fog, beside the road and taking up most of the small rocky plateau, they came upon a barnlike building with a red-painted gambrel roof and wide welcoming doors, swung open: judging from the various garments draped all over them, a clothing store! And what a commanding location.

"Bandits, or business?" Ciam asked dryly, making a beeline to their front yard.

"Same difference," she answered. She dismounted, waited while he parked the moped, leaving the engine idling. Then, him hugging hands under his armpits and exaggerating the chatter of his teeth, he joined her and they hurried into the store.

A wonderfully warm cave stinking of raw leather and tobacco and coffee. The heat's source seeming farther back, they headed that way directly, pushing through racks of smelly sheepskin outerwear. Then they burst into a space dominated by a large old-fashioned wood-burning iron stove. And, radiating a ruddy glow under its rusty brown shell, was it ever working.

From behind a long counter, their thin black hair scraggly around pallid faces pinched suspicious and wary, an unsmiling couple watched them.

Ciam asked jokingly, "Say! You got some heat to go?"

The couple's expressions never changed. Slowly they looked at each other, then returned to their stolid gazing.

Sassela avoided Ciam's rolled-up eyes to her, addressed the man spongily: "So, how much are your coats?"

He regarded her, a technical expression in his eye, like a tailor assessing a fit. The woman answered, "Wheech?"

Sassela shrugged. "Any one."

"Wheech?" said the woman sharply.

Any possibility of Sassela doing business instantly vetoed, she nevertheless reached around to the nearest rack, held up a coat's sleeve. "This one," she said.

The man spoke briefly in their language. The woman interpreted, "One hun'red dollars. American."

Sassela swallowed her shock at the obvious heist-price. "That's nice," she said. The shabby thing wasn't worth ten!

Ciam called from farther down the counter, "You sell hot milk?"

The woman shook her head.

Ciam again: "Coffee?"

The woman nodded grudgingly.

"Well, can we have two really velly hotty ones?" ordered Ciam.

Lips pursing, the man started toward a black-bottomed kettle on a hot plate set on a low shelf against the wall.

Ciam sauntered over, put his arm around her waist. "I think they're contrary to you coloreds," he whispered.

"Ain't it obvious?" returned Sassela in the same soft tone, "'N fact, I don't even want their coffee. Let's just leave."

"No, no. Hold up, sweet stuff. You right, but we still want their heat. Not so? Coffee only keeping us here longer. Just don't turn your eyes while he makes it. Remember spit and milk same color." He flashed her a grin, gave her a squeeze.

"Don't be disgusting. But sure, I forgot how cold you must be."

"Won't be for long," he said, and jammed his crotch against her butt.

"Stop, Ciam," she said, and rumped back before leading him nearer to the man fixing their coffees.

"No milk, please. Leave them black," she said, and opened her purse for some drachmas.

The woman took the money, gave back change; never did blink her caustic stare.

The bike was dutifully puttering away, and chilly-assed Sassela aboard the freezing backseat, they were quickly off. Maybe warmed up by his chance to annoy the shoddy shop couple, maybe the caffeine, Ciam was once more in high spirits. When Sassela pointed out that they were not retracing their route, he yelled, "Most certainly not, my lady. It's a shorter way to Hut going down this side of the mountain."

"You studied the map?"

"I've a magnet in mih mind," he boasted.

So Sassela gritted her teeth as down the mountainside he buzzed them, faster than the whisking wind.

Then, suddenly sensible, he put the engine in neutral, and they coasted along quietly through a softer breeze. Then Ciam began singing a Latin tune about bandits, needful of many shouts of "Ole!"

A good soldier, she tried dutifully, but couldn't get her heart into it. Third chorus she quit.

Around a turn, they came into a hamlet: low simple houses hedging the narrow cobbled roadway. Ciam engaged the engine, slowed to a deliberate meander. As they wound along, warmly dark-garbed natives greeted them variously with surprise, amusement, concern. Some waved, some cheered them on with heartening *Ola!*s.

Steering with one hand, Ciam waved back madly, smiling with chattering teeth only she could hear.

Finally out of the village, he speeded up again, until she clung to him dearly, praying the gods to forgive his foolhardiness. A desperate plea as she could feel his shivers again.

Nearly down the mountain, they came upon a jeep parked beside the road. They slowed down, looked it over. In the front seat were maps, measuring equipment, pens, a thermos flask.

"Let's hijack it," Ciam joked.

"Not if he could help it, I don't think," said Sassela, pointing. Fifty or so yards away, she had noticed a man in a field. He looked professional, sensibly dressed in khaki, black high boots, binoculars and camera hung around his neck. He looked a tourist content and warm, getting his money's worth.

He acknowledged their attention with a wave.

Sassela waggled a hand at him.

Ciam yelled, "Yo! Bro!" Off again they went.

Several kilometers on, almost to flat land, the breeze more merciful, they were purring along when the moped's engine coughed, and barked, then choked, and sputtered ominously silent.

Sassela looked about: nondescript scrub and olive trees beside them. Behind and in front, empty roadway narrowing. The cloud-covered light said late afternoon. The prospect overall was bleak.

Ciam checked and tried and twisted things.

"Oh, boy!" he finally exclaimed. "Guess what. We're out of gas."

Sassela moaned, screwed her eyes tight shut. "Oh, God. What's to do now?"

"Guess we just gotta walk. And push."

Nothing else. So, Sassela at the moped's seat, they set to. A slight downgrade and improving temperature made for easier work. Although Ciam's face was showing strain, and he didn't sing anymore.

It seemed that they'd walked a thousand miles before, totally exhausted and numb beyond plain cold, they pushed the moped into a village. Just as—salt in the wound—the well-equipped man in his jeep rumbled up behind them.

Suddenly animated, shoving her to it, Ciam hissed, "Sass, Sass. Stand in the road. Make that man stop."

Momentarily reluctant because of her scant and inappropriate clothes, she nevertheless turned, faced the slow following jeep with her arms spread appealing. It braked full-stop. She went to the driver's window.

"Can I help?" the man asked, in proper though accented English.

"Oh, I hope so. We have had problems with the moped, you see. . . ." And Sassela related their story. He listened in silence, only the glint of his glasses interrupting his gaze on her. And, perhaps moved by their misadventures, he offered assistance and know-how.

"There is a place. Right here. Two houses away," he pointed across the road. "I will park." His lips squeezed the "w" closer to a "v." "You meet me there."

The flood of relief came close to warming her.

25

An anthropologist researching the area, he was German, his name Reinhard Schultz. Reinhard, he insisted to Sassela as the three of them crowded through the door. "I recommend this place. Let me suggest a soup to warm yourselves. Here they make a good soup."

Seemed the folks about knew him as a scientist, and held him in much respect. Truth said, the genial innkeepers—a bearded man, his buxom wife, and a skinny, bright-eyed, teenage daughter—treated him like royalty. As his special charges, Sassela and Ciam got their propers: everybody beaming amusement and concern; the wash-up accommodations first class, warm water, perfumed soap, fluffy white towels in upstairs bathrooms with spotless toilets.

Wondering how much Reinhard's generous German marks contributed to this reverence, Sassela used the facilities, washed face and hands, smoothed her hair, got herself feeling human again.

Ciam was not back when she returned downstairs,

but Reinhard was waiting. Tensely, it seemed. "I have ordered some hot soup for you and the, ah, young man. Yes?" he said. The gleam behind his glasses asked questions about Ciam, declared he was making a move.

"Ciam's his name. And that was very kind of you." Sassela smiled, uncomfortably aware of his bright roving eyes, self-conscious of her large nipples still prominent from chill. But then the tip of his tongue slid out like a pink slug, flicked at and missed the sweat beads rimming his upper lip. At such a giveaway, she could meet his burning eyes confidently. In this storm, her mind said, even a sleazy harbor is haven.

He brought his chair close as she took a seat at the table, and seeming fluent in Greek, immediately became a font of knowledge, explaining everything. Sassela listened politely to the inn's history since before the Second World War. Then she was told the significance of various bric-a-brac about the stately room.

Mind-dulling stuff, and she welcomed the innkeeper's interruption when he appeared with a tray bearing a shotglass of golden-colored liquid.

"The drink is raké," Reinhard said. "Say with accent on the 'e'. Rah-ké. You see?"

"Rah-ké," repeated Sassela dutifully, and sipped the viscous brew—sweetish, yet harsh on her palate.

He smiled approval, continued, "It is self-made, you see. Home brew from the cellar, even. With blueberry, figs, fruit, walnuts. Like ouzo without the aromatics. Ah-ha."

Mouth formed for courteous response, Sassela was distracted by a bumping and tumbling and a muffled squeal from upstairs, the vicinity of the bathrooms. Reinhard, facing the staircase, glanced meaningfully at her, then eyed the second floor. Catching the inference of his look, Sassela swallowed a catch of annoyance: Yes! Ciam was not yet back, and neither was the innkeeper's daughter anywhere to be seen. Once again he had proved his callowness.

The wife appeared from the kitchen with another tray, this one with two large steaming bowls. Split-pea soup fragrant with cardamom and other herbs, mouth-watering. The woman placed one bowl before Sassela, the other before the empty chair opposite. Just as, from upstairs, came a yell—Ciam's voice—a scrambling rush, then he pell-mell down the stairs.

Sassela looked for his pursuer. None to be seen; although he brought to the table the smug grin of a fox who'd just beaten the trap.

The innkeeper's wife sighed, "Ahhh—" caught Sassela's eye. "Keeeds," she remarked with a smile of parental understanding, then added, *"L'espiegleri. Ne?"*

Sassela smiled back vacantly, her mind awhirl at how Reinhard had explained her and Ciam. What kind of couple? She shot a self-conscious glance, and noticed him exaggerating with his lips, silently mouthing a word. But she still didn't understand.

Ciam, meanwhile, had pulled his bowl of soup nearer his chin, stirred up a steaming spoonful. "Just what the doctor—" sly eye to Reinhard "—ordered," he said.

Reinhard acknowledged him with a curt nod.

Although so quickly Ciam was back concentrating on sip-swallowing his soup, Sassela wondered if he'd caught the cool animosity in his benefactor's response.

Afterward, the missus brought them coffee and candied preserves. Pointedly speaking to Sassela, Reinhard identified with authority, "'Sweets,' this is the name."

"In the Caribbean we have the same thing," observed Ciam. "Same name, too."

"Ah-ha," said Reinhard flatly.

Never did the skinny innkeeper's daughter show her bright-eyed face again.

*　　*　　*

Despite Sassela's offer, Reinhard settled the bill, suggested he ride her home in his jeep. Again speaking
directly to her, he said, "Your, ah, companion can gas
the moped and follow us to your hotel."

"Nope," said Ciam vehemently. "I not riding that
bike no more. Be too cold, anyhow."

"Can you borrow warm clothes from someone?"
Sassela asked Reinhard.

He shrugged, smoothed his hair delicately. "We are
near sea level, now. Not much cold. The road is easy to
follow," he said.

Ciam turned abruptly, went and looked out the window.

Sassela watched Reinhard solemnly study his back.
"Can't we find him some warmer clothes?" she
repeated.

"Who?" he said. "This is a small village, without a
clothing store."

Ciam joined them. "I know how to do it," he
declared. "I could hold the moped in the tray of the
jeep."

Sassela looked at Reinhard, said quickly, "That
sounds good." She didn't want to ride alone with this
man.

Cool eye on Ciam, he said, "But can it fit?"

"Sure," said Ciam.

Sassela brightened her voice. "Let's give it a try," she
said, and started for the door.

Once outside, Reinhard got into the jeep behind the
steering wheel, his attitude clearly expressive of a man
in his rightful place, and who wasn't budging. Sassela
went with Ciam to assess the job at hand.

The sleek moped they'd been riding all of a sudden
seemed cumbersome, heavy—and clearly longer than
the jeep's tray.

"It'll fit diagonally," said Ciam.

"Yeah," Sassela agreed. Noting silently that it'd be a close fit. And that, for better room, two bulky canvas bags there would have to be shifted around.

The moped was, in fact, enormously awkward and heavy. Ciam huffed and strained to lift and then maneuver it handle-first into the jeep's tray. What muscle she could, Sassela helped out, but felt herself more of an encumbrance. So she gradually adjusted her efforts to guidance and encouragement while leaving the bull work to Ciam's stalwart determination.

It never left her mind though, that Reinhard might've left his steering wheel and come lend a hand.

At last it was done, moped and Ciam secure in the tray, and they drove off. Right away, prematurely pressing for advantage, Reinhard began: "I am an anthropologist, and for data I specialize in cemeteries. I study habits and customs. Mundane matters. The—" he searched for words, his stubby fingers off the steering wheel, spinning circles, engaging her curiosity, "—common information. From their graves, I get indications of mortality, of epidemics from their death age. Also we may learn ideas of their wealth. Certainly their gender. All because of their burial customs, you see? This material I make my scientific view. I pigeonhole the culture, you may say. From their graves I recompose their myths, their habits, their rituals to honor departed. I study very carefully. With insight and luck, maybe my graves will give me robust lives. Strong lives, and yes, in a manner, even souls. Ah-ha! Yes, sometimes among my graves I have found a soul—"

Reluctantly, Sassela found herself taken with his absorption, his spirited eloquence. *Night of the Living Dead* shading her mind, with a skeptical lilt she said, "You found a soul?"

Reinhard turned his attention from the roadway,

regarded her steadily for a moment, looked back at the road while he took several deep breaths, his face pinking. As if adequately braved, he continued, "I say to you, more than one time I have seen my own. Yes, it is most true. Most personal—"

He pulled a handkerchief out of his inner jacket pocket, carefully wiped his brow, then remained silent.

"You were saying about your job—" Sassela nudged.

All the cue he needed: "No, no! What I do is not best described as job. Calling is maybe better. I am a small bit of a great science. You see? One of many small stones building the mountain. Or even taking it apart, eh? You see?"

"How you mean?"

"It is how we work together. That is the essence. Like worker bees, from many different flowers, we return all to one hive. Bring everything we gather. You want to hear this? Let me say it. Only yesterday, I'm going to my site, and there's a butcher at his job. Ah! Grand it was—" he glanced at her, eyes sparkling behind the rimless lenses "—grand. He hung the swine. Big as himself, this one. Squealing, squirming in the air. A death dance, as the butcher, certain with his holds is helping the balance with his belly. His apron is a bloody mess, he hugs close the animal. His eye is level with the jugular. The shining steel of knife. He gathers to apply—"

"No! Stop!" Sassela interrupted, horrified. Shook her head firmly. "I don't want to hear."

"Oh!" exclaimed Reinhard, fisting the free hand he had been gesticulating. "I am most sorry for offending. Forgive me, I did not think. This is not pleasant. No?"

"No, it's not your fault. I'm squeamish. Always have been about blood. It just turns me off."

A while of quiet; then Reinhard started talking again: travel in general, the beautiful countryside, inoffensive neutral matter. None of it registering, as what with the warm cab, the engine's steady drone, she was close to drifting off. Stray thoughts entered her mind: of Ciam's comfort in the jeep's tray. Was he holding up against the wind? Was he cold again? Was his stubborn choice to come along the better? Then she remembered the embarrassing tumbling upstairs at the inn, and didn't feel so caring. She'd have to ask what that had been all about, but later.

Eventually, by routes Sassela couldn't figure, they pulled up at the rental place. Ciam dropped off the moped, picked up his bicycle, put it in the jeep's tray. Then ten minutes more, they were at the trace leading down to Hut.

"This is your hotel?" said Reinhard, amusement bubbling in his throat.

Defensively, Sassela declared, "A house is what you make of it. Don't you think?"

"Ah, yes," he allowed, the amusement no better hidden.

"Well, I can't thank you enough for everything. You saved our lives, you know. What can I say? Except that you were an angel of deliverance."

She heard the crunch of gravel as Ciam jumped off the jeep and started off down the track for Hut. Knew he wouldn't be saying "Thanks" to Reinhard. She levered open the door, turned back and stuck out her hand. "So, I'll be seeing you," she said.

"Of course," he said, gave a limp handshake. "I'll drop by soon. See how you are, have a drink, okay?"

"Sure, anytime." She got out, thunked the jeep's door shut. "Our house is yours."

He smiled briefly. "So good day, now." The engine engaged. The jeep surged off.

Sassela went down the track.

*   *   *

In the tired evening, she found Ciam a-soak in a shallow pool, head raised safely on a flat stone, his eyes closed. Shoulder barely nudging his, she directly joined his warm vote for R&R. Wasn't long before she heard a soft snore saying he had fallen asleep. She shook his shoulder gently. "Ciam!"

He shuddered, opened his eyes blearily.

"Let's go in, hon. Before we fall asleep in the sea," she said. Helping him to his feet, she put an arm about his waist and led him up the twilight beach.

He stood slack as a zombie while she dried him off, raising each arm, rubbing with the towel, then releasing the limb to fall back, hang loosely. And when led docilely to the bed, he merely standing there, she had to roll him in.

Not long after, she slipped under the covers and into the sleep of the exhausted.

26

Next morning, Sassela was aware—in that semiconscious way—when Ciam did not return to bed. No bother to her, though, this morning everything was postponable. She languidly chalked up his absence to youthful resilience, then remembered the misadventures of yesterday and that she was cross with him. Drowsy as a yawn, she dropped back into the balm.

The day developed shapelessly—a relief after the previous one's doings. Without energy, Sassela lazed about, rousing herself just enough to make a journal entry:

Dear Di,

The recent mountain adventure has disclosed various aspects of our guide. He has worked hard for us, showed strength and courage, yet on the other hand, his behavior regarding a flirtatious innkeeper's daughter has provided reason to question his loyalty, and put the group's self-esteem at risk. All in all, this ecological adventure, after turning this way and that, now seems to be shifting in a negative direction.

Bfn. Sss.

She wasn't hungry that evening; had a nibble and a glass of retsina. "Oh, I'm fine," she assured Ciam when he asked, having proposed a trip to town. "Just feel like staying in."

He sprawled on the bed, looked at her suggestively and patted beside him. "Want to climb over here?"

Not in the least interested, Sassela offered instead, "If you only want to *give* a massage, I might."

The pout in his manner was immediate. Without a word, he sort of wriggled his attention to the hill-view window.

Sassela drained her glass, halved it again from the near-empty bottle.

"You never want to do anything," he muttered.

She heard, but to make him repeat himself, said, "What did you say?"

"Is no fun 'round here any—"

"Depends on what you mean by fun. Not so?"

"No. I talking 'bout how you so grumpy all the time—"

"Grumpy! Me grumpy? Who's the one always striding off for any reason at all. Who's the one always embarrassing me—"

He scrambled up from the bed, "You still going off on that? I was at a loss. A little girl like that, I never realized what was going on. So what you wanted me to do?"

"And yesterday, with that innkeeper's skinny daughter. I suppose you were at another loss."

"Is that what you talking about? We was just play-ing, just messing around."

"Can't you even admit how you were selfish and childish embarrassing me like that in front of a stranger, abandoning me to his company—"

"Seems to me both a' you were getting along very well enough."

"Damn you to even dare insinuate—" she screamed, incensed.

He drew himself to the edge of the bed. "I'm not sug-gesting anything," he mumbled quickly.

To help manage her temper, Sassela strode to the sea-view window, stuck her head out, and freed her loosened hair to the cool, cool breeze. Slowly moving her neck, giving her tresses their sway, she heard the bed creak, and paused.

"Listen, Sassela," she heard him say. "I'm sorry, okay. I guess I threatened your dignity. Later."

"Sure—" she began, but by the time she had turned around, his huffy back was beyond the closing door.

She was in bed, as if asleep, when, very much later, he returned and silently crept in. After which they slept as if on separate mattresses.

27

Next morning's clouds were low, turbulent and gray, setting a mood. Snug in the covers, Sassela thought cynically, maybe two weeks was the natural limit for this kind of fling. And they still had four more days to get through. She squeezed her eyes tight, tried to recover her doze.

The afternoon followed drizzly and cool. They stayed inside, courteous with each other, Sassela straining to marshal the basics of two-man canasta. Ciam, withdrawn, was a patient teacher, explaining preliminary details while he shuffled the cards—a new deck, slick and lively, though no match for his slender, caging fingers.

They heard a motor approach and stop. Then the crunch of expensive, high-top boots coming down the track.

Sassela caught Ciam's leery eye as he murmured, "Someone's accepted a habit."

"Won't last long, I don't think," she said, as came Reinhard's call: "Hallo the house!"

"I'll get it," said Ciam.

Sassela buttoned up Ciam's long-sleeved shirt she wore, wished she'd put on a bra.

Ciam pushed the door open. Mangling an Eastern European accent, he said, "Welcome to my laboratory, Herr doctor."

Reinhard entered hesitantly. "Good day, my friends. I was passing—" as usual, pinching his "w" to a "v."

"Sure, sure," said Ciam expansively. "Once you're in the neighborhood, why not. What can I offer you? Some brunch, retsina? Maybe a spot of peppered caviar?"

"Well, thank you," said Reinhard doubtfully. "I have a bottle of amontillado. Very good. Maybe we share. Yes?"

"Yes, of course, Reinhard. Have a seat. Let me get cups," said Sassela, and went to the sink as he drew a bottle from his canvas carryall, dropped the bag by the door.

Ciam offered his chair and went to sprawl on the near edge of the bed.

Reinhard sat. "You enjoy playing the card games?" he asked.

Sassela waited a pause for Ciam, then past his silence, answered, "I'm only beginning to. Ciam is teaching me canasta."

She returned to the table, set down cups. When she glanced at Ciam, she met deliberately averted eyes. "Do you know canasta?" she asked.

"Of course," said Reinhard as he poured the sherry. "I played this game most nights throughout my student's career. Yes, with the practice I am good."

From the bed: "You played for fun, or money?"

Reinhard looked startled, said quickly, "No, no. Only for fun. I am more scientific, gambling is difficult."

Quirky to his discomfort, Sassela prodded, "Reinhard

is more of a scientific speculator than a gambler. He assumes from evidence and reconstructs past lives—"

"—for the advancement of Western civilization, right?" backed up from the bed.

"And the cause of knowledge," Sassela concluded. She took Ciam's cup to him, winked with mischief, returned to her chair.

"No, no. It is not fair," said Reinhard, pink-faced, his hands of well-fed fingers raised shoulder-high in protest. "Knowledge is important to all, to everyone on earth. Particularly—" he mouthed every syllable, quickly at ease in the explainer's role, "—particularly, my friends, if the so-called global village is to evolve. My field is the force of superstition. Hidden, yes. Subtle, yes. But yet most significant. Ah-ha! Let me show you a modern superstition changing a history, shortening a world—"

He paused, looked from Sassela to laid-out Ciam on the bed, then aimed his thesis back at her. "Europe before 1914 was the star on the stage of world affairs. Everything modern began there. Economy, culture, inventiveness, political dynamism. Yet by 1945, Europe was reduced to a peninsula on the western side of Asia. What did us in was a superstition that we were natural masters. 'Leaders of the free world' became an acceptable statement. 'Third World' became an accepted political salve to explain away theft of natural resources and neglect of native peoples' societal systems. Folk superstitions, I mean, the primaries of human ethics. So this now is my interest and research. I see it inevitable that stiff-necked, modern civilization will bow again to the ancient ways. I am a student of the advance guard. I learn and try to understand so I can educate those who seek these other ways of knowing."

"Well," said Sassela, at a loss for appropriate response, as cynical Harry surprised into her mind. She wondered briefly how he'd react to this scene of the "oppressor" giving nativeman his propers.

"Seems to me either you're an intellectual mercenary, or you're picking sides with the angels," said Ciam. He had gone over to the beach-view window, and spoke as if to the scenery.

His rudeness, no longer good-natured, made Sassela suddenly impatient with him. Here was Reinhard in sensible manner developing an intelligent conversation, about relevant matters. And all Ciam could do was sulk at the window like a surly child. What was it with him? "How do you see that?" she challenged sharply.

A swift glance at her. Hurt? He said, "Obvious to me."

"Knowledge is neutral. It has no preferences," declared Reinhard. "Look at me. I inhabit cemeteries. There I am a presence. I study the sites for decoration, for inscription. I get lives from that—"

Ciam was fidgeting with the window, swinging it all the way back so it banged against the wall. Rudely banging it again and again as Reinhard went on speaking about his research. Sassela wondered at his restlessness. Were his own Caribbean heritage and superstitions biasing him against Reinhard? She recalled him passionately telling of his birth that night by the fire, his eerie moodiness afterward. Maybe it was the subject of conversation that forestalled a bantering mood with Reinhard. But just then, Ciam broodingly slammed the half-window, declared, "Yo! smart guys. See y'all later." And through the door with a squeak he was gone.

"He does not like me, you think?"

"Nothing personal, though," said Sassela. "He gets that way."

"Youth!" said Reinhard, with such disdain that Sassela squirmed at not launching a defense. Instead she prompted, "So, you were saying about—?"

"Experience. Mature, tried and true human experience, and how we go about accumulating it. You ask
maybe, what is the nature of this drive for knowing? I
say it is of the soul, and I say this drive consumes.
Consumes the student, his time, his period of significance here. As it consumes any true student. For the
banker student, it could be the buy and sell, the com-
pounding of commerce, the promise of market values.
For the baker student, it might be the fluffy world of
flours rising and falling. Such a one is run by leavens
and hot ovens. Peculiar, no? But, there is also the magical scent of fresh bread and sweet pastries. And what
could match this? You see, for every true student there
are compensations. No?" He reached a handkerchief
out of his jacket, took his glasses off and wiped his
shining face.

Which changed him altogether. The gleam from the
lenses gone, his small face lost authority, became inno-
cently fervent, fueled by higher commandment.
Without the intensity of blood and guts.

"—ah?" he persisted.

Still distracted by the change his glasses made,
Sassela had lost track. "I guess you're right," she said
safely.

He spired his stubby fingers, looked at her as if well
satisfied. Then he put his glasses back on, got up and
went to his duffel bag left just inside the door.

Sipping her wine, Sassela watched him rummage
within the bag. He returned to his seat, put a pint of
brandy on the table, and with hands spread generous,
proposed, "If it is not an insult, I would have a drink of
this now. And I much wish that you would join me." He
indicated the bottle with an urbane nod.

"Sure," said Sassela, gracious to his gallantry, "with
such highly stimulating company, I would be honored
to."

From the kitchen area, she could only scrounge up a handleless teacup. So Reinhard emptied his teacup out the hill-view window, and there, before that spare vista, they toasted to health, and wisdom, and Greece. The brandy was smooth, each toast re-stoking the glow it set off in the pit of her stomach. With every toast, though, Reinhard seemed progressively needful to put hands on her: friendly around her shoulders, familiar about her waist. Finally, his quick camaraderie becoming repellent, she said, "I need retsina. Let me get a bottle," and slipped out of his grasp, crossing to the cupboard, stepped up on her chair to reach the wine. And there he was, quickly after her, steadying the chair, his head somehow managing to nudge against her buttocks.

She slashed her arm downward, shoving him away. "What the hell d'you think you're doing?" she yelled.

"I, ah, overbalanced," he mumbled, sweat popping from his red face, eyes everywhere but hers. "I missed, ah, tried to hold your chair—"

"With your face up my butt? Huh?"

"I didn't mean, intend—"

"Yeah, right," Sassela stepped down, eyed him sarcastically. "It was an accident, huh?"

As soon as he sat down again, she went to the sea-view window, made much show of searching the beach this way and that. "Ciam should be here soon," she observed.

Reinhard got the intended message. Face still reddened, hasty to his duffel, he zipped it up. "Ah-ha, I think maybe I will go now," he said. "It was good, the drink with you. We will again, I hope. Yes?"

Tone seeping sarcasm, Sassela said, "Sure, drop by anytime. Remember, my house is yours." She pushed the door open.

Not touching her at all, Reinhard slid by, up the track to his jeep. Door closed again, sharp in the back of her nose, a bitterness tainted the room.

*   *   *

Spiteful and half gloating, when Ciam returned, Sassela told him about the awkward try.

"I'll break the underhanded shithead!" he shouted, rocking the table with the slam of his fist.

Sassela shifted her chair safely away, regarded him calmly. "Why the rage and violence? He didn't do any-thing. And I can handle myself anyway."

He eyed her shiftily, not daring to accuse. But his mind was in his red wild glare. "Let him cross mih path again, he'd find out 'bout handling."

"Sit down, Ciam," Sassela told him tiredly. "Start acting your age. Nothing happened, I said."

He gave her a long look. "I don't feel to sit down. Especially not where your beau warmed up with his sad, droopy ass."

"Why don't you go take a walk then?" she said sar-castically.

He threw her a caustic look. "Maybe you're right," he said, and left.

Sassela gazed at the closed door, shaking her head, slowly blowing out her sigh. It was growing boring, this cryptic game-playing, his childishness. And *she* was not a kid. She sipped her retsina, mentally composed the statement for her journal's next entry: essentially, that she was near ready for normalcy.

Late afternoon he returned repentant, and Sassela, indifferent to all but peace and quiet, allowed him his will, which led to more retsina by the beach, and a strenuous tanning session. Afterward, the cool sea breeze mixing with the warmth of the fading sun rays produced a soothing balance on her sweaty skin as, her face against his chest, Ciam's blood pulsed strong, and mysterious. Outside the contented blackness of her closed eyelids, the waves lashed listlessly, and growled and grunted like happied appetites.

She broke the quiet: "Don't they sound like belly growls?"

He didn't respond.

"The waves, I mean, sometimes almost like they're purring?" she said.

"Don't know if you know, but you almost right," he said gravely, far, far away from Sassela's mood.

"How you mean?"

"Is not purring. The sea sighing tears. Is how the sea does cry a sound to ears and heart. A feeling sound like now. Girl, is a sad, sad sea we hearing." So solemnly he spoke, she rolled off his chest, looked at his face.

The brimming eyes she met confused her. What tender spot of his past had she pricked to have resurrected this melancholy? He lay blankly staring at the sky, chest heaving, blurting out his heartfelt: ". . . alive with longing. Like yuhself, like a swamp, a forest. Leh me lend you an idea. Suppose de sea does miss every single drop of water leave it? And I mean every one. So yuh thinking even mist and clouds and rainbows. And yuh thinking them as tears from a sea pining, from a mother patient and biding for she fluids to return to bosom, return from them unnatural places like rocks and empty air. Yeah, this sea sighing, sounding cries for she life that she missing. She liquid blessings. Yeah, Sassy, sea could be a sad, sad place."

Mindful of his outbursts, Sassela eyed him warily. "Ciam," she said, "you're very weird. You know that, right?"

As if she'd never spoken, he addressed the purpling sky: "Yuh ever get to wondering why every natural body ketch a yen when they close the sea? The water in you feeling the same call. Is why seawater warm can pleasure right through your skin—"

"Ciam! Is it your Caribbean talking here? Seawater

in New York is a chill seventy degrees, warmest. Your theory could account for that?"

He shrugged. "I don't have to. Not to somebody who only believe television."

And to her utmost surprise, he upped and stiff-backed toward Hut, naked buttocks shedding black flakes on the gathering evening.

Sassela shook her head resignedly. She was past fed up with these petulant suddens of his. It seemed that ganja darkened his moods, shortened his temper, made him grim and mopish. Briefly, she thought to follow him up to Hut, talk it out with him. But the sun was just about done, and the purple shades of evening sultry, and dried sweat and flaky sand all over her. So instead she went for the towels, draped to dry on some large boulders. The departed sun, as usual, had pleasantly warmed the waist-deep pools into a balmy salt-soak; soothing indulgence Sassela was prompt to enjoy.

28

Ciam was normal the next morning. Up before her as usual, his proposal was a day of touring. Relieved by his better mood, Sassela was all "ayes."

They biked in and once more collected the moped from Gregori's, set off for the other side of the island. No houses, no people, no trees, it was Nature's rough side, got to by jolting rutted roads no car could ever use. After an hour of rugged holding on, Ciam parked them by the waveless sea. Sweaty and hot, Sassela doffed her shoes, answered the water's call to her feet.

This was a black, remote place of towering crags and bare, gnarled cliffs kneeling into a placid glittering sea. Strangely moved, she stood peaceful at water's edge, on the empty black-pebbled beach, the wavelets lapping cool at her toes. The silence was complete, as if they were on a world all alone.

He must have read her mood and mind. She felt his hand boldly lifting her skirt, fingers smooth between skin and panties, pulling firmly down. She wiggled help to them, twisting, looking at him. Hard and naked as the rocks. His eager breath soft on the open beach. Then freakily, she couldn't wait either, turned and flung her arms around his neck, hopping onto him, skirt raised high, legs spread wide with wet, naked welcome. Quivered as he slid right in.

Although, awkwardly a-stagger from the pull of her hanging weight, and gravity, and passion, still well inside her crevassed clasp, he fell down on her, juicing her up, while the smooth-pebbled beach became brace for her arched back, imprinting bruises from the fervor as he shot into her. And, like a lush flowering flame, she bloomed in orgasm.

Caprice of passion, perhaps. As she floated emptied to the might of pleasure, wisps and notions flitted through her mind: a conceit of life-force shared in honor of gaunt gods at this bleak place she'd come to. Then with a dismaying twinge, past vision's realm she got a surreal glimpse of the locale: as a scene bare of human identity, a desolate vista surrendered to isolation, and absolutely contrary to the lonely privacy she so cherished about her New York.

Suddenly chilled, she had Ciam take her out of there.

Sassela woke before dawn anxious and tingly to subtle differences. The crisp air tasted sour and metallic deep down her throat. A tender fullness of her breasts drew attention to their weight. In tiniest ways she felt changed, more delicate of texture. A sharp word could cut. A sudden tear might drown her spirits. Puzzling her mind, she couldn't figure why.

It wasn't a sleepless bed. Wrapped warm in the sheet as she had been, Ciam remained soundly at it. Reasonable enough! Not sensible to her body systems, though. Since her time lapse had adjusted, she was popping up her usual perky seven—this queasy morning an offbeat from her rhythm. Although right now, other body functions were reliably pressing.

The rickety privy didn't put her off anymore.

Especially early mornings, when there was not the slightest smell, no buzzy flies. Nowadays, for minutes after business was done she'd sit ruminating: on the ingenuity and humor of the builder—his use of the tireless sea as night-soil remover, the chairback and armrests for the seat around the doughnut. The shack would appreciate some renovation, though. That last passing shower had showed up significant leakiness— especially one particularly cheeky dripper which annoyingly splattered the bared and vulnerable bum.

Wouldn't be much to the job. A sheet of galvanized metal or plastic, some two-inch nails, a carpenter's hammer. Time was I'd have tackled it myself, Sassela mused—and contexts interconnecting, all at once her bowels slackened, pooping a little fart as she divined reason for her morning's unease.

Memory presented twenty-year-old Sassela summer-job sweaty in yellow, oversize coveralls, her hard hat like a blue bird in lacquered sheen. Ready in hand, head and claw, her carpenter's hammer. Life was adventure, this job was fun. Provided energy, zesty sunshine, tangy air, plus college credits for the community work. And a major major plus, at the door of the site's makeshift office, Mr. Rafe Abent, outstanding in dark suit, red-patterned tie, his style cool as a summer stream. Look at him and forget the hot, bright morning. He was boss. Sharp eyes glinting clear intelligence and authority, he pointed out things to the uniformly sunglassed foremen. They nodded to his expertise. Engineer Rafe Abent, black and brainy, authority in shining clothes. Beautiful, and carrying it easily. A man who spoke stuff once and it was followed through, made done. A pharaoh.

Sassela guessed that day there were no other seats free. Because, at the lunch table, he sat next to her. Chatted nicely, beyond the usual silly compliments. In the natural flow, she agreed to same time, same place the next day. He said it, and it was so. That was his way, intelligent and wise as twice her age. His insights soothed, grooved her into wisdom, made her mature, free. Next date she advanced to visiting his bachelor's apartment, an Upper East Side town house.

The car that took them there was foreign, with leather seats cool and yielding. The stereo system, not to be seen, sounded magnificent. The luxurious ride never let in street noise and, as if on a dreamboat, they were soon at the town house. "Company pays," Rafe said, as he spread his arms wide and laughed richly. Famous pictures on the high walls. Persian carpets underfoot. Smart old-fashioned music. Big leather-covered chairs. Fat crystal glasses. Top-quality drugs, legal and otherwise.

She had felt so shrewd at having dressed to impress: flared purple satin pants, halter top just a tease small.

No surprises followed. Company probably paid for the abortion, too. There were other costs, though. Like the mental taxing which, despite all of Rafe Abent's assurances, only Sassela paid.

He'd said, "It's your body, isn't it?" and he'd said, "It's your right!" and he'd said, "It is your decision." Hadn't he?

Sassela never knew any of it for certain. On her part, three weeks late for the first time, a lot of it went fast, the balance made vague by worry. But Rafe Abent, with authority, kept on talking, talking, talking. So what else to do?

In his foreign car with the cool leather seats, quickly they were at the place he took her. Welcome smiles were cold as their silvery gurneys. Quick were their professional eyes to the signature on the check Rafe Abent handed over. Then their clammy, touchy gloves. The chill sting of needle. Cold guck. Then, without a gasp, the hungry speculum, its dreadful silver jaws a-widening.

Cold and fear, a bleak unknowing pause. Then, blearily, she heard their instant-hearty voices: "You're going to be fine!" and "Is there an escort meeting you?" and "Need a car service?" Every courtesy crisp as frost.

They might've, could've murdered a part of her. But mercy, the event was professional, went fast, was already far ago, long away. A shivery blast of one year's summertime, at the edge of memory, fogging out. Except for one profound certainty. As etched in her will, cold and hard like an icicle, was the vow: *Never would she go through that again . . .*

Abruptly, Sassela caught up with her runaway train of thought, wondering why it was leading her down such pregnant tracks. She left the latrine, anxiously trying to recall her usage of the contraceptive sponges, and readily found misses and gaps. Yesterday's spontaneity at the bare, black beach, for example.

You can't get pregnant overnight! her other mind argued. Maybe the queasiness was only food poisoning, it suggested. But all day through, a piercing flash in tanning time, an inedible morsel at dinner, her disquiet persisted.

29

Vague unease chased her about in dreams that dissolved from memory when her eyes finally opened to morning's light. Then Ciam awoke with a rigidity problem that delayed breakfast until Sassela limbered it for him. And then, greedily, table turned prop, they tried for a second solution. Afterward, while eating, they planned the remaining day: Sassela wanting an hour or so to catch up on her journal, Ciam one-track-mindedly recommending nude sunbathing or swimming, plus dollops of any other fleshy diversions.

"Just two more days' vacation, my honey swamp," he reminded, his stunning smile returned. "Then it's back to old, cold, ordinary Apple."

It made sense to her. He didn't have to point out that journals have no say, and would wait. "Meet you in a short minute," she promised. "I'll just headline the stuff, and fill in later."

Already stripped while she answered, hand shyly cupping his response, he went naked to the call of the drawling breakers.

And so proceeded an uncomplicated day, everything easy as planned, many forms of frolic sampled, subject only to *randy interruptus* as their moods would ebb, or flood, or flow.

Evening, like a voyeur creeping, surprised them dozing on the slated sand. Snoring softly from a drooling gape, Ciam seemed totaled. Sassela, however, was refreshed; felt strong and, as her gut's growl reminded, ravishingly hungry. Were it the era of genies, and had she the cork to a sample, she thought, he certainly would've been sent for a service of those loosen-a-button Harlem church dinners: those with brisket of beef and racks of ribs and greens and cornbread and hot gravy and some red hot habañero pepper and something dangerously calorific like a custard milkshake to wash down some straightforwardly sinful dessert like chocolate cheesecake and slices of ripe papaya—

"Hungry?" Ciam asked, rousing her from gourmandizing fantasy.

"You kidding? Hungry's not close," she agreed.

Without further discussion they went to Hut, washed and dressed, then rode off for the bright lights.

They stopped and studied windowed menus at two other places. Either offering was solid staple stuff: broiled fish, pita bread, feta cheese, red wine, goat milk, and one or the other stew. Good filling food for students, or folks vacationing from tight pockets. But, with Hut a freebie, even money-minding Sassela admitted she was well under budget, near vacation's close and at the end of a perfect one after a flawed yesterday. And it seemed that all this and whatever else well-qualified her being fancy hungry. So, hobbling her misgivings, she was the one who suggested the garish arena with its excellent, four-star fare, despite the risk of encountering Fifina.

"Nah!" he protested immediately. Too quickly, it seemed.

"Afraid you can't handle that ill-mannered child?" she prodded slyly.

"No, I'm not!" Ciam declared hotly.

"Take it easy, I'm just teasing," she said, feeling even better about her challenge.

Safety in numbers, though, she chose a table in the main hall, near the waiters' station, and they were promptly attended. They chose directly, passed up the usual prerequisite viewing of the meal. In short order their selections arrived: abalone soup, an excellently done fluffy rice pilaf, and for the entrée, poached sea trout steaming delicately with rosemary and other aromatic nuances.

Quickly and cordially went the business of suggesting and pouring and serving and setting of glasses and plates. Then, mutually intent on the purpose of their outing, conversation choked under as they both became rapt with consuming the savories. And every dish and dainty, every dab, without exception, was grand.

Satisfied belches discreetly done, they were waiting for dessert—raspberries with cream topping—when she caught sight of the imp, sauntering toward their table. One look at her manner, and with a qualm, Sassela knew she was in for a reckoning.

The first difference she noticed was the set of the brat's hair; she'd let down its thick, luxurious abundance to fall way past her buttocks, where the ends were gathered, short-braided, and tied with a scarlet ribbon starkly contrasting with all else of her costume—ankle-length dress of black, glimmering, satiny fabric, shiny black shoes, frilled socks. The ensemble, on the brief figure, suggested a ridiculous midget queen of spades.

Sassela coughed her helpless snigger into her hand,

and said, "Well, little Miss Fifina, aren't you all dressed up today? You look almost grown. Where's your—" She paused; her worst suspicions made her balk at saying "father," but "waiter" and "carrier" weren't right either. "—your guardian?" Then she met the child's marble-cold eyes, and the flat female challenge in them.

Barely head-high with sitting Sassela, the child stared defiantly as she seemed to study and assimilate response. Then, in a thin reedy scream, she launched her assault. "Man is no guard me. Is my place here. Is me boss, me queen. Not you, okay. Now you not stay here. Go! Go!"

As she spoke—arms akimbo, tiny hands fisted, full mane a-tremble from her snaking neck, foot stomping tantrum tempo—she gradually drew closer to Sassela until, her back to Ciam, she was barely elbow-distance away. And, in that moment of partial privacy, the angry, childish face underwent a grotesque readjustment: wrinkling under suddenly shrewd eyes, a violent grimace scouring wickedness around her mouth, and unnaturally aging the whole face into a sneer of hideous menace, like some ancient, horrible mask on an evil doll.

Then in a flash the look was gone. Done with her imperious commanding, the little creature flounced back and climbed into Ciam's lap, pulling his quiescent arm close around her belly. "You go now!" She pointed a finger at Sassela.

A look to Ciam for assistance saw him just sitting there, smiling ambiguously, letting the little monster stroke his neck, and the back of his hand. There in the central hall of the gaudily lit, public restaurant, the whole tacky scene was happening again, and making no sense at all.

"Ciam! What's going on?" she appealed.

Yet, as if dumb, he just sat there impotently, his look empty as the moon. And when she stood up and crowded her face into his and tried to meet his eyes, their shutters had returned.

Sassela couldn't deal anymore. She grabbed her purse abruptly. "Ciam, let's get out of here!"

Secure on her lap-seat, the creature said, "No!"

Not that Ciam had made the least attempt to move, which only frustrated Sassela back down into her chair. So then, drawing a deep, defensive breath, she searched hopefully about for the stern waiter. No sight of him, although everyone else had now made her debacle center stage. Not only adjacent diners, but many of the overcostumed waiters were passively watching the scene, and showing no intentions of interfering.

She hissed desperately at Ciam, "Look here, Ciam. I'm not taking any more of this, okay. I'm going to get up, and I'm going to walk. If you're with me, come. If you're not, then, good night!"

Without meeting her eyes, he said, "All right, Sass, you better go. I'll handle everything. Just take it easy."

So Sassela gathered up her purse, and her scarf, and her shattered dignity, and walked away; through the glare of electric stares, out of the garish, glittering, disgusting place. And outside, she didn't once think of waiting for him.

She rode hard, working anger into sweat, and by the time she was back at Hut, was calm enough. But not to sleep. She put away the bike, stripped and went for a swim, self-consciously keeping on underpants even in the evening's private rock-pools. She splashed into the refreshing water, her prudish Aunt Maisie's voice sounding in her head: "There's dirty about in Denmark." Which, Sassela had to admit, did not nearly describe the atmosphere in this particular precinct, was not even close to envisioning the corrosive creepiness generating her anger and humiliation.

Certainly there was something sexually unnatural here: that stern waiter-man as a dumb brute mounted by his impish mistress. She with her penchant for bare-back riding. With a quiver, Sassela remembered the glimpse of ancient evil in the little face. Whatever else, that girl was definitely more than a simple child. But what was she about? Which question, of course, brought to mind her own demon lover, Mr. Ciam Turrin. Much less, yet regretfully more than she had bargained for. But tonight had been the last straw with him. Though oddly, she didn't hate, or even regret him. She had taken her shot at a good time—but he had turned out fickle and weak, and more than anything, untrustworthy. She sighed, yawned tiredly. All in all, she mused, holiday's end was seeming more and more a savior. There remained only tonight, tomorrow, its night, then Sunday morning's flight back home.

Lulled to dozing with her legs in the balmy pool, Sassela eventually roused and dragged herself to Hut and into bed. Snuggled under the covers, she fell asleep immediately. . . .

. . . *there in the diamond desert, in desperate circumstances, harbor at hand, she opens her bloody pouring eyes, beholds an enormous terrarium . . . dark evergreen lushness in a giant transparent blimp afloat eye-level above the glistening diamond-sharp sands, which never cease lacerating the soles of her feet as she cranes to view the spectacle inside . . . there the impish girlchild and a grinning curlike Ciam reclining naked as eggs next to a languid stream gently a-gurgle . . . as Sassela's eyes rain red anguish, the carnal child mounts Ciam and begins writhing obscenely, the lavish vegetation a fine screen detailing action silhouettes . . . while, staring from the glaring, brilliant desert, with excruciating slowness, Sassela learns that she isn't really thirsty for the comfort of their beguiling brook . . . it is only that she is cold, so*

very cold, that her shivering is shearing her bloody feet,
gnawing away right through to her frigid white bones . . .

She awoke, cold indeed, as she'd wrestled the covers
completely off.

Restlessly tossing, Sassela listened to the night:
sounds morosely different from her Harlem. Here,
Night's interruption was a monotony of waves lashing
the stolid shore, indifferent as Time, as irrelevant. Here
noise was nothing crucial. No wailing sirens. No por-
tent. No random explosions bearing exciting possibilities like gunshots? Or firecrackers? Or even auto-
exhaust backfires? Here were no such trite or true
uncertainties. The vital signs here were crickets screech-
ing automatically, and the stupid peeping of stupid
frogs: moist, scared, tiny things like the quivering,
opalescent fragility Ciam had handed her one evening.
Here life was creatures such as these, insignificantly
directed by ever-crashing waves, vaguely beautiful and
numberless.

She pulled up the rough covers against the shudder
of this dreary prospect, and while warmth stingily crept
back, the horrid dream eddied away from memory.
Then slowly into snugness again, she fell asleep
soundly. Although off and on half-waking, vaguely
aware of the lonely bed, her other mind did wonder,
Where was Ciam?

30

He never came in all the night. Morning come, Sassela woke and managed breakfast: boiled oatmeal on the kerosene stove. With a spoonful of honey, it was enough. Then she went to the cove and the peaceful sea. His sudden broodings as catalyst, Sassela had got to watching the waves, thoughtfully noticing. Better afternoons, she had gone to the high bluff at the end of the cove's crescent, and in a rocky lee of the hill, contemplated the enigma of the ocean's face, the nuanced messages on its ever-rippling surface.

Today the wind was up, gusting, boisterous as kids at recess. As she puffed her way up the bluff, the gusts tussled and tossed with her, flagged her about like clothes hung on a line. Then, from her cozy spot, she watched the wind play the sea, too. Wrestling with the wavelets. Rushing them hither and thither. Quivering them on the swelling sea in swirls come quick and gone. Swarms of them, like goose bumps along a fleshy course, rippling along for many, many meters, racing each other away.

Never before had Sassela seen wind as carefree and fun; it was this sea that showed her. This sea, its body vast, endless and mysterious in just being there. This primary womb, essential mother, full of life with life its own. Despite the bright, warm sun today, deliciously the riddle chilled her.

Returning from her midday stroll, Sassela saw what seemed to be a bag at their drop-off spot. Curious, since Yiorgis had already done his last delivery. It was from Reinhard. His research ended, he had dropped off extra supplies for them: chocolates, a bottle of red wine, a flask of brandy. Stuck between them was his good-bye note in firm, square handwriting: "So long, my friends. Be careful."

About to return it to the bag, she noticed writing on the other side: a mysterious stick-figure sketch of a small person with triangular breasts riding a bull with a crying man's face. Sassela's heart thrummed with alarm as the simple picture immediately recalled the image of Fifina riding the waiter's shoulders after their first disturbing encounter in the restaurant. But, she wondered, did Reinhard actually intend this as a warning? She shook her head, determinedly forced the morbid conjectures from her mind.

Midafternoon she went up to Hut, and Ciam still was not there. She made a snack, then prepacked her suitcase, assembling whatever mementos and not-to-be-forgotten bric-a-brac. Then after a fitful nap, she went back out for a final meander.

Around two hours later, wistfully braced by the countryside's stark beauty, she felt ready, and with well-devised confrontation strategy, returned to Hut. Quiet and empty it was. So she checked for the bicycle. No, he had not yet come in. She shrugged her frown away, poured a glass of retsina.

Looking out the sea-view window, sipping her wine, Sassela knew a first seepage of sympathy for him, a softness for the massive embarrassment attack he must be suffering, the guilt that must be keeping him away. Although, mind set regarding him, she couldn't help but muse coldly, He did build this uncomfortable nest. It was meet that he roost in it.

Sultry after the wine, she undressed and started for the cove nude under the towel, but halfway along, she remembered the voyeurs and returned to Hut for her flankless one-piece. She wiggled into it, went in the briny. But even for flopping in the water, the suit was uncomfortable as it suggested: the crotch slipping up her buttocks as if aiming for a split. So she went to the best-protected rock-pools, took the silly thing off and soaked in preferred nudity.

She didn't return to Hut until near sunset, yet still no sign of him or his bicycle. A glance at the track up to the roadway reminded her of Reinhard and his last presents, and the macabre stick-figure on the back of his message. Then, abruptly, an intuition set off tremors in her stomach: Ciam wasn't going to come in. She knew it truly as the electric alarm that had seized her being. And despite everything that had happened between them, her heart began pumping hard with concern for him.

Sun well set, the done day bleeding reddest rays, Sassela went searching him out. She biked into town, where another holy day had passed on to a festive evening of bazaars and puppet-shows, various tourist-aimed entertainments. The place was bouncing—locals, visitors, businessfolks celebrating. Even the severe clergy in their forbidding black and brown garb were kicking their heels. Most of the action was crammed into one six-block stretch. In the busyness of the distraction, hoping for success, shying from checking the light palace, Sassela set to prowling.

Systematically, she went inside every store, eating place, drinking spot. In the electric-lit streets, looking for brown skin, she peered at each encountered face. In every group of strollers she gauged each walk for Ciam's. Luckless time passed; she noticed the evening's festivities seemed to be winding down. This stirring more anxiety, Sassela began asking about. Approaching anyone at all, touching her own skin, questioning, "Did you see a brown man?" or "Did you see a black man?" or "Did you see a black American?"

Response from the populace—locals, tourists (European mainly)—didn't vary much. Those who didn't understand her language just smiled themselves away, and those who did pause to listen hadn't seen him. Most blankly avoided her bother. Then she happened on the friendly charm vendor.

"You seen my young man?" she asked.

"The beauty boy-man? No, no. He not come today. Maybe I take him, eh? *Ne?*" she said, with a suggestive, cackling laugh.

"No, no," said Sassela, "I don't mean now, today. Since yesterday, last night, he's gone, and didn't come back to Hut—I mean, to the house."

Ears perked, the old vendor eyed her. "Since last night? You no see beauty boy-man since last night, and alla day?"

Relieved that at last someone understood and could appreciate her concern and urgency, Sassela said, "Yes, yes. That's right. Not today either, and since last night. We had a fight, sort of, and—"

The old woman misunderstood again. Grinning broadly her sparse browned teeth, she drew close and nudged Sassela. "He alla time ready, and you no wanta alla time, *ne?*" And again her suggestive cackle.

"No, no, no. It's not that. We quarreled in the bright-lights restaurant. A little girl there, a spoilt, rude brat, and Ciam—"

The old vendor suddenly grabbed onto her arm, staring. Then in a quavering voice, the old lady exclaimed, "The small one? Fifina? The *Daeva*? Ohhhhh! Fifina take the beauty boy?"

And as Sassela nodded, the woman's eyes swiftly filled and spilled, and she looked away. Soft and sadly her croaky voice came: "She got him good. One night and one day?" She shook her head dismally. "Too much. He no good no more. She take your *palicari, ne*."

Puzzled, scared, still fishing for insight, Sassela added information. "My flight's tomorrow, you see. Ten-fifty in the morning—"

The vendor interrupted with a dismissive wave of her hand. "He no go. *Daeva, lamia* got him. He no good for you no more."

Sassela felt like she was climbing a greased pole with "make sense" the prize atop, her most extreme efforts getting her nowhere but down. Seemed this kind old woman, the only person who could understand and share concern, was deluded, convinced that Ciam couldn't or wouldn't leave because he was enchanted, or enslaved, or kidnapped. Her implication being that the admittedly deranged little creature, Fifina, was responsible.

Sassela figured to clear up the misunderstanding: "It's not like that. He's probably embarrassed and gone off roaming in a funk—"

The vendor cut in, exclaiming, "La! The ram-ring! You put it on him? Eh? The charm ring. He got charm on him? Eh? *Ne?*"

Sassela now remembered their first encounter and the charm she'd bought; rather than confessing she'd never intended to use it, she answered as if doubtful, "I don't know for sure. He might have it on. I don't know."

A malicious finality to her tone, the old vendor said, "No, no. No fool me. You no believe, huh? Now you find out true-true. *Ne*. Know for sure." And in sudden huff, she went behind her stall.

Scared by her abruptly dismissive tone, Sassela reached over, grasped the vendor's sleeve. "Don't go. Please," she begged. "Please tell me, tell me what's going on. I really don't understand what's happening. Where's Ciam? If you know, please tell me. Please. Nobody else is saying anything to me." Tears of frustration flooded.

Maybe they greased the vendor's tongue. She shrugged her sleeve free, peered rheumy eyes at Sassela. "Hmmph!" she sniffed, and began gathering up her wares, wrapping them in cloths, folding them in a large sheet. Without looking at Sassela, she said, "He, your *palicari*, Ciam, he now juice bullock. The *lamia* got him. She drain young mans' ballos. *Ne*. For sure she drain them. No more jam-jam in your *palicari*. No juice. Same all here young mans. They go 'way fast or *Daeva* take them. Then *Daeva* milk them young mans' jam-jam, *ne*, she stay look like child. *Ne*, like *mekré*. You wanta know, eh? Is young mans' juice, they life juice. She live on—"

"Not now! Not now!" Sassela burst in, compelled to stop the superstitious jabber. This was not what she wanted to hear. "What're you saying? Are you trying to frighten me? Are you talking about that little girl, Fifina?"

The vendor jerked tight the knot of her big bundle, turned on Sassela in a fury: "Fifina! Fifina!" she screeched. "Little girl? *Demon!* She just same so when I was *mekré*. Look—" blood-red glare in her eyes, she pulled the sleeve up a ropy, yellowed arm, "—look, me *mekré*? young? Eh? No, no. But she Fifina stay *mekré*! She *lamia*, you hear me? *Lamia!* She got my *palicari*, too. Yeh! Long time now same *Daeva* take my pretty youth-boy."

The madness was too much. Sassela whirled away,

groped for her bike. She hopped on and rode away to escape, to dry her eyes in cool air. She pushed hard on the pedals, furiously pumping her legs, feeling the muscles burn. Fast as she rode, though, she couldn't pedal away an eerie sense that the vendor *was* sincere, had suffered loss. It'd be impossible to fake such bitterness and hatred. And whatever drove the old vendor's deluded passion, Sassela had to acknowledge one glaring observation: she had never seen any young men Ciam's age in town.

She found herself topping the hill overlooking the rustic town she'd escaped, at the branch of the road leading down to Hut. Panting, Sassela dismounted, let the bike fall in a heap. She inhaled deeply of the cool night, and looked about, recovering her breath. She wondered suddenly, Why was she running away?

The place, nestled cozily between the sea and sudden hills, was little more than a village, its white rooftops and walls tranquil and silvery in the moonlight. Right on the bay, the imp's electric-excess hellhouse was mercifully dark. An arch with crucifix and bell identified a church. A low, rectangular, dimlit complex housed government offices—she had exchanged money there. A church and moneychangers officially promoted it to town status. Yet its people, the tenor of everyday life here, suggested the village was unconvinced of its changed role, had remained unadvanced. Uncomfortable experience reminded that the smaller eating places still lacked indoor plumbing. Every house Sassela had seen had animal pens in the backyard. Everyone seemed to bake bread, the bakeries' supply to tourists running out by midmorning. In general, Sassela reflected, these were simple folks leading a simple, natural life. Their heightened susceptibility to superstitions was not surprising. She, on the other hand, was a trained educator from the heart of the sophisticated world. She had done courses in psychology, had read from L'il Abner to Zen, was familiar with scientific method and Sherlock Holmes. And now, being confronted with a missing person, she'd be damned if she abandoned the job because of local folktales.

That she had worn sneakers, jeans, and a heavy long-sleeved green shirt made her well-dressed for checking out hunches. Coasting back down the hill, she decided to scout around the last place she'd seen Ciam, the restaurant. So when close enough, she laid the bike in roadside shrubbery, and set off on careful foot.

Making a wide circuit to approach the restaurant from the opposite side, she was nearing the large house from which she had seen the lamia-girl and her mount emerge, when an approaching figure crossed the road and went to the back. Heart racing expectantly, Sassela slunk between the roadside shrubs, and crouched down to watch she didn't know what. Shortly thereafter, another figure came hurrying up the road and also turned off for the back of the house. A brief while more, another shadowy shape followed suit. Then, in a bit, another. Sassela grunted satisfaction at the pattern, and waited minutes more for as long as she could. Finally, curiosity spurring, she set off a-crawl on hands and knees behind the shrubbery, intent on inconspicuously crossing the road to sniff out this late-hours convention of shady figures.

Stealthy as a ninja, she got around to a large, slope-roofed room extending from the main house. Light at the bottom of a closed side door suggested where the figures had entered, and her ultimate target. Undecided still, she squatted in the shadows keenly searching every direction. From her position she could keep eyes on the road in both directions, as well as on the side door; but to approach it closer would blind her to late arrivals. Playing safe, and figuring she had the time, she settled on remaining put for another few minutes before committing herself to checking the door. And just then there came a tinny bleat, a narrow sound—Ciam's unmistakable, jolly-paunch laugh; but a twisted, tortured version, beastly and shrill, more akin to a ram-goat's vapid bleat. Its tone set goose bumps rising along the back of her neck, and then Sassela recognized what it was: a suggestion of helplessness to an extreme terrible passion exactly on the edge of reason.

More than afraid now, with a quick lookabout, she abandoned the shadow of the shrub, and scurried over to the shed. The door of thick, solid wooden slabs had no keyhole, but by leaning her ear to it, she got some sounds of what was happening. She crouched down and listened. In company with Ciam's cry, there was grunting and snorting and flesh-slapping and panting and, occasionally, a chorus of sighs. And intermittently through all this, encouraging, urging, demanding, the authority conducting the show was the distinctly pitched voice of the Daeva-girl, Fifina.

Sassela became overwhelmed by a craving to see. As if some mystical element held her bound, nothing else mattered. She had to get a peep. She rose, jammed an eye to the chinks between the door's sturdy slabs, one, another, yet another. No go; each seam was too narrow but for light. She tried her eye around the door's middle hinge, the sounds inside whipping her on. Then she scrambled to the unprotected, uncovered corner of the shed, searching frantically where the boards met. A foot from the ground, she saw an eye-sized crevasse, and swiftly, she was flat on the dirt at her spy-hole, chin rutting a furrow, butting her eye to the crack at the door's bottom, stealing sight of the private ceremony.

The splinter of vantage showed a group of standing backsides with hands uniformly clasped behind. Pathetic hands folded over weary mens' rumps. Broad and flat haunches, maybe a dozen or so in sight. Commonly clad in wornout work-clothes and coveralls, from elbows to knees, plain squat behinds, their attention transfixed by some spectacle before them. The hands, by themselves, betrayed and displayed total involvement. Stern, implacable hands some. Soft, pudgy others sweated and twisted and wrung. Large, harsh ones tightened into brutal fists. One calloused pair that twitched and cradled, gripping each other dependently. Another, knuckles frozen with lit cigarette, pale smoke rising thin, unwavering, straight up as a spike. Oppressed hands they all seemed—filled with despair and helplessness. As if beyond their variety, some common shackle, some discomforting focus yoked them together like a team of dumb draught beasts—or petty prisoners in punishment stocks—clenched to attention, hot and wetting themselves.

Right then Sassela heard Fifina's demonic scream: creepy, carnal, crying orgasmic triumph. And as her heart quavered at the sound, a hand gripped Sassela's shoulder harshly.

Fear sucked into her like gravity; undeniable, having its way, its terror empowering. She wrenched herself away and up, twisting her body savagely, and the clutching hand lost grip, and the sting where it had been quivered of freedom. Of flying, wanting to go. But only a moment, and again she was snatched. Hard hand around her neck forcing her to turn, see her captor.

Amid the stench of alcohol, a shiver within the frenzy, she glimpsed into the stern waiter's sharp, strangely youthful eyes. And again, within her soul, fear swelled mightily; a wave of whirling energy in which she writhed and twisted and wrenched about, until, well out of his grasp, she was racing pell-mell, hoping for the road.

A powered rush of giant strides, exhausting effort. A

desperate glance behind. He wasn't following. Although far from certain, she still didn't slow down, pumping, forcing past her legs' and lungs' protests begging her to stop. And when their desperation gave, on will alone Sassela only slowed, and strained to keep up a ragged jog.

Until vaguely, in a blank nightmare of search and movement, she was at the bike. And finally, pedaling free, a sharp breeze in her face, she was flying away from there.

Once inside Hut, she latched the door, collapsed sweating on the bed. Catching her breath, her reason, concentrating, she tried to recall what had just happened. Nothing concrete, she had to admit, calming little by little. Only his laugh to prove Ciam's presence. And all that slapping and sighing and female come-crying might've been anyone's sounds of an illicit sex-show. Maybe she was the one in trouble here: for trespass and escaping arrest. The stern waiter with the young eyes had certainly seen her face to face. What would be his response?

Pacing the small space like a turkey in a cage, she was suddenly aware of how primitive and cramped and vulnerable Hut was. Everyone in that village probably knew she was shacked up here with Ciam. Everyone! She shuddered, clasped her hands, and pulled tightened knuckles to her mouth. What was going on with Ciam anyhow? she agonized. How had it come about? What should she do?

Maybe he'd just turn up. She stared at the flimsy latch on the door willing this, wishing fervently that he would; even sulky and mean. Then, for the first time, she realized how fragile the door was—any firm stomp easily would break it. She here alone, a stranger, anyone could apprehend her. She wouldn't know who was authority, who was not. Her anxious mind strayed to her New York apartment, its solid door, double locks, its phone and 911.

She lay down, but more and more the bed grew antsy as, tightly scrunched in a fetal ball, she rolled and shifted from side to side. No better comfort anywhere. Then suddenly she choked up, heaved close to tears at bitter truths: she just wanted out of this damned idyllic vacation. No dream time, this wasn't at all her expectation. What she really wanted now was home, Harlem. With familiar creature comforts, well-used and dependable. Yes, even Harry. It was as her Aunt Maisie said: Strange aloes were never as sweet as homegrown sour grapes. "Yes! Home," she sobbed, startled at her own anguished voice.

And, by and by, drained of even worry, she surrendered to fractured sleep.

31

Awoken in deep night, she knew a breathless sense of wrongness, even beyond being out of place, and alone. Long anxious heartbeats, it came to her: the quiet was total. But for her quick close breathing, there was nothing to listen to. Nothing outside but a quivering stillness of spooky vibrations, ominous and biding. Suddenly short of breath and damp-eyed, she fought an urge to burrow under the rough covers and forced herself up instead. Protests creaked from the big rude bed as she swung her legs down, testing the hardwood floor with her bare feet. The cool was pleasant underfoot as she went to the window and swung it open.

Her blinking eyes caught reassurance from the moonlit version of the familiar goat track to the gravel road, a silvered negative of it. A clean gouge, liquid pale where the path bent midway climbing up the hill, the scratchy, aggressive shrubs softening to a mysterious fan-brush shadow. Then, as her ears grew attuned, gradually she could hear the hiss and swish of a gentle sea. And the soothing screechy cricket families. And the frogs throaty with eternal beeps. All peaceful, steady, cool.

Not too long, growing drowsy, she turned from the window with a sigh, and firmly composing mouth and mind, returned to a more restful bed. . . .

. . . *a vacation beach, the Caribbean maybe . . . coconut trees behind them, she is trying to shoot pictures of Ciam and Harry . . . the light is flickering weirdly, bright to glaring, blues to violet, tones unbelievable, angles never proper . . . she moves in for a closeup and then she could see right into their faces, the eyes of their faces, slipping through their eyes into their minds . . . in that realm of their heads she sees what goes on for them, sees exactly as they see . . . herself with another woman, both of them naked, prancing around a bonfire like natives, lewdly grinding against each other . . . and suddenly she recognizes her partner! the sluttish Fifina . . . who begins to lick Sassela's sweating, hairy belly, the pelt down her inner thighs . . . all around, pants-less men-slaves wearing red and white waiter jackets, shackled together hands to their drained-out balls with a thin silver chain, somberly watch, and in rows and rows behind, a multitude of black-shrouded women hand about a vacant Ciam with his cock like a passive pike as they tear into it, rending him apart, greedily ripping with sharp, white rodent's teeth, consuming him . . . even as, scissored at their thighs, flesh against flesh, shamelessly rubbing, approaching explosive orgasm, she and her partner wildly dance sexual abandon, and coming in naked from the night, prancing to a quick calypso rhythm, Nollis Pabois is chanting in gleeful baritone: "As love is death, so let we die! No life as this, then make—" and everything is blurring lost in most pleasurable pain as she vacuums in breath, stocking up for absolute exhaustion . . .*

And clammily a-sweat, writhing and choking from the clasp of her imprisoned soul, Sassela's eyes popped open to the dawn of her departure.

It was still dark outside, she saw, as with alternate reality came a sweet surge of relief. Then as quickly, she remembered: last night, Ciam and Fifina. And that horrible experience combined with the murky terror of the just-now dream engulfed her once again, veering her to hysteria, to a hoarse, gasping emptiness. With a flailing witless motion, she swung herself off the bed, the jolt of her feet to the floor hurting, sharpening her mind and marshaling her.

She released her breath in a guttural sigh, and for a moment sat slumped at the bed's edge to reason comfort to herself. She had come for a vacation, and it had gone wrong. The rest of it, the complications, she should just evict from her thoughts. So she gathered herself up, took cool steps to the hill-view window.

As she gazed up from this deep bottom of the sky's starry basin, Sassela found odd comparison to her high-rise view of Harlem; the buildings' windows enigmatically agleem with myrriad brilliant souls. Pointlessly? Or was it just her, she asked her cynical other. Here, from the base of this glowing bowl of faded Grecian night, the bewildering question remained: Was there purpose to the lights? She turned from the window. Time to finish packing.

The flight was scheduled for ten-forty. Yiorgis had promised to pick her up at seven. Based on his grocery deliveries, Sassela felt certain he'd be there. She glanced to her wrist—for the first time since that day she'd put away the timepiece—then went to her ready suitcase. She took the watch from the small side-pocket, strapped it on. Phosphorescent spots showed five-thirty. She lit a candle, slid it into the tall glass on the bare table. Then planning what to leave behind, what to take, she paced the flickering dimness competing with dawn.

Five minutes early, Sassela was waiting at the roadside when, heart a-flutter, she heard the engine and
Yiorgis's taxi came rattling around the corner. It
stopped, and he was out of the car, vigorous as the brief
swirl of dust it'd stirred up.

"Good morning, good morning. So! All is ready. We
are good. *Ne?*" he greeted, manhandling the lightened
suitcase into the car trunk.

"Good morning," said Sassela. "Thanks for coming—"

"And the boy, Ciam?" Yiorgis interrupted, a questioning look down the incline to Hut. "To the airport, no?"

Sassela avoided his eye, reached for the door's handle. "I don't think so," she said coolly. "His plan was
staying on. He's not in now, though." She opened the
door, got in.

A pointed blank spaced their courteous flow. Then
Yiorgis slammed her door firmly shut. He got behind
the wheel, drove off. As soon as he was done with shifting gears, pleasantly enough, he asked, "Had a good
vacation?"

"Yes," she answered, again coldly, and feeling his
eyes on her through the rearview mirror, she opened
her pocketbook. "And how much would it be to the airport?" she asked.

"Four thousand drachmas, ma'am," said Yiorgis, his
voice immediately reserved, subtly contemptuous.

"Thank you," said Sassela, and rummaged within
her pocketbook, checking tickets and passport, counting up the drachmas. Maintaining passive distance.

His disdain didn't bother her, she told herself defiantly. All she wished was to be out of the benighted
place. And who in hell was this yokel to judge? It was
her *vacation*, after all.